REDEMPTION

REDEMPTION

David Berardelli

REDEMPTION

GRAVESTONE PRESS

PART 1—IN THE DARK

Chapter 1

It was a pleasant week for early October in Orlando, Florida. It was comfortably cool at eight o'clock that night when Justin Greer got out of the rented compact, left the faintly lit parking garage on Robinson, and went down the block that led to the bar where he would find and eliminate his latest victim.

Although he was never told much about his assignments, he was informed that this victim frequented Gina's several times each week and spent approximately one hour in the place before leaving through the rear door.

Even though these briefings always left out the most pertinent details, Greer knew it didn't take a brain surgeon to figure certain things out. This could easily be a drug hookup—possibly Colombian weed, or coke. Distribution in the Central Florida area had become rampant during the last several years, with talk of a major dealer making regular exchanges in this area.

Not much else had been said to him. The victim's real name wasn't even mentioned. Only his nickname, Shooter, and a general description, was disclosed. Even so, it didn't take a genius to see through something like that. The man either smuggled guns or earned his nickname by injecting himself with drugs. If he was buying and distributing, he was also carrying around sufficient firepower. And if he'd been distributing for any reasonable length of time, he was to be considered extremely dangerous.

The bar, thick with the gray haze of cigarette smoke and the pungent, irritating mix of perfumes and colognes, was already booming by the time Greer stepped inside. Most of the clientele looked to be in their mid- or late twenties; the others, hookers and the slightly older business crowd. Greer squeezed his way through, to the hectic bar at the other end of the room. The juke exploded with loud, muddled nonsense that sounded like someone skinning a live cat.

No one gave Greer a second look. He was wearing a plain gray tee shirt, black leather vest and jeans. His Marlins baseball cap was stuck low on his head, covering his forehead and short light-brown hair. He went up to the bar and barely gave the large-breasted blond hooker a second glance as he lightly brushed her bare knee.

"Want company tonight, baby?"

"I'm busy," he said. "Thanks anyway."

"I can make ya feel real good…"

"I don't wanna feel good tonight, thanks all the same."

She muttered something and lowered her lavishly painted lips to her umbrella drink.

The bargirl, her skinny arms covered with tattoos, rested her elbows on the counter. Greer saw that many of the customers were hoisting umbrella

6

drinks, so he ordered one. He knew he didn't have much time, but since he had to blend in, he had to make his brief appearance convincing. While the girl went to fix his drink, Greer used the bar mirror to survey the room. Although he'd never actually seen a photo, he'd been told Shooter was about six-two, slender, combed his long dark hair straight back, and wore tight dress slacks, casuals, a dress shirt with the top three buttons unbuttoned, and a gold vest.

No one in the crowd fitted that description.

"I don't see him," he muttered, lowering his head.

"He's already out back, scoring," came the reply from the earpiece in Greer's left ear. "Better hurry."

"How many are out there?"

"Three. There's one standing at the end of the dumpster, looking bored, but he's definitely keeping an eye out. Shooter and his supplier are standing in front of it. They're about sixty feet from the rear door. They'll see you the moment you step outside. If you keep low, the nightlight over the door might not light you up much."

"What about the noise coming from in here?"

"Open the door once the song finishes. And make sure you pull it shut the moment you step outside. Do it fast."

The girl brought over his drink. Greer had a sip, grimaced at its sweetness and dropped a ten-spot on the counter. While she scooped it up, Greer forced his way back into the crowd and went searching for the restrooms, which led to the office marked *MANAGER*, as well as the rear exit.

***

The two figures were standing in front of the dumpster.

Shooter, the taller of the two, held his hand out as the guy facing him handed him a large plastic bag. Shooter took it, opened it and studied its contents. He then lowered his pinky inside the bag. A moment later, he pulled his hand out of the bag and sampled the miniscule amount on the tip of his pinky. The other guy mumbled something. Shooter handed the guy a wad of bills he'd removed from his vest and shoved the bag under his left arm.

The instant just before Greer could pull the door shut, the juke started back up inside the bar, disrupting the silence. The two turned sharply in his direction.

Greer suspected that the guy standing at the far end of the dumpster would pull a weapon. Greer had already pulled his own weapon. "They made me," he whispered, his pulse racing.

"Give us a moment," came the reply in Greer's earpiece.

"Don't take too long."

"You lost?" Shooter asked in a loud, high-pitched voice.

Greer didn't reply. He was confused, wondering why Shooter hadn't already pulled out a gun. Neither had the other guy, or the one standing at the end of the dumpster. Greer had dealt with drug runners before; they were always armed to the teeth. Why these two hadn't already started shooting was something he just couldn't get.

"I'm about to kill that streetlamp," his earpiece said. "Give me five seconds."

"I asked you a question, dude!" Shooter was getting agitated.

"I know," Greer said. "I heard you the first time."

"Well?"

"I'm thinking up a really good answer."

Shooter groaned and shook his head. His buddy said, "You a fuckin' narc?"

"Not exactly."

"Whaddya mean, not exactly?"

"Get ready," came the earpiece.

Everything went dark.

Loud gasps resonated simultaneously.

Greer crawled over to a stack of old crates and palettes and squeezed between two crates. Just as he brought up his automatic, he saw two figures disappearing behind the dumpster. Shooter stood in the same place, his head tilted as he tried penetrating the darkness.

"Hit the light," Greer told his earpiece.

"When?"

"Right this second would make me a very happy man."

The streetlamp blipped, showing exactly where Shooter was standing.

Greer pumped a .45 round into Shooter's head. The boy was slammed against the dumpster, his head whacking its heavy metal side with a dull thump. He went down hard, his slender form barely making a noise on the concrete slab.

The other two vanished.

Still hidden between the wooden crates, Greer listened to the heavy silence for a minute or so before getting back up.

"Is he down?" asked his earpiece.

"Yeah."

"Get out now. ETA for OPD will be two minutes."

Greer listened for another thirty seconds before getting back up. He rushed back to the metal exit door and cautiously nudged it open. All he heard from inside was the irritating juke and the ecstatic screams from the crowd. He slipped back inside and instantly became invisible within the quivering mass.

Just as he opened the door to the front entrance, he heard the approaching sirens.

Chapter 2

Greer made it safely back to the parking garage just before nine-fifteen. Street activity was almost nil; so was the traffic in the parking garage.

No one gave him the slightest glance.

As he approached the rental, he used the key fob to open the trunk of the rental. Keeping his eyes and ears alert, he took off his cap and leather vest and dropped them in his black leather overnight bag. He also removed the .45 from his waistband and placed it in the bag as well. Then, satisfied he wasn't being observed, he closed the trunk.

After one last quick scan, he slid behind the wheel of the rental. Using the interior lights and the visor mirror, he ran a comb through his hair. Then he pulled out of his spot, coasted down the ramp, paid at the gate and eased back onto Robinson.

Heading east, he drove straight to the rental agency on Semoran Boulevard, completed the paperwork for the return of the rental and went back outside. His black Honda Accord sat in the rear lot, between a maroon Ford pickup and a white Lexus. He put his bag in the trunk. After giving the lot and the busy highway a thorough scan, he got in the Honda, left the gravel lot, pulled out onto Semoran, and made a left at the first light, which took him back downtown.

His one-bedroom apartment, located on the second floor of a refurbished eight-story brick building on Church Street, had been his home for the last five years. He locked the door behind him, went over to the cabinet above the sink in the tiny kitchenette and grabbed a bottle of Absolut vodka. He poured two inches into a glass and downed it in one swallow. Then stood there, leaning against the counter and hating himself for what he'd just done, what he'd become.

He managed to empty his mind of what had happened in the last hour, focusing instead on the strong drink that would ease the throbbing in his temples. It didn't quite do the trick, so he poured another inch. A moment later, he closed his eyes and smiled as the familiar comforting mellow drifted warmly through his tired limbs. Sighing, he went back out into the living room and collapsed on the sofa.

Once he finally began to relax, he grabbed the remote from the coffee table and switched on the TV. Turner was playing silents, but he wasn't in the mood for a silent movie. He got up and sorted through the DVDs from the pile on the table next to the TV. Bogart came up. *Conflict*. A moody 1946 film *noir*. An excellent movie. Tense, but something that had always relaxed him. He slipped it into the player, went back to the kitchen and splashed another inch of warm vodka into the glass.

The movie started the moment he sat back down. He sipped the drink, sat back, closed his eyes and felt his body melting softly into the cushions.

By the time he'd drained his glass, he discovered that he couldn't keep his eyes open. He slipped off his shoes, lay on his back, closed his eyes and prepared his tired brain for the soft, caressing nothingness of sleep.

***

Early the next morning, Greer's earpiece buzzed, waking him instantly. The voice said: "You have a new assignment."

He sat up and rubbed his eyes.

"Are you awake?" asked the voice.

"Yeah."

"Are you ready for your next assignment?"

"Uh…yeah."

"You sound not quite alert. Drinking again?"

"I'm fine."

"That's not what I asked."

"I had a couple when I got back home last night."

"You can't be hungover. You've been told this before. You've got to be one hundred percent sober, one hundred percent ready to—"

"I needed something to help me relax."

"This is an important assignment."

"I'm *not* hungover, dammit."

"See that you aren't. And keep the attitude to yourself."

He was getting angry. He knew that their threats were supposed to frighten him, but he'd been at this much too long. However, he didn't think it would be very bright to tell them that their intimidation tactics no longer worked. It would be much better if they learned this important tidbit on their own. "What's the assignment?"

A pause. "You're *sure* you're ready to work?"

13

"Just give me the details."

***

The two-story townhouse sat in a grove of trees on Rockledge Road in the Lake Underhill area, not far from South Conway.

Greer parked his rental, a light-blue Camaro, halfway down the street. Before getting out, he slipped on his Miami Dolphins baseball cap and sunglasses. With his gray shorts, athletic shoes, dark-blue polo shirt and lightweight maroon jacket, he could easily pass for a Florida tourist.

However, the .22 Beretta automatic resting in its plastic bag in the harness stitched into his jacket hardly qualified as standard tourist garb.

"Whatever you do," the voice in his earpiece had told him earlier that morning, "do not touch the gun. Wear gloves when removing it. Be very careful how you handle it when you position it."

An hour earlier, Greer had, as instructed, found the gun in its designated locker at the Greyhound Bus Terminal in downtown Orlando. The key to the locker was "accidentally" dropped at his feet on the dirty tile floor as he went inside the crowded building. It had happened much too quickly for him to identify the person in the fast-moving crowd. Greer wasn't surprised. His handlers went to great lengths to accomplish their tasks, hiring only the best talent money could buy.

Greer didn't waste time wondering about their tactics or resources. For one thing, he didn't care. The only thing that concerned him was picking up the Beretta and taking it to the townhouse precisely

14

at 2:15, when the residence would be vacant. He knew nothing about the owner of the townhouse. His instructions were concise, but always vague. And they were never to be questioned.

Greer didn't care about any other details. The only thing that really mattered in this case was that he didn't have to kill this man. This pleased him.

Despite what he did for a living, Greer actually hated killing people.

The key to the townhouse lay underneath a potted plant in the center of a group of nine that had been arranged neatly in front of the living room window. After putting on his gloves, he picked up the key and went up the three concrete steps leading to the front entrance. He gave the area a quick scan. No one was about. He pulled open the screen door, used his lockpicking tools to unlock the front door, and slipped inside. While he stood in the center of the rubber mat, he gave the premises a cursory once-over and pulled off his shoes.

Other than the quiet hum of the air conditioner and the slight popping of the refrigerator, he heard nothing. He noticed a few abstract pictures on the walls, four open doorways, and some expensive-looking furniture while working his way down the hall to the master bedroom. He was very careful not to trip on anything or accidentally brush against something. All sorts of people would be examining this place very shortly. He didn't want them to find evidence of anyone else being here.

It took him less than five minutes to find the hiding place for the Beretta. Using a different pair of gloves, he pulled the tiny pistol out of its harness, removed it carefully from its plastic cover, and positioned it. This done, he hurried back to the front door, put his shoes back on, stepped outside and returned the key to its former position beneath the plant. Then he turned and went down the walk.

He was about to cross the street when a slender figure with flowing red hair approached him.

Startled, Greer forced himself to look straight ahead.

His instincts told him this girl could be a potential eyewitness. He didn't want anyone remembering him. He'd learned long ago that if you didn't look directly at someone, they found it difficult to identify you.

Still avoiding her eyes, he took another step, until he was just a few feet from the curb.

The young woman kept coming.

If he could just take two or three more quick steps, he'd reach the curb. Then she'd see only his back.

One more step…

Despite his instincts, his professionalism, as well as his growing paranoia, he discovered that his feet had stopped moving. There was something about this girl that had made him forget about his precautions. He didn't know what it was. A sense of warmth, perhaps? A feeling that there was something special about her?

Whatever it was, something about her made him stop cold in his tracks to let her pass. And in the next moment, she turned his way.

16

He found himself staring at a young face obscured by a pair of large-rimmed sunglasses. The brim of her light-blue baseball cap came down so low, he couldn't see her forehead. She wore no lipstick, and the collar of her lightweight jacket was pulled up, hiding her neck and cheeks. She had a slender frame and long legs concealed in dark-blue sweats, and walked quickly, with a spring in her step.

In spite of her slender legs, he discovered that he couldn't stop focusing on her face, and realized that although he couldn't see her features, he suspected that behind the dark shades, a pair of beautiful blue eyes had somehow seen directly into his soul.

***

Unable to move, Greer watched her as she marched briskly to the end of the block. She stopped at the intersection and looked both ways before crossing the street. He admired her slimness, the quiet energy of those long legs. He couldn't stop staring at her hair as it bounced across the top of her shoulders.

Briefly he thought of Sharon, his ex-wife. Sharon and her thick dark-brown hair, her steel-gray eyes. Her smile, which had the natural ability to turn from sizzling to glacial in the blink of an eye. Most of all, her talent for evaluating him at a glance, then dismissing him completely by turning away.

He continued watching the redhead until she'd disappeared behind the bushes lining the front yard at the next block. Only then did he realize that he still hadn't budged.

Cold reality quickly slammed into his consciousness, bringing him back to the present, and he suddenly remembered that he had to make tracks.

After shaking himself back to a fairly presentable state of alertness, he crossed the street and went down the block, where he'd parked the Camaro. His thoughts lingered on the redhead as he got behind the wheel and fired up the ignition. He was about to pull out when his earpiece buzzed.

"Have you finished?"

"Yes."

"That was a five-minute assignment. You should have checked in five minutes ago."

Before replying, he considered his options. He couldn't possibly tell them about the redhead. There would be all sorts of irritating questions.

Anyway, it wasn't anyone's business. And since he'd completed his assignment successfully, a minor delay should not be of any concern. To anyone.

"Just making sure no one saw me," he said.

"Seriously?"

He flinched at the doubt he'd sensed in the voice. Doubt meant trouble with these people. Serious trouble. He knew right then that it was important to get them to focus on the main issue.

"I had no problem planting the Beretta."

"The details were carefully planned and worked out. No one is supposed to be there for another

18

thirty minutes." A pause. "This is why you needed to get out of that neighborhood in the timeframe allotted you."

Greer didn't reply. There was no need for anyone to know why he'd stayed put for just a couple of minutes longer than he should have. The assignment hadn't been compromised. He'd gone right in and planted the gun. Didn't touch anything, and left his shoes on the mat in the foyer.

And if he stopped to stare at a good-looking young woman for a moment or two later on, it was no one else's business.

Confident he hadn't messed up anything, he put the car into gear and eased away from the curb. He was confident that he'd dodged their personal questions with enough subtlety to keep them off his back. At least, for now.

However, the moment he reached the end of the block, the voice came back. "Have you decided when you're going to tell us about the redhead?"

Chapter 3

Greer's heart raced.

He hadn't seen anyone else in the area or noticed any camera activity. How the hell could they possibly know about the redhead?

We know everything.

Once again, their arrogance thundered its way into the picture, and he was reminded yet again of how drastically his life had changed the day they'd first contacted him. All he remembered from that first encounter was the dim figure in a gray suit stepping silently into his hospital room. And telling him how grateful the country was for his excellent service. How valuable he still was. How capable. And how the country desperately needed his services.

The days quickly meshed together, and then another dim figure entered his life. And then another. And then several doctors studying him with their instruments and monitors. Asking him questions, giving him advice, suggestions. Telling him how much better he'd be after a few sessions of therapy. And once the therapy was finished, they'd released him, told him he was good to go. And that they'd contact him when they needed him.

Just a couple of days after he'd moved into the modest Orlando apartment provided by them, the first call came, from someone he'd never talked to before, who didn't even have a name. The call had come from a small plastic earpiece he discovered by accident in his shirt pocket.

The first thing this mysterious voice told him was to place the piece in his ear and keep it there. Then all would be just fine and dandy. He'd never have to worry about anything again. Life would quickly become wonderful. But he'd have to obey them completely. They'd know if he didn't. They'd know, because, as they'd told him time and time again, they knew everything.

And they knew about the redhead.

He waited a few moments for his pulse to settle down. His thoughts spun wildly, and he discovered that his brain had stopped working.

Was another blackout coming on? Very doubtful, but it was still something to fear.

"I'm driving," he told the voice. He'd said it just to remind them. In case they wanted to show their superiority at the most inopportune time.

"We're fully aware of what you're doing."

Maybe he wouldn't black out again. They'd no doubt realized that forcing a blackout on him right now, as he was driving a rented car on a busy street, would create all sorts of problems. It could cause an accident and kill him. It might even kill someone else. Or make other irritating complications. Questions. Unwanted attention.

All the things they didn't want.

He took long, deep breaths to calm down. When his brain finally resumed its normal process, he realized that he might be able to squirm out of this. The important thing was, of course, not letting them know they were intimidating him. Intimidation gave them the advantage. They were experts at it. After all, they'd had years of experience perfecting their craft.

After a few more deep breaths, he decided to proceed with this the best way he knew. "What redhead?"

A pause. "You know better than that. If we know something, your only option is to tell us everything. You know very well what happens if you lie to us."

Don't ever lie to us…

You don't want the blackouts to start up again…

Once they start, we're the only ones with the power to stop them…

"Are you talking about that young woman who was walking down the sidewalk while I was leaving the house?" he asked.

"You know full well what we're talking about."

Although the voice was flat and as disinterested as always, Greer could feel the arrogance coming through. But he knew he shouldn't weaken. Once he did, everything would go downhill.

"I have no idea. I don't even know why we're talking about this in the first place. What is so damned important about a young woman I don't even know walking down the street in the middle of the afternoon? There are other people living in this neighborhood, you know. Just because you assigned me to be there at two o'clock in the afternoon doesn't guarantee there won't be anyone else in the area. I counted twelve houses on each side of the block. That comes out to at least twenty-four, perhaps forty-eight people, possibly even more, living on that block alone. Not everyone living there works the same hours."

"We are quite aware of the number of people living in that neighborhood. We're also aware of who is working and who is not."

"Then what's the problem? Why take issue with this? All I did was stop for a moment or two to let one of the locals pass me on the sidewalk. Is that a crime?"

"The problem is, you were seen watching her when she passed you. That was not part of your assignment."

"I know exactly what my assignment was. I did it, didn't I? And without a snag. What more could you possibly expect from me?"

Silence.

Greer felt his heart racing once again. In spite of his struggle to stay in control, the voice, as always, reigned supreme. This was already turning bad. If he didn't fix things, it would turn abysmal in a heartbeat. He had to come up with something that would pacify them. It sounded simple, but he knew from painful experience just how impossible such a task could be.

"Well?" the voice finally asked. "What have you got to say for yourself? Explain why you didn't leave when you should have."

"First of all, I'm a human being. A man. I was watching a young woman. Get it? Man? Woman?"

He waited for a response. He heard only silence. They were listening. In this case, they were waiting for him to slip up. "For one thing…"

Then he stopped and analyzed the situation. Why did he have to explain himself for something he should not feel guilty about in the first place? He didn't actually *see* the girl, did he? He glimpsed her hair, her cap, her sunglasses, her jacket, jeans, athletic shoes. Nothing else. Nothing they could consider threatening…

"We're waiting…"

"For one thing, I didn't really *see* her."

"Explain…"

"If I was being observed, you already know the answer to that."

"We're still waiting for an explanation."

"Maybe it would be easier if I gave you a description of the person you seem to be obsessing about. Would that help?"

A pause. "It might…"

"All right. About five-seven or -eight. Red hair. Light-blue baseball cap. Sunglasses. Lightweight jacket. Jeans. Athletic shoes."

Silence.

"That's it."

"Just what are you getting at?"

"I didn't see her *face*. What I saw was what I just described. I couldn't ID her if you grabbed her and stuck her right in front of me."

More silence.

"Is that all you wanted to talk to me about?"

"You're missing the point."

"What *is* the point?"

"The point is this. It doesn't matter if you can't identify her. *She* can identify *you*."

Despite his growing fear, he knew better than let them know what was going on in his head. "You're totally wrong."

"And why is that?"

"This girl didn't even see me."

"And how would you know?"

"For one simple reason. I turned away from her when she came closer. I only turned back in her direction after she'd passed and had gone a fair distance away."

Silence.

Greer kept the Camaro in the steady traffic heading east. His hands had turned white as they gripped the wheel. His heart pounded heavily. The silence turned thick. And deafening. And grew unbearable by the second. If he didn't hear anything shortly, he feared he'd come out of his skin. But he forced himself to keep a firm grip on the wheel, breathe normally, and try not to kill anyone on the highway.

After several minutes of total silence, Greer decided they'd chosen not to pursue the matter.

He took the Camaro back to the rental place to turn it in. Once his nerves had settled down, he decided to stop at the first steak restaurant he came to. He'd done a damned good job; he deserved a T-bone, baked potato, and a mug of dark beer as a reward.

The moment he stepped inside his apartment two hours later, he collapsed on the couch with an old movie—a 1940's Cary Grant classic—lulling him to sleep.

Chapter 4

Waking early the next morning, Greer sat up on the couch and struggled to sort out what had happened the night before.

Some hazy memories trickled back. The townhouse in the Lake Underhill area. The .22 Beretta he'd placed in the top drawer of the bedroom nightstand. The slim redhead...

Most of all, the redhead.

Then, as that warm image drifted by, that other memory, cold and frightening and unrelenting, bullied its way through.

"Have you decided when you're going to tell us about the redhead?"

And what he'd told them

("This girl didn't even see me")

to get them off his back.

Had it worked? Had they believed him? Had they thought for even one moment that he might actually be telling them the truth?

All he knew was that a young woman had crossed his path and, for the first time in years, he'd felt something he hadn't experienced in a long time.

Was it a reminder of his loneliness? Was it a yearning? His hormones coming out of their self-imposed hibernation? A sense of bonding with another person? The feeling that he'd detached himself from the human race and, for the first time since Sharon had walked out, experienced a strong compulsion to return to it?

All he knew for certain was that, for the first time since he'd come back from Germany, that single brief encounter had made him feel like a human being again. A human being with urges. Needs. And all this reminding him that the heart that had been beating so distantly inside him for so long had suddenly made itself known again.

How could that be?

How could he have experienced so many emotions in a single moment?

He hadn't actually *spoken* to her. Hadn't *touched* her. He hadn't even had been close enough to smell her fragrance.

And, as he'd told them, he'd never even seen her face.

But whatever happened had obviously stirred something inside him that had been dormant for a long time. And in that single moment, he realized that, in spite of every disgusting thing that had happened to him since he'd first gone to Iraq more than ten long, difficult years earlier, he still remained among the living. A living, breathing man who, in the blink of an eye, had mysteriously come back from the land of the dead.

Suddenly overwhelmed by this unexpected flood of images, he got up from the couch and staggered into the bathroom. For the next ten minutes, he stood under a warm shower, his eyes closed as the soothing stream cascaded onto his face and body, revitalizing him.

After a breakfast of scrambled eggs, toast and coffee, Greer, still obsessing about the redhead, decided to drive back to the Lake Underhill area. He knew that his chances of bumping into her again were slim at best. However, the mere thought of returning to the area where he'd first seen her brought about a warm feeling that made his spirits rise.

For some inexplicable reason, he felt like doing something out of the ordinary. Something that might make him feel better about himself and things in general. He hadn't heard from his handlers since their last exchange and decided that what he'd told them had satisfied them. They hadn't called back, so he figured he was off the hook. The silence also told him they didn't have another job for him. They almost always called in the morning for an assignment. This gave them a couple of hours to finish arranging the details. And since it was now almost ten o'clock, he guessed that he was free for the day.

After squirming into a light-blue polo shirt, jeans and tan casuals, he grabbed his wallet and keys from the kitchen counter and headed for the front door. He pulled it open, he took one step out into the hall, and stopped cold. Then stood stock-still, wondering what he was doing. After a few moments, he discovered that he was gazing at the peeled plaster wall. And the fire extinguisher in its glass box a few feet farther down.

The first waves of depression rushed in. Then, realizing the futility of his latest decision, he closed the door behind him and stood facing the living room couch, telling himself over and over that he was an idiot.

What made him think even for a second that he could just leave, get in his car and look for a young woman he'd stumbled across during an assignment? A woman who'd almost compromised his future? A woman his handlers somehow knew about as well?

They'd rake him over the coals, then put him on probation for months, which would automatically be tacked on to his five-year commitment with them. And then they'd keep an even sharper eye on him.

They'd told him in the beginning that he would be under their control. From then on, personal relationships were out of the question. And for the next five years, they owned him. And where he lived. And everything he did. When his contract was up, he was free to do whatever he pleased, provided he signed the disclaimer preventing him from acknowledging their existence. To anyone.

Five years of his life. Unless, of course, he did something really stupid—like what he'd almost done just minutes ago.

If they decided that he hadn't acted in any way that disobeyed orders or threatened their existence, his contract with them would be up in just six months.

But then what? What would he do then?

How would a man with his specialized skills function in the outside world? What good would these skills be? Could he sign up with an employment agency? Could he list any of the things he'd learned in Survival School? Jungle Training? Desert Training? Sniper School?

It was painfully clear that his experience would not be in demand in the private sector. The civilized world would fear him, want him gone. Out of sight, out of mind.

He'd be thirty-five years old, with no marketable skills, no references, and no prospects. His future would be bleak, at best.

As another wave of depression surged through him, he plodded into the living room and collapsed on the couch. He wanted a drink but decided it was much too early in the day. Later, after lunch, he'd suck down a belt or two to help rid himself of this sudden attack of hopelessness.

An hour or so with a book, maybe?

Unlikely. He didn't think he could concentrate long enough to get through a page.

Music, then?

Judging by his dark mood, he couldn't imagine what he could listen to that might lift his spirits.

He picked up the remote and aimed it at the TV. Just then, his earpiece buzzed.

His pulse hammering, he sat back and willed his nerves to calm down.

"What are you doing at the moment?" the cursed voice asked.

"I'm in my apartment," he replied, struggling to keep the contempt out of his voice.

"We know where you are," the voice replied. "The question was, are you involved in something right now?"

Briefly he considered lying to them, telling them he was about to have breakfast. Or take a shower. Or getting ready to do his laundry.

He knew that wouldn't fly. They knew what he was doing. He didn't know how they knew, just that they did. For the last four and a half years, he'd periodically checked the apartment for bugs, but hadn't found any evidence whatsoever. But he knew how they worked. He strongly suspected that they could have someone come in every other day and move their equipment whenever he was out on assignment.

"I was about to watch TV," he said flatly.

"Then you won't mind leaving your place in the next fifteen minutes."

Of course I'd mind, he wanted to say. *I mind everything I do for you people. I hate you and want you out of my life. I know I'm forced to do your dirty work for the next six months, but I don't care. I don't like what you've made me do, what you've turned me into. I don't want to talk to you anymore.*

But he knew how they'd react if he told them how he felt.

"Another assignment?" he asked tiredly.

"Get in your car and be in the front lot at Fashion Square Mall in thirty minutes."

"And then…?"

32

"And then you'll receive further instructions."

"Thirty minutes? That's kind of pushing it—"

The earpiece went dead.

***

Greer pulled into the front lot of the crowded mall at 11:13, precisely thirty minutes after receiving his latest instructions. Since the lunch hour had already begun, heavy traffic made the trip more hectic, but he managed to get to his destination with seconds to spare. As instructed, he took the Honda to the front lot and coasted halfway down the aisle that led to the glass doors of the front entrance.

His hands trembled as he parked facing the huge building. He was always nervous before a job, especially when he had no idea what the assignment would be. He'd wanted to ask questions but had been told that questions were not allowed. Questions irritated them, made them even more difficult to work with.

But this didn't change the fact that he hadn't wanted to come here. He knew something terrible was going to happen. And that he'd be the cause of whatever it was.

He flicked off the ignition and sat back in his seat. He needed a few moments to empty his mind. To take a few deep breaths, close his eyes and think of the ocean, or the mountains. He liked emptying his mind before he was forced to do something bad. However, the moment he'd sat back, his earpiece buzzed.

"You've arrived."

As always, they knew exactly where he was. This was obvious, since they'd buzzed him the moment he'd parked the car and flicked off the ignition.

But he knew better than voice his views. He didn't want to anger them.

"I'm here," he said.

"Are you ready for your instructions?"

"I'm here," he repeated, trying to keep the contempt out of his voice, yet knowing he didn't really care if they sensed it.

"You're to go inside and directly into the center of the mall. Walk over to the bench facing the front display window of the drugstore and sit down. There's a kiosk just eight feet from the bench. A young woman will come out. Make sure she has an accident."

He wanted to ask what sort of accident.

The voice continued, immediately answering his question. "A fatal accident. Her car is a three-year-old gold Hyundai. It is parked one row down from where you've parked. East of your car."

"A fatal accident," he muttered, growing nauseous.

"One that will not raise suspicion."

He swallowed. "Just how…when should I—"

"You know better than ask questions."

"Yeah. I know."

"If you'd waited ten seconds, I would have finished your briefing, and your question would have been answered. Understand?"

"Yes."

"You will be told the moment this female leaves the store."

The earpiece went dead.

His nerves jumped like short circuits as he got out of the Honda, closed the door and shuffled unsteadily down the aisle that led to the store. He felt as if he were approaching an awaiting guillotine. Killing someone you didn't know was bad enough. But when the intended victim was female, it made the task infinitely worse.

He tried convincing himself that whoever this female was probably deserved this. She could be a very bad person. She might even have committed a terrible crime inside the store. After all, she was considered an enemy of the state, wasn't she? Otherwise, his handlers wouldn't want her dead.

He forced himself to believe that he would make this as painless as he could for her. He didn't care what she did; she didn't have to know what was happening, and she surely didn't have to suffer.

He was very good at making accidents happen. He'd done things like this a few times before. He didn't enjoy doing them, but he always worked quickly so he didn't waste time agonizing about them.

He took the seat facing the store and tried to empty his mind. Trying once again to think past this horrible task. To accomplish this, he focused on what he'd have for supper. The movie he'd put on

(*Cary Grant?*)
(*Audrey Hepburn?*)
(*Spencer Tracy?*)

when he fixed his meal and brought it over to the couch. The drinks he'd have before shuffling off to bed.

Thinking of everything but the task at hand…

Then he saw the familiar figure coming out of the store. The red hair. The sunglasses. The baseball cap.

The earpiece buzzed again. The cursed voice said, "That young woman is your new assignment. Follow her outside and do your job."

Chapter 5

Erika Young hurried out of the drugstore as quickly as her legs could carry her.

She had no idea Yvonne Michaels was working at the store. If she had known, she wouldn't have even gone into the place. She'd only gone in for a few essentials—and, of course, to see if she could find any of her favorite films on DVD. She'd been to the DVD outlet earlier but hadn't seen anything interesting. Nothing she couldn't do without.

These days, she was heavily into fantasy. She figured it was because she appreciated escape more than ever. She particularly enjoyed the *Lord of The Rings* trilogy and had wanted to buy the three Hobbit prequels for a good price. She hadn't found them yet but knew that she would have probably already added them to her library if she went out looking more often.

These days, she didn't go out in public at all. She knew that wasn't a good thing, especially since she was only twenty-two and had the rest of her life ahead of her. But she hated people looking at her and wanted to scream her lungs out when she caught them staring.

This convinced her even more to consider buying her DVDs online.

Yvonne Michaels was one of those people who seemed to enjoy making life miserable for everyone else. Yvonne had been extremely popular all through high school. As head cheerleader and girlfriend of the team's football captain, Yvonne was voted best-looking, most popular, and most likely to succeed. Just why she was working at the local drugstore was anyone's guess.

But that was her business. All Erika cared about was Yvonne seeing her. The moment she glimpsed Yvonne leaning against the counter, popping gum and running her cultured nails through her long black mane, Erika dropped the toothpaste and spare toothbrushes into the bargain bin, turned and hastily made tracks toward the EXIT sign.

Erika didn't know if Yvonne or anyone else would even recognize her these days. With her baseball cap, sunglasses, and collar pulled up, she hoped no one would know who she was. Which was perfectly okay.

Erika left the store and told herself she'd never go back. She had no idea what Yvonne's world had become, just that the girl had a gargantuan mouth. Erika knew that if Yvonne had seen her, the news would spread like wildfire and people would be yapping about her again.

The moment she left the store, Erika sensed something was very wrong. And when she glanced to her right, she realized the source of her suspicions.

It was the guy she'd nearly bumped into yesterday afternoon on Rockledge Road. The guy who'd stopped just as she was about to bump into him. The nice-looking guy who'd turned away the moment their eyes met.

His turning away had made her wonder if he'd seen her face. To play it safe, she'd grabbed her collar and pulled it up.

Yes, this was definitely the same guy.

And now, here he was again, this time sitting on the bench next to the kiosk, watching her as she came out of the drugstore.

The moment she'd glanced at him, a strange sense of danger came from out of nowhere, making her blood turn cold. She suddenly realized that she was being bombarded by a bevy of strong emotions so powerful that they made her shudder.

Fear. Anger. Outrage. And a self-loathing as intense and as penetrating as anything she'd ever felt before.

Every emotion, dark and deep and sizzling hot—oozed from him, turning his outward image into something so dark, she couldn't begin to fathom what crippling disaster was going on inside him.

Her first instinct was to walk over and ask if he was all right. Not so long ago, she might have actually considered doing just that.

But not now.

The decision was instantly made for her. When the hot viciousness of the darkness smothering him drifted her way, she knew she had to get away. She had no idea why this stranger, this man she'd seen briefly only once before, would pummel such horrible emotions at her. She also had no idea why she was able to sense these feelings in the first place. She only knew that whatever the reason, it had made her queasy. If he was crazy or unbalanced, it wasn't up to her to help him. It wasn't that she didn't *want* to help him, or anyone else who needed it... But in this case, she somehow feared that this guy was beyond help.

And with this in mind, she turned left and, increasing her gait, joined the staggered groups of customers and tourists making their way for the glass doors nearly a hundred yards away, which would take them to the front lot, where she'd parked her car.

A minute or so later, when she finally reached the doors, a kind, considerate elderly man coming in smiled and held it open for her. As she nodded her thanks, she could tell without even turning around that the man possessed by all those intense, devastating emotions was right behind her.

***

Struggling to keep the panic away, Erika focused on getting to her car as quickly as possible. The mere fact that she could plainly see it parked just fifty yards away sent waves of warm relief shimmering through her.

But even so, she couldn't ignore what was going on behind her.

She sensed that he'd narrowed the gap. She couldn't help wondering if this was going to be a mugging, a carjacking, or something worse— something that might send her to the hospital. This area wasn't noted for violent crime, but no place was immune to anything these days, and she knew to be cautious. She carried a small cannister of

40

pepper spray in her bag but didn't want to use it for fear of hurting anyone. She realized how lame that sounded, but it was how she felt. Right now, she had to face the frightening realization that her only option might be to disable the man following her whatever way possible.

Keeping close to the small groups heading off to their vehicles, she continued walking briskly down the aisle, totally obsessed with doing whatever it took to reach her Hyundai. She'd wanted to call 911 but didn't want to cause attention to herself. And she didn't want to alarm the man. Judging by the vicious signals emanating from him, she didn't want to do anything that could feed the anger consuming him.

She had to get a firm grip on the pepper spray but wanted only to use it as a preventative tactic. If things went the way she hoped, all she had to do was turn around and hold it out in front of her. Most attackers would know what it was. They'd anticipate the pain and agony associated with it and would make tracks. Hopefully, this was all she had to do. She really didn't want to hurt him. Although he'd been transmitting scary vibes, she'd sensed confusion, even torment, amidst the hatred and the anger.

As she moved closer to her car, she opened her bag, pulled out her keys and also the pepper spray.

Please don't make me have to spray him, she thought furiously, her pulse fluttering wildly. *If only he'd trip or something... Then I just might have enough time to get in my car and—*

The harsh thump and subsequent grunt directly behind her destroyed her concentration. Her heart thrashing, she spun around.

The man was lying on his side on the pavement.

Chapter 6

Stunned by the sight in front of her, Erika quickly forgot all about her original plan. As she watched him right now, he no longer appeared threatening or dangerous. He had become just a guy who'd suffered a mild mishap and needed help.

Should she? Or shouldn't she? After all, he'd been stalking her, hadn't he? And while doing so, he gave off a ton of scary vibes.

She knew she should call nine-one-one and tell them she was being stalked, and that her stalker—

Where was her proof? Just her word alone that the man was following her? Was she really certain he actually *was* following her? Or was this all just her imagination?

Of course she was certain. He'd been giving off those nasty vibes, hadn't he?

But what else could she tell them? That in the last few minutes, she could sense vibes, emotions? Feelings? His anger? His torment?

They'd consider her a nut job.

She couldn't very well tell them—or anyone else, for that matter—that just a very short while ago, she'd started picking up things she couldn't explain. And although she could describe what these things were, she had no idea where they were coming from or why she was suddenly able to pick them up.

She decided it best to keep all this to herself.

So then, what should she do?

Calling nine-one-one was out of the question. Her best bet was to get in her car and drive away. This guy could just forget about her and focus on someone else. Or go home and forget about his career as a stalker.

She continued watching him, especially his eyes. He was avoiding hers while he struggled to get back to his feet.

When he gets back up, he'll come after me again—

No. He wasn't doing that at all. She sensed that he wouldn't. In fact, she suspected that once he'd straightened, he'd walk away and forget all about her.

But none of this helps me cope with the fact that I'd somehow made him trip and hurt himself...

She shoved the pepper spray and her keys back into her bag. Then, ignoring her shaking limbs, she cautiously went over to him.

Still watching her, he struggled to straighten, using the bumper of the parked Dodge Ram pickup for leverage.

"I'm sorry, but I—" She stopped herself. She'd almost told him what she'd been thinking. Best keep it inside and forget about letting anyone else know about it. For one thing, he probably wouldn't believe her. And if he did believe her, he'd think she was crazy. If she kept quiet, this might just turn out all right. She wasn't quite sure how she knew; she felt that things wouldn't be so bad if she kept cool about it and didn't arouse anyone's suspicion.

"Are you all right?" she finally asked.

"I think so..." His eyes stayed on her as he tentatively shifted his weight. His gaze didn't move from her as he straightened. She knew that touching him would be a mistake. For one thing, she didn't like touching anyone these days. For another, she didn't want to get too close. Though she'd caught no further darkness emanating from him, she reminded herself that he'd been following her. And the fact that he hadn't explained himself or his actions suggested that his motives were probably not at all honorable.

She sensed only confusion. And fear—which made no sense. She was grateful that the dark emotions she'd experienced earlier had vanished, but it just wasn't clear where this strange sense of fear was coming from. Or why it was growing. Only moments ago, it appeared to be slight, distant. But right now, his fear had increased in darkness and intensity, and she could see it clearly in his eyes.

"Are you sure you're all right?" She could come up with no logical explanation as to why he feared her, and had no idea how she could find out without asking him. She knew how it would sound for a young woman to ask a man such a question. She didn't sense anything the day before, when she'd first seen him. But right now, the look in his eyes and the sudden paleness of his skin told her this man, for some reason she could not begin to comprehend, was scared to death.

As a precaution, she held up her right hand to cover her cheek—just in case he'd glimpsed her scars.

"My ankle...I don't know how I managed to do it, but..." Just then he stopped talking and began looking around. She wasn't quite sure, but he acted like someone might be watching him.

"But what?" she asked softly.

He continued looking around. She wondered if he'd zoned out. But just when she was about to repeat her question, he said, "Just being clumsy, I guess. Wasn't watching where I was going..."

"Would you like me to call nine-one-one?"

Again, he didn't respond right off. But after another quick scan toward the busy lunch traffic on Colonial, he turned back to her. "No. I'm...okay. I'm fine. Listen...I really need to—"

A slight buzzing sound stopped him cold.

For a moment she thought she might have heard a bee flying around. The traffic whizzing down Colonial made it difficult to hear much of anything. But one thing was certain: the moment she heard it, he'd stiffened sharply, and his head jerked to the left. It was almost as if he'd been tapped with an electric prod.

"Are you *sure* you're okay? I mean really? I could call—"

"No!" He backed away, a little too quickly, nearly losing his balance. "I'm fine. Really." Smiling, he held out his hands as if to ward her off. She couldn't help noticing that his smile was forced.

It made her wonder if he was actually trying to hide his fear. "Thanks…for caring."

"But at least let me take you to—"

"No. I'm okay. Really!"

He darted between the pickup and another parked vehicle, making his way for a light-blue late-model Honda. He scrambled to get in, fired it right up and pulled out like a jackrabbit, zipping down the aisle and then making a sharp left. Squealing rubber, the Honda dashed to the side entrance, which would take him west, back to Colonial, or south, down Maguire.

Confused, Erika watched as the Honda pulled out recklessly into heavy traffic, scurrying down to the light. It immediately made a quick right, which would take him straight to town.

She stood in the same spot, wondering what on earth had just happened. What would make a man act like that?

What had scared him so much?

And what on earth was that weird buzzing sound?

After agonizing over this a while longer, she decided it best to forget about it. The man obviously had major problems. It wasn't up to her to try and figure out what they were.

She turned and walked back to her own car. She hadn't taken more than a few steps when she somehow sensed someone a fair distance away, watching her.

Chapter 7

Considerably unnerved by the Mall incident, Erika pulled up the paved drive of her parents' home just fifteen minutes later. As she got out of the Hyundai and went up the steps leading to the front stoop, she found that she could not get the event out of her mind. No matter how hard she tried to analyze things, it made no sense.

First of all, the episode the day before, which seemed to have started it all, defied every conceivable sort of logic. She thought she understood why the man had stopped to let her pass on the sidewalk. Her first impression, of course, was that he was a gentleman—a sort of person she rarely saw these days. He'd no doubt stopped to let her pass because he didn't want to be rude and step right in front of her. Case closed.

However, she could see no reason why he'd remained standing in the same place until she'd reached the next block.

Had he been so appalled by her appearance that he couldn't function? So disgusted by her scars that his brain had turned to mush?

Or had he actually *liked* her looks?

It wasn't *that* much of a stretch, was it? Before her accident, she'd always considered herself reasonably attractive. She'd been blessed with good hair and even turned quite a few heads with her eyes and smile—and also her long, slender legs. But even so, she'd never rated herself so breathtaking that the mere sight of her would turn the average man into a babbling idiot.

It had to have been the scars that had made him stop stone-cold.

But logic told her that this just couldn't be. For the last two years, she'd been painstakingly diligent about keeping her appearance hidden—her collar pulled up, the sunglasses and cap added for more complete anonymity.

What happened yesterday had to have been caused by something other than her appearance. Something else had obviously taken place. Something strange and frightening.

But the incident at the Mall, as she left the drugstore, had terrified her down to the bone. The man's violent emotions, registering clearly in his eyes and body language, made no sense. What was wrong with him? What were his intentions? Why would he have singled her out?

Did he want to rape her? Mug her? Take her car?

Why would he want her car? He had his own. It was a Honda—just like her old one. And it was parked just one aisle down from where she'd parked the Hyundai.

The message was both clear and terrifying. He was after *her*—*not* her car.

Once again, the horror and total weirdness of the situation caused a jolt of ice to climb up her spine.

She'd made him trip. She had no idea how she'd done it. All she knew was that she'd somehow made it happen. Just one moment after she'd visualized it, it had actually taken place.

Just as she'd imagined. Just as she'd wished.

How was this possible? How in heaven's name could she *wish* such a thing to happen?

Had she caused it? Or was it simply coincidence?

And how in heaven's name was she suddenly able to sense the emotions coming from another person?

The thoughts swept through her, and she wondered once again if she'd imagined the whole thing. For long moments she stood staring at the front door of the house, not seeing it. Her vision immediately clouded over, and she found that she wasn't seeing anything. All she could do was wonder what had happened. If the strange man at the Mall was somehow connected with the monster that had nearly killed her two years ago.

Later, after the shock of the situation had run its course, she blinked herself out of her fog and focused on the front door again. And remembered where she was. And what she was going to do. Then she noticed the diamond-shaped window on the front door. And the front stoop. And the flower garden beneath the living room window Mom had been painstakingly trying to maintain for the last several years. Then her hand. And the keys resting in her palm. And then she realized she'd finally come back to the real world.

Sighing tiredly, she tried to insert the key into the lock. Missed. Tried again. Missed again. Frustrated, she closed her eyes and took in some fresh afternoon air to calm down. *You can do this. It's very simple. Just slide the key into the latch, turn it clockwise, then turn the doorknob.*

She really could do this. She'd done it hundreds of times before, hadn't she? It wasn't complicated at all. And she was very smart. An independent young woman.

She finally managed to unlock the front door. Relieved, she slipped inside, closed the door and stood quite still once again, thinking about what had just happened.

I made a man trip. He was following me. I visualized him tripping, and it actually happened.

I imagined it. It happened. Just like that.

She turned to Dad's pride and joy—the Sanyo widescreen he'd bought last year for Christmas— and thought about turning it on without picking up the remote.

Concentrate. For some strange reason, you can do stuff like this now.

Make believe you want it on. Visualize the History Channel, the Hallmark station...

Nothing.

She closed her eyes and tried again. *On. Turn on. Switch yourself on!*

She waited ten seconds. Fifteen. Twenty. Then she opened her eyes.

The set remained black.

What was going on? Why did something work before and not now?

Was it because she'd been stressed at the Mall? Frightened?

Did stress and fear have everything to do with this strange new power?

Or was this just coincidence after all?

Maybe she hadn't done it at all. Maybe she'd just thought she'd caused it because she'd somehow picked up on it the moment the man tripped.

It was possible, wasn't it?

After another minute or so, she decided to stop agonizing over all this. She was wasting the day worrying about something that no longer mattered. Anyway, it was time to find something to eat. Then head off into her room, log on, and start editing that paper Edwin Porter, the English Lit student at Rollins, had sent her. This was a fairly good gig— twenty-five bucks a page, which resulted in a hundred and fifty bucks. Dad couldn't quibble about something like that, could he? Especially when she gave him half—which had been their agreement since she'd graduated from high school.

She went into the kitchen.

Mom, as usual, had left a scribbled note on the refrigerator door.

Chicken salad sandwiches in the Tupperware on second shelf, sweetie.
Be home @ 4.
Love ya,
Mom

She just wasn't in the mood for chicken salad. Besides, Mom always put too much garlic in with the mayo and the dill relish. Erika found a thick slice of Monterey Jack, a large pickle, a paper towel and a can of Sprite, and headed off to her room.

And hoped she could concentrate on the paper, rather than what she'd imagined happened at Fashion Square Mall.

Chapter 8

Later that afternoon, after Erika had finished her cheese and kosher dill, she suspected once again that someone was watching her.

What was it this time? Just more paranoia to make things slightly messier? Some residual nonsense fueled by what had happened at the Mall?

Or had it something to do with what happened the day before, on the sidewalk?

Whatever it was, she knew she shouldn't just discard any of these suspicions. Since yesterday, these feelings had been growing and had never been wrong.

This told her the obvious.

Someone was watching the house.

"I can't take this anymore," she said aloud. Then, struggling to keep her wits about her, she wondered once again what had happened to mess up her life.

If things kept moving on their present course, she'd soon be ready for the rubber room. She hadn't slept very well the night before and thought she'd actually dreamed of heavenly spirits visiting her just moments before she'd forced herself awake. She'd even dreamed that some familiar voice was talking to her in the darkness, telling her things would turn out okay.

Dreams. Heavenly spirits. Bizarre thoughts. And, as if that weren't enough, a strange man seething with rage following her out of the Mall.

What was going on?

What did she have to do to break the spell of whatever madness had suddenly taken hold of her life?

Her cell phone buzzed, and she cringed as if she'd just been zapped with a cattle prod. Suddenly angry at herself, she grabbed her cell. The ID display said: *MOM*.

Sighing in relief, she waited for her pulse to settle down, then brought the cell to her ear.

"Hi, Mom."

"Hi, sweetie," Mom replied in her usual cheerful voice. "Home right now?"

"Yep."

"Working on something?"

"Yep." She could tell by her mom's tone that she was probably going to be hung up at work again. Mom worked for an insurance company on the second floor of one of the office complexes on Maguire Boulevard. As head transcriptionist, she frequently had to put in an extra hour or two of overtime. Many of the employees were young females, and pregnancies and emergency visits to the hospital happened all the time. And whenever someone didn't call in or had to leave early, Mom or one of her subs had to stay and handle things. Mom enjoyed the overtime, of course, but since Dad demanded that his dinner be ready at precisely six-thirty, Erika had to jump right in and take over.

55

"What's going on?" she asked. "You gonna be late?"

"Maybe just an hour or so. Do your mom a big favor. Take those T-bones out of the freezer and put 'em in on the bread board—would ya please? We've got four hours. Since I just bought 'em yesterday, that should be enough time to get 'em thawed out. Okay?"

"No prob."

"Thanks, sweetie. By the way, how was the chicken salad?"

"I wasn't that hungry, so I just had some cheese and a pickle."

"Ya sure that'll hold ya?"

"Uh-huh. See ya when you come home."

Erika put down her cell and went back to the term paper. The moment she began scouring the first paragraph of the third page to hunt for typos, fragments and misspellings, a strange feeling

(it's the same guy)

brought back her earlier sensation of being watched.

She stopped what she was doing and sat bolt upright. And scanned the room. Then closed her eyes and waited for the fluttering in her limbs to settle down.

A voice in her head?

Was it her own thoughts?

Or was she actually hearing voices?

Wasn't the episode earlier, with her stalker tripping, more than enough to keep her in a state of permanent confusion?

56

Just moments ago, the voice had popped right into her head. It was almost as if someone had slipped into her mind and tried talking to her. She'd initially hoped it was her own voice but realized that she'd been concentrating on something else at the time. And as she thought more about it, she decided that this wasn't much different from her dream the night before.

This left her with the same unsettling conclusion: What she'd heard was something she couldn't explain.

It's the same guy.

What on earth did that mean?

Was this the same guy who'd followed her at the Mall?

Or was this something else?

The same guy… It meant that the man out there right now could be the man she'd encountered at the Mall.

But why?

If someone was actually watching the house, why in heaven's name should she care about this person's motives? Why waste her time wondering who was out there? Why put herself through all sorts of turmoil about all this? She had things to do—a paper to work on, a couple of T-bones to take out of the freezer.

If the voice she'd just heard was right, and the person watching the house was the same man who'd followed her out of the Mall, why should she care who he was? Or why he was following her?

She wondered for a moment if she could be facing someone with limited intelligence.

The facts were painfully clear. For one thing, he was now fully aware that she'd spotted him. They'd actually met and had even spoken to one another. She knew what he looked like, how he was dressed. Even the car he drove.

To make this even worse, he'd hurt himself. Tripped on his own two feet and went sprawling to the pavement. He should consider the experience a very bad omen. A clear sign compelling him to stay away.

But even if he was unable to read the signs, he'd have to be a moron not to realize that there was no reason at all to follow her around. She lived a quiet, solitary life, posed no threat to anyone, and had no enemies. She spent most of her time in her bedroom, working on term papers, listening to music and watching her favorite movies on DVD on the thirty-inch widescreen Mom and Dad had bought her for her last birthday. It was a quiet, predictable, and somewhat boring existence, but it suited her and she'd grown quite fond of it.

She didn't deserve any of this. But if there was actually someone out there watching the house, she had to face the fact that she was the only one who could deal with it. Dialing 911 might not work in this case. What would happen when the cops showed and couldn't find anyone out there? Would she be known from that point on as the girl who cried wolf? Would the police brand her and her parents a family of fruitcakes? People to ignore? To stay away from?

Would she be able to live with something like that?

She had to fix this herself. By herself. For herself.

That was the solution. The only logical one. And she told herself she could do it.

Erika pocketed her cell, logged off, got up and went over to the clothes tree next to her bedroom door. She put on her cap, grabbed her sunglasses from the shelf and shrugged into her lightweight jacket. She left the room and went down the hall, to the living room. Before opening the front door, she made sure the brim of her cap was pushed down, the sunglasses in place, the collar of her jacket pulled up.

The same guy, huh?

Her blood was up, and she didn't care *who* belonged to the voice—if she'd even heard one in the first place. If that really was the same guy out there, she was going to have it out with him, one way or the other. She hated stalkers. They were bullies, and she'd always loathed bullies. She'd learned years ago that she was quite capable of facing a bully, and if she stood up for herself and didn't let the fear take over, she'd never be intimidated.

The horror she'd gone through two years earlier, appalling as it was, had given her a renewed love for her freedom and independence, and she wasn't about to let anyone take it away from her.

Her heart pumped madly as she stepped out into the warm, sunny afternoon. Seeing and sensing nothing, she went down the front steps and stood quite still, listening to the air. This time, she sensed something farther down the block, to her right.

Gathering courage, she marched down the front walk, turned right and continued briskly down the street, until she spotted a glimmering silver Challenger parked along the curb, in the middle of the block. For some reason she couldn't quite comprehend, something about the car kept her full attention. This could possibly be the car in question. And if she was correct, her stalker was sitting in it.

I don't know how I know. I just do.

Fired up with a renewed energy, she kept up her pace. And when she reached the rear of the vehicle, she glimpsed someone in the front seat, behind the wheel. The passenger window was more than halfway down.

Silently she moved closer, then peered inside for a better look.

It was the same man, all right. The same guy she'd nearly bumped into the day before. The same guy who'd followed her from the drugstore at Fashion Square just a few hours ago and tripped following her to her car. He held a pair of binoculars in his hands and was watching her house.

A fresh batch of anger shot up her spine. Without hesitation, she stepped up to the side of the vehicle, bent and, in a loud voice, said, "See anything interesting?"

The binoculars dropped. The man gasped. His eyes bulged. He sat frozen in the seat.

Erika's anger dissolved, turning into cold fear the moment she noticed the gun and silencer on the seat beside him.

Chapter 9

Stunned, Greer remained frozen in his seat, gawking stupidly at the girl staring at him from the sidewalk. As before, her face was concealed behind sunglasses, a baseball cap, and the collar of her jacket. But just then, her jaw dropped, and he realized that she'd just seen the pistol and silencer resting in full view on the seat next to him.

She began backing up.

His pulse hammering, he discovered that he still could not move. He could only watch her as she moved away from the car. The chaos in his head had turned into a dark gray fog. He had no idea what he could do or say. All he could think of was how everything had turned into a nightmare in one split second.

They hadn't accepted his explanation

("I tripped in the parking lot")

of why the Mall incident had ended so badly. All they seemed interested in was that the girl was still alive.

"Since you couldn't handle your earlier instructions," the voice had said less than an hour ago, "we are now forced to rely on your sniper experience. This has to be done within the hour."

His instructions, plainly put, dictated that she had to die. But he knew that he could no more kill this innocent young girl than he could purposely run over a stray dog. His orders left no wiggle room for debate. Even so, for the first time since he'd started working for them, he knew there was no way in hell that he could possibly go through with this.

But the message registered coldly.

He had to go through with it. Otherwise, they'd retaliate immediately. It was bad enough that he'd failed so miserably at the Mall when he'd tripped over his own two feet out in the parking lot. They would not tolerate another mistake.

But just then, after she'd turned and began running away, common sense took over, and he knew what had to be done.

Shaking himself out of his trance, he picked up the gun from the passenger seat. Then, just as he brought it closer to his face and pressed the cold end of the silencer to his right temple, his earpiece buzzed.

"Have you completed your assignment?"

His heart hammering, he forced himself to block them out. And positioned his finger snugly on the trigger. Just a slight pressure was all that would be required. The pistol had a hair trigger. All he had to do to end all this was—

"Why aren't you answering?"

Just a little more pressure, and—

"You've got exactly one second to respond."

Holding his breath, he forced his wet eyes shut *(it's the only thing I can do that makes sense)* and, gritting his teeth, began to increase the pressure of his finger against the tiny crescent of metal that would set him free—

The blackness came immediately.

***

As she ran, Erika snatched her cell out of her pocket, nearly dropping it when her trembling fingers wouldn't cooperate. Using both hands, she somehow managed to keep it in her grasp.

It was difficult getting her thumb to function. She knew she needed to stop running to dial properly, but she didn't want to be too close to the Challenger when she made the call.

Her fear had clicked into overdrive. She knew nothing about firearms but had seen tons of movies and could tell that the long-barreled gun she'd just seen was probably designed for distances. And although she had no idea what the thing's range was, she was reasonably certain that she was much too close right now to give the gunman a problem.

Once she'd reached the end of the street, she stopped running and ducked behind a gray SUV parked along the curb. Terrified that the maniac might start shooting, she pressed the number 9 with her quivering index finger. Then she managed to find the 1, punching it as well.

Just as she was about to hit the 1 a second time to complete the call, she stopped. And, for the next few moments, wondered what in heaven's name she was doing.

Something inside her

(that strange voice again?)

had sent her another message.

Was it a voice? Or just a gut feeling?

Whatever it was, she strongly felt that she shouldn't make the call.

64

What was going on? Why on earth should she feel this way? The man had been *stalking* her, for God's sake. He was sitting in a car just down the block from her parents' home, watching the house through binoculars. And he had a long-barreled gun and silencer lying on the seat beside him.

So why shouldn't I get the police out here?

She had no quick answer. All she knew was that her gut instinct had decided that she shouldn't make the call.

Was there any reason why she shouldn't get the cops out here to arrest him?

What if he needs help?

Once again, her inner senses weren't making the situation simpler.

Of *course* he needed help. It was logical, wasn't it? He was a *maniac*, for God's sake. He'd been stalking her and would have kidnapped her or done something much worse if he hadn't tripped outside the Mall. And now he was sitting in a car down the street, watching the house. And he had a gun. And a silencer.

What sort of maniac is he? she asked herself.

One who needs my help...

That cursed inner voice again.

What if it was wrong? What if her intuition had gone haywire? Why should she endanger her life by walking back to that car just to see if her instinct was right?

Do it...

Why should I?

You'll soon see...

65

Crouched behind the SUV, Erika struggled to decide what she should do. And wondered why she should risk her life trying to help someone who, judging by the obvious, fully intended to murder her.

The cursed inner voice told her she'd soon see...

She'd certainly find out if she went back there. She'd know one way or the other.

But what if she was wrong?

She'd end up dead. And she'd deserve a Darwin Award for doing such a stupid, lamebrained thing.

You won't know until you check it out...

"I'll probably end up with a bullet in my head," she muttered, expecting a reply. But after hearing nothing, she sensed that it might actually be all right if she went back and checked. It was a strong feeling, and very clear as well.

She remained crouched behind the SUV another minute or so, waiting for this latest feeling to vanish, or drift away.

It didn't.

After more intense deliberation, Erika tiptoed down the block. Her cell gripped tightly in her hand, she cautiously approached the Challenger. Her heart thrashed wildly with every step, but she managed to keep her feet steady, making sure she could spin around and haul ass at any given moment.

Twenty feet away. Fifteen.

Ten. Eight. Five.

All the while, her gaze stayed fixed on the rear window, her total attention on movement inside the Challenger.

There was no movement, and her senses did not change.

Three feet from the rear bumper. Then two. Then one.

Her feet stopped moving. Her heart pounded. Her body trembled. The phone had grown warm and moist in her palm.

Silently she crept up to the side window and peered inside.

The man was slumped over in the seat, his eyes closed.

He didn't move.

Chapter 10

A soft voice came out of the blackness.

"Are you awake?"

As comforting as the voice was, he didn't want to answer. He wanted to stay in the darkness. It was nice there. Nice and quiet and warm, with no evil voices sending him places to do bad things.

He thought he was dead at first, that he'd shot himself. After all, he'd taken the gun and put it up to his head. It had a hair trigger, too. Every gun he'd ever used since Iraq was equipped with a hair trigger. It somehow made the process more efficient. Quicker. With no complications. This way, he had much less time to think about what he was doing.

He feared that he remained in the world of the living. The soft, soothing voice had clearly demonstrated that when it had asked if he was awake. It wasn't the same evil voice that, for the last five years, had made him do all this killing. This voice didn't sound evil at all. It was caring. And reassuring. And above all, female.

But if he wasn't dead, how could he explain what happened? Had he entered some temporary plane between life and death? A strange place where the soul is evaluated and then cleansed before being sent to its eternal rest?

Was this Limbo? Purgatory?

Or was he still among the living, slowly coming out of his unconscious state?

His thought processes had finally started coming back together, giving him a better perspective of what had actually happened.

Another blackout, of course. It made the most sense. They'd stopped him from killing himself. They wouldn't tolerate his voiding of his contract with them. They'd simply turned to their technological resources and prevented him from doing anything stupid by switching him off.

"Are you awake?"

That voice again. That same soft, comforting voice.

He wanted to reply but discovered that when he opened his mouth, the only thing he heard was air trickling weakly out of this throat.

But he had to try. To let her know he was still alive. That he could still communicate. And think coherently. And make her understand that he wasn't dead.

"They...won't...let me..." His voice was barely audible. The tremendous effort had exhausted him.

"Don't try to talk," the voice said.

He struggled but couldn't manage a reply. Just another weak dribble of air.

"Can you hear me?"

Taking a deep breath, he managed a slight nod.

"Should I call nine-one-one?"

The image put him in an immediate panic. If he hadn't been immobilized, he most definitely would have forced himself up and out of the car. But since he couldn't even raise his head or open his eyes, he had to lie there helplessly and wait.

But at least he could move his head.

"You don't want me to call nine-one-one?"

It took a superhuman effort to enable him to shake his head. He could move it only an inch or so in each direction.

"Are you gonna be all right?"

Once again, he summoned all his strength and managed a miniscule nod.

"All right, then. I've got to go."

He didn't want her to leave. He didn't want to be alone when they found him here. They'd take him back. He didn't want them to take him back. That's when everything would turn bad again.

"No…pl-please…don't let them…" Exhaustion returned quickly. He could feel the darkness getting heavier.

"Don't try to talk."

He tried desperately to move his hand. To reach out for her. He wanted to touch her, hold onto her. The darkness didn't seem as frightening while she was close. Somehow, things didn't seem quite so bleak.

But his body had turned numb.

If only I could open my eyes…

I need to see her…I really need to—

"Before I go," the voice said softly, "I have to say this. I don't know why you've been following me and I don't care. I want you to stop doing it right this second. I have no idea who you are or what your problem is, but don't you ever come near me or my family again. Understand?"

He tried once again to open his eyes, but whatever they'd done to him was more than he could overcome. Apparently he'd come out of it a little too soon, long before his body was able to recover. Possibly because her voice had disturbed him. He opened his mouth to tell her what was going on. Why he'd been forced to do this. Why he didn't want to do anything to her. And, of course, why he'd tried to prevent all this by killing himself...

Most important of all, he wanted to tell her that this was not his idea. He hadn't wanted to wake up at all. He wanted to be dead so he could not hurt anyone ever again—

A moment later, he thought he'd gathered enough strength to say something. He wanted to tell her he had nothing against her. Other people were responsible for all this. And, most important of all, he never wanted to hurt her in any way.

The next image flashing into his head made him cringe.

The gun.

The moment they walked over to the rental and opened the door, they'd see it.

And his employers would turn this into a final endgame.

Then, just as the panic began taking hold, another heavy blanket of total darkness came out of the vast emptiness of his mind, turning everything black again.

***

Erika slammed the door shut. Before moving away from the Challenger, she gave the man one last glance. He seemed to be sleeping soundly.

"Just remember what I said," she whispered, glaring at the motionless figure. "Don't *ever* come near me or my family again."

Moments later, she heard the distant sound of an approaching vehicle.

Chapter 11

Crouched behind the giant rosebush in her front yard, Erika watched the silent police car, lights flashing, slowing down, and stopping beside the Challenger.

As she watched, she couldn't stop wondering if something was very wrong.

For one thing, she couldn't understand how this had been called in so quickly. How anyone could actually see that the man had collapsed behind the wheel, or noticed a strange car parked along the curb. This was a fairly quiet street. She hadn't seen any passing traffic since she'd approached the Challenger. And she was sure the neighbors couldn't see anything. The houses were just too far from the street.

The more she thought of it, the more she realized how lucky she was that she'd managed to get away before the driver of the squad car saw her.

The rosebush—as well as the trees lining the street—blocked much of her view, but she still had no trouble watching the two blue-clad figures getting out.

She expected them to pull their guns the moment they saw the man slumped behind the wheel. The gun and silencer would be in full view, telling the cops the man was extremely dangerous.

But this just didn't happen. Although the trees along the walk obscured her view, she clearly saw

73

that neither cop had moved quickly, or pulled their weapons.

Something just wasn't right...

Maybe they'd figured that since he was unconscious, he wouldn't pose a threat. They could confiscate the gun and silencer right off, without risking their safety. However, they'd have to open the passenger door to do that. But neither had opened the door.

In this scenario, they'd no doubt cuff him while waiting for the ambulance. Again, this could not be done unless a door was pulled open.

So far, no ambulance had shown up. No backup. Judging by what she could see, both cops stood calmly near the Challenger, talking on their radios. One looked around while the other watched the Challenger.

About a minute later, a plain white van appeared, slowing down and stopping directly behind the squad car. Two men dressed in dark clothing got out.

Keeping close to the rosebush, Erika moved to her right for a better view. The bush was much too thick to afford her a sufficient perspective. She had to move to the far end, nearly exposing herself to the street.

Even so, her new position didn't give her a clear view. The trees obscured much of the activity, but she was able to see one of the men from the van pulling something out of his jacket pocket. A sudden glint reflected from the afternoon sun suggested a badge.

She saw little movement for the next minute or so and wondered if she should sneak down the grassy knoll for a closer look. A palmetto farther down would conceal her.

Her trembling knees convinced her to stay put. She asked herself why she should even care. The man had been *stalking* her, for heaven's sake.

However, the van had shown up, complicating things. She strongly sensed that it would be a ginormous mistake to walk right over and start asking questions.

She suddenly remembered the buzzing sound she'd heard at the Mall. And her heart skipped a beat.

What in heaven's name *was* all this?

She didn't have time to analyze the situation. In the next few minutes, the squad car pulled away and turned off its lights. The other two stayed near the Challenger, watching. Finally, one of them got back in the van. Erika no longer saw the other man.

The Challenger pulled out of its spot and hurried down the street.

The van also began moving.

Then, except for the sounds of seagulls coming from the lake, and the distant traffic roaring down Lake Underhill Road, she heard nothing.

Erika waited another minute or so.

Silence.

Her thoughts raced as she hurried back to the house.

***

Greer awoke in darkness.

75

His thoughts muddled and cloudy, he waited for the nausea to pass before trying to sit up. Things seemed worse this time. The last time he'd blacked out, the nausea took a minute or so to pass. This time it seemed to be taking much longer.

He lay there for several minutes, his eyes closed while waiting for the nausea and the cloudiness in his brain to subside. When he began feeling better, his thoughts cleared and he grunted into a sitting position. Then, after taking a few moments to adjust, he rubbed his eyes. Once they'd cleared, he scanned his surroundings.

He was sitting on the couch in his living room.

And what did he expect? They'd given him another blackout. Just pressed whatever button was required to kick his ass right out of commission. They were experts at this. And when they were satisfied that he was sufficiently harmless, they picked him up and took him back to his private prison. Case closed. Over and out. A minor problem solved.

They knew how to fix problems. They also knew how to fix things quietly, without anyone else knowing what was going on.

And if anyone ever found out what was going on, this problem was fixed as well.

Experts. Cold. Calculating. Lethal.

Slouched on the couch, his elbows resting on his thighs, he gently massaged his temples to coax his brain to start functioning again. The moment his thoughts began to return, the image of the young redhead flashed brightly, and his nausea came right

back. And he knew right then that what he'd done—
or, rather, had *not* done—was not going to end well.

Then, as the panic quickly grew, his earpiece
buzzed.

"Have you recovered?" the voice asked.

The anger returned. He decided to let them wait
for his reply. He was in no hurry to respond to them
anyway. Hell, he didn't want to respond to them at
all.

"Yeah," he said finally. "It took longer this
time."

"We decided to give you some extra time to
think things out."

His hands had become tight, painful fists. He
wanted to visualize the man's neck trapped
helplessly in his hands, but since he had never seen
any of them, envisioning such an image proved
impossible. "Very considerate of you. But it's kind
of difficult to think things out when you're
unconscious."

"Turn on your TV."

"What?"

"Turn it on now. And set it for DVD mode."

He wasn't in the mood for their games. He
needed a drink and wanted to lie down and forget
the last twelve hours. "I'm not exactly in the right
frame of mind to—"

"Do it. That's an order."

His pulse racing, he forced himself to unclench
his fist. Then he picked up the remote and did as
they'd ordered. The image coming from the
widescreen made him shudder.

The picture showed him lying on the ground in prone position beside a parked van, a sniper rifle resting on a bipod in front of him. The camera taking in the shot from six or eight feet behind and a foot or so above him shifted to his right. Seconds later, the next shot moved in closer, showing him aiming the rifle at a middle-aged man with thick white hair walking toward a shopping mall and then suddenly collapsing to the pavement when his head exploded in a horrible splash of red mist.

"Why?" he asked, his teeth clenched. He found it difficult—almost impossible—to turn away from the screen. His eyes just wouldn't cooperate. He switched off the DVD and dropped the remote onto the table in front of him. "Why show me this?"

"To remind you."

"Of what?"

"We'll let you figure it out. We realize you're still slightly off your game due to your recent blackout—"

"I'm thinking pretty clearly right now, thanks very much."

"This is good. Then you won't need much of a—"

"I was once a sniper. I used to kill people. You don't forget shit like that. But that doesn't mean you like it. And I didn't. I hated it. It was a job—nothing else. And when I did it in Iraq, I only did it to keep my buddies—as well as innocent people—from being killed."

"You are still a sniper. This is the reason we hired you. And, just in case you might have forgotten, you have been killing people ever since."

A heavy surge of heat rushed up his spine. It took all the willpower he could find to stay relatively calm. "What does that have to do with—"

"You obviously need a refresher course. This will bring you back."

"Back?"

"Where you need to be. Your place, your standing. What you're capable of. Where your loyalties lie."

"Why must I be reminded of all this when I—"

"Because of what happened just a few hours ago. You have obviously forgotten your place. You need to be reminded of your contract, your debts. You owe us. You know that. You also know what we've afforded you. Because—"

"I get it, dammit."

A pause. "Do you?"

"Any idiot with a braincell or two would."

"Are you absolutely sure? If you're still even the slightest bit hesitant about what is required of you, you should continue watching the DVD. It'll remind you of more than a dozen other assignments that you handled quite well. Extremely well, in fact—"

"As I just said, I don't *need* to be reminded." He glared at the remote. He wanted to snatch it and slam it against the living room wall. But he knew it wouldn't accomplish anything.

79

"If this is the case, then we would enjoy listening to why you bungled that last assignment you were ordered to—"

"I didn't bungle anything!"

"If this were the case, the female you were ordered to eliminate would now be dead."

He didn't reply.

"We would like to hear your explanation of what happened."

He sat back and closed his eyes. They wanted to hear why he'd chosen not to pump a bullet into the skull of an innocent young redhead and then drive away as if nothing had happened. Why he considered it wrong to murder a young girl who, as he saw it, was no threat to anyone. They were so evil and so completely out of touch with reality that they needed to hear such an explanation. They were simply incapable of figuring it out on their own.

"We're waiting."

"Before I say anything, I need to know why this young girl was selected in the first—"

"We don't provide explanations. You've known this from the beginning. We simply give out orders. You follow them and everything will be fine. When you don't do as you're told, we have a problem. You know what will happen the moment we consider you a problem."

"Vividly."

"We're still waiting for your explanation."

He leaned back and stared at the cracked plaster ceiling. He knew how they operated. He also knew that nothing he said would matter to them. But he had to tell them something that would keep them off his back for the time being. They weren't exactly the most patient group in the world.

"I'm sure you realize," the voice said suddenly, "that if you persist in becoming a problem, we will be forced to terminate your contract."

"Somehow, that doesn't seem so damned bad right now." He didn't know why he'd said that; he only knew that he'd meant every word.

"In this case, another asset will be assigned, and we're certain that your replacement will be successful in carrying out the contract."

The reality of it slammed him brutally in the chest. In simple terms, if he didn't eliminate the redhead, they'd turn him off permanently and then assign someone else to take care of her.

"Did you hear what we just said?"

"I'm not deaf, you know."

"Then tell us what we need to know. Why did you deliberately disobey orders and sabotage your last assignment?"

His thoughts looped as he struggled for an explanation. Whatever he said would have to be good. And believable. And logical. Otherwise, they'd press their appropriate buttons and he'd cease to exist. And then they'd proceed with the elimination of the redhead.

He decided to tell them the truth and see where it went from there. "She snuck up on me."

Silence.

A moment later, the voice said, "Go on…"

"That's the extent of it."

"*This* was why you chose to bungle the assignment?"

"As I've already told you, I didn't *bungle* it—"

"She's still alive, is she not?"

He didn't reply. He should have known this would not work.

"A simple explanation of what happened will go a long way in our final judgment of this matter."

"I was watching the house, and the next thing I knew, there she was, standing beside the car, staring at me. Then, just a couple of seconds later, she ran away."

"And why did she do that?"

"I guess I scared her." He didn't want to tell them she'd seen the gun.

"She saw your firearm, did she not?"

He felt his heart sputter. His palms were sweating. "If you'll…if you'll just let me—"

"It was on the seat beside you, was it not?"

"Listen. I—"

"You're a professional killer. You always have your weapon within reach. This is how you work. This is how you've managed to stay alive all these years."

"But—"

"This is why she ran, isn't it? And why you bungled the assignment. She saw the gun, panicked and ran, and you no longer had a clear shot of her."

"Please. Listen to me…" He knew what they were about to do. He also knew that he had to do something—anything—to change their decision.

"We're listening…"

"I can make this right."

"You obviously don't have any idea of the gravity of this situation."

"If you'll just hear me out—"

"This female was marked for elimination the moment she saw you. You have created an extremely difficult and dangerous condition for all of us. She lives with her parents, and we've got to assume that she tells them—"

"You can't possibly know that she told them anything!"

"To act on the side of caution, we have to assume she has. And if so, you have placed not only this agency in jeopardy, but also this female's family."

"No!"

"And to end this the only sensible way possible, we've got to—"

"I know I can make this right." His heart pounded wildly. "I promise I can."

A pause. "And just how could you possibly do that?"

He took a breath and waited for his heart to settle down. He had to think of a way out of this. Otherwise, the girl—as well as her parents—would be eliminated. "I'll do it. I'll get it done. I will. I really will."

"But if she's told her parents—or anyone else, for that matter—"

"She hasn't."

"And how could you possibly know?"

He decided to try a gamble. What did he have to lose? "Check on it yourself. You've got access to everything, don't you? You know her name, her address—everything about her. Check her phone records. If she hasn't made any calls in the last half-hour—"

The earpiece went dead.

It took him considerable effort to stand up. His knees kept buckling. He finally made it, then staggered over to the kitchen, opened the cabinet and grabbed the vodka bottle. He poured two inches into a glass and downed it in one swallow. Then he poured more and tottered back to the couch.

For the next twenty minutes, he sat very still, the empty glass heavy in his hands as he waited for the final blackout to come. Just sat there, hating himself for what he'd let himself become. For what he'd been doing the last five years.

I've got to stop this. I can't let them order me to kill anyone anymore, and I certainly can't murder that girl. She's done nothing. She doesn't deserve this. And if there's any way in hell that I can stop them from hurting her or her family—

His earpiece buzzed.

"We have checked her phone records."

"W-Was I right?" His voice was shaky.

"There was indeed a conversation."

Greer swallowed audibly. His pulse hastened. He could barely get the word out. "And…?"

"Apparently the conversation with her mother did not indicate anything of national concern."

84

"Good. Great." He wanted to celebrate. To actually start breathing again. But something in the man's voice told him this wasn't the right time for celebration. "Then her parents ...they aren't exactly a threat, are they?"

"Your original assignment still stands."

He began trembling again.

"Her parents arrive home in two hours. You have exactly two hours to finish your assignment before they come home. Otherwise, we shall have to make other arrangements."

Click.

His heart raced as he fell back onto the couch.

For the next fifteen minutes, he stared at the dark emptiness of the ceiling and wondered how in heaven's name he was going to make this right.

Chapter 12

Erika found it impossible to concentrate on the paper she'd been paid to work on. Her thoughts kept returning to what had just happened down the street.

It just didn't make any sense.

There were cops at the scene in just minutes. A gun and silencer were visible on the front seat of the Challenger, but the cops didn't seem to care. That is, not enough to open the passenger door, confiscate the firearm and arrest him. Then, just a couple of minutes later, a van showed up, and two slender men dressed in dark clothing got out. And within five minutes, everyone had left the scene.

Weird.

This made her aware of other things that seemed even weirder.

The quiet buzzing sound she'd heard when she'd confronted the man outside the Mall. How he'd immediately turned deathly pale and scrambled into a Honda just moments before tearing out of the area.

Then: that brief flash when one of the men from the van took something out of his pocket and showed it to the cops.

This reminded her of the spy thrillers she'd seen on TV and on DVDs. Good cops. Bad cops. Undercover cops. Confidential Informers. Spies. Traitors. Double-crosses. Terrorists. Bombers.

Other things registered, and her thoughts began spinning wildly.

Badges. Listening devices. Earpieces. Wires. Binoculars.

Long-barreled pistols. Silencers.

James Bond. Jack Bauer. Jason Bourne.

Suddenly nauseous, she sat back in her chair and took a few deep breaths in an effort to calm down. It was important to focus. She just couldn't let her imagination get the best of her. But no matter how hard she struggled to clear her mind, the obvious question remained.

If that guy really is a spy or government agent, why on earth is he interested in me?

She'd never associated herself with subversive types, gangs, or radicals. She'd gone through sixteen years of school without forming any worthwhile friendships. She hadn't trusted or confided in anyone in the last two years. She was a loner and had every reason to be. Why would anyone be even remotely interested in her?

Fighting to push the panic away, she concentrated on keeping her thoughts in check. And soon found that she needed to look at this in some semblance of order.

Then, taking a deep breath, she closed her eyes and forced herself to concentrate.

When exactly did this nightmare begin?

Yesterday. It all started two streets down, when she was taking her afternoon walk. She'd just finished retyping a term paper for a Rollins student and was ready to start on the other one she'd been paid to work on. She'd seen a man about thirty-five years old come out of the house where Ernest Lohman lived. She didn't know Mr. Lohman and recalled seeing him only a couple of times out in his back yard, mowing the grass, or trimming his hedges. However, Dad knew him. Just a few weeks ago, he told her and Mom that Mr. Lohman, who was a developer, was causing problems for some people who wanted to turn a condemned city block south of downtown Orlando into a high-rise. Apparently Mr. Lohman wanted to do something else with the property and was making a lot of important people angry—

Oh my God...

The man she'd nearly bumped into the day before had just come from Mr. Lohman's home. And ever since, this same man had been following her.

Her pulse racing once again, Erika logged out of Word and started researching the most recent articles from the *Sentinel*.

***

Greer slipped through the trees lining the street and snuck up the path that led to the redhead's house. Then, crouching close to the base of a large rosebush bordering the southeast corner of the property, he scanned his surroundings.

No one was about. This was good. He'd been extremely careful when he snuck out of his apartment, flagged down a cab and had the cabby drop him off two blocks away.

We have eyes everywhere.

His body shivered with rage each time the phrase slipped into his head. They'd jammed that same image into his brain dozens of times during the last five years.

We know everything.

That was something else they wanted him to remember. They used it to intimidate him. It was how they got him to do their dirty work. Their evil.

But they were wrong. They didn't know everything. They knew he was a sniper, but what they did *not* know was that a sniper's greatest strength wasn't his weapon. Or his excellent eyesight. Or his gut instinct. Or timing.

A sniper's greatest strength was his anonymity. His ability to hide in plain sight.

That, and his patience.

He'd always prided himself in his talent for becoming invisible. For sneaking somewhere amongst the enemy, setting up, killing the target, then getting out without ever being seen. Sometimes the sneaking-out part would take a few hours. Other times, it could take days—even weeks.

The best sniper knew when to get out. Carlos Hathcock was the best of the best. Ol' White Feather would lie half-submerged in swamp water for days before deciding the perfect moment to get out. The man would go for days, even weeks, lying among the rice patties, deadly poisonous snakes slithering all over him, the Cong stepping on him as they desperately hunted for him.

The best of them knew when to stay and when to get out. That's what made them good. It also helped them survive.

He glanced at his watch. 5:07. Not long at all before the girl's folks arrived home. If he wanted this to happen the way it should, he had to start moving.

He had no idea what he would do when he actually saw her again. All he knew was that he had to tell her what was going on. Why he'd been following her. Then, maybe with her help, he could find some solution for both of them.

He spent the next five minutes watching the street, the houses, the driveways. When he was confident no one was watching, he moved away from the rosebush.

Just then, traffic sounds resonated half a block down the street.

Struggling to stay focused, he squeezed his lean frame back into the rosebush and waited.

It was the rush hour, and he had to wait another five minutes for the next lull. But while he waited, he strongly suspected he was being watched.

Taking a deep breath, he squirmed even further into the rosebush. And waited.

And hoped he was being overly paranoid.

***

Erika had been researching the Net for the last twenty minutes but hadn't come up with anything useful until she clicked on the option that took her to the obituaries. The name instantly caught her eye, and she cringed in her chair.

*Ernest Lohman, 64, local land developer,
dies in freak gun accident.*

The article read:
*"Orlando Police have investigated the death of
the local developer and ruled it accidental,"* Alden
Maylor, Lohman attorney and family spokesman,
said this morning, following a brief investigation.
According to OPD, Lohman was cleaning the
compact automatic weapon in his bedroom when it
accidentally discharged, striking Lohman in the left
eye and killing him instantly.

Doris Oppenheimer-Lohman, Lohman's wife of
39 years, was immediately notified at her place of
employment in downtown Orlando, as were
Lohman's 36-year-old daughter Chris, their 38-
year-old son Ernest, Jr., and Lohman's mother, who
presently resides in the Allen P. Hurst Home of
Assisted Living in Altamonte Springs.

Lohman's widow, as well as both Chris and
Ernest, Jr., were shocked to hear the news. "I didn't
think my father even owned a handgun," Ernest. Jr.,
said. Daughter Chris substantiated her brother's
statement by saying, "My father hated guns. I mean
really hated them. He'd lost a good friend just
before high school graduation when his buddy
tripped over a deadfall while carrying a rifle during
hunting season, and the thing went off, killing him."

A brief investigation was begun to look into the
matter but called off due to budget cuts and lack of
manpower.

Erika sat back and stared suspiciously at the screen. Something was very wrong about the article and also the incident. Something very obvious. Dad had spoken fondly of Mr. Lohman a number of times. Dad said that the man was friendly and very soft-spoken. The type who could never hurt a fly. According to Dad, Mr. Lohman contributed large amounts of money to St. Jude and The Shriners.

"I didn't think my father even owned a handgun."

"My father hated guns."

Yes. Very wrong indeed.

Erika sat back and closed her eyes. Almost immediately, the image of the man leaving Mr. Lohman's house the day before appeared. The same man who'd purposely avoided looking at her. The same man who'd been waiting for her the moment she came out of the drugstore at the Fashion Square Mall.

The same man who'd followed her out of the Mall, into the parking lot.

The same man who, just a couple of hours ago, was watching her house with binoculars. With a long-barreled gun and silencer lying on the seat beside him.

No! This can't be!

She stood up and looked about the room. Suddenly everything in the room seemed strange, unfamiliar. As if she'd never been in here before. Her first thought was that she'd been working too hard. She wondered once again if her imagination had been going haywire. It occurred to her that, instead of looking at things logically, as she should have been doing all along, her thoughts were coming up with things she couldn't possibly grasp.

She suddenly suspected this same man was lurking outside her house.

"I'm going out of my freaking mind." She moved away from her chair and hurried out of the room.

On her way down the hall, this strange feeling grew, and she visualized that the strange man stalking her was now crouched in Mom's rosebush in the front yard, watching the house.

"This is *way* too much. *Way* over the top. These thoughts just aren't real. They can't be. How in heaven's name can I possibly imagine someone out in the front yard, hiding in the bushes?"

She stopped in the kitchen doorway and struggled to clear her mind. Was what she'd just glimpsed in her head actually true? Or was her imagination working overtime? How could she possibly visualize something like that in the first place?

It's true, isn't it? she asked herself.

Yes, her gut instinct told her.

Frightened, she reached into her pocket and grabbed her cell.

Her next visualization told her that the man hiding in the bushes was frightened and needed her help.

Why would he be frightened? Why would he need my help?

She remembered how he'd reacted at the Mall. And how the buzzing sound she'd heard had instantly given him a fit. And how he'd run from her. And scrambled into the Honda. And pulled out of the parking space. And into traffic, like a bat out of hell.

Her gut told her once again that she needed his help.

Erika stood stock-still, her pulse pounding.

What should she do?

Listen to this feeling? Trust her senses? Her gut?

What if I'm wrong?

What if you're not?

Groaning, she pocketed the cell. For the next five minutes she remained in the kitchen doorway, her body stiff, her eyes closed while she struggled to desperately clear her mind.

Then, suddenly, the image came to her in one big, bright blast.

It told her that she had to somehow deal with this right now. She had to find out, once and for all, what was going on with this man.

And this meant leaving the safety and security of the house.

Chapter 13

Greer's pulse raced when he heard a car door slamming shut. Gently nudging a cluster of roses, stems, and long, needle-sharp thorns away from his face, he peered around the bush.

The Hyundai's taillights came on. The engine grunted to life. A moment later, the vehicle slowly began backing down the drive.

He dropped down into a low crouch. Gritting his teeth, he squeezed as much of himself into the center of the rosebush as possible. Thorns and stickers poked and stabbed his flesh.

The Hyundai drew closer.

Fighting to ignore the sharp, tingling pain in his hands, forearms and face, he gingerly turned his head to face the inside of the bush so he couldn't be seen. The vehicle continued creeping dangerously close. Then, just as it was about to pass, it stopped.

Greer froze. His pulse hammered.

The quiet whine of a window rolling down sent shivers down his spine.

"Get in." It sounded like the redhead.

Startled, Greer slowly turned his head toward the Hyundai. And stiffened.

She was sitting behind the wheel. As usual, she wore her baseball cap, dark shades and lightweight jacket with the collar pulled up. Although he couldn't see much of her face, the ends of her mouth were pulled down, suggesting a frown.

"Get in. *Now*."

His thoughts spun wildly. None of this made any sense. He wondered if he'd gone insane.

"C'mon!" She gestured toward the car with a slight jerk of her head.

His thoughts continued to whirl. Totally confused, he hesitated, not wanting to move.

She gazed at him, this time without the frown. "Someone's down the street, watching us. He won't be able to see you if you get in the back, on my side."

Greer still didn't budge. This had become much too bizarre to analyze, or even understand. How did she know someone was watching? Even so, why would she do this? Was this even happening?

"Do it. *Now*!"

Just as he opened his mouth to ask what was going on, she said, "If you wanna get us both killed, stay right there. Don't move. Just stay put and be an even bigger jerk than you were at the Mall."

That was enough to force him to make a decision. Bizarre or not, this was making just enough sense for him to do as she'd just said. He dropped to his knees, crawled over to the Hyundai, reached up, carefully eased open the door, slipped in and pulled the door shut behind him.

The redhead immediately backed down the driveway and put it in gear. Then, heading west, the Hyundai hurried down the street.

***

She drove quickly, changing lanes often and zipping through red and yellow lights. She drove like an automaton, not taking her eyes from the road and not uttering a word.

Lying on his side in the back seat, his heart thrashing, Greer decided it was time to find out what was going on.

He propped himself up on one elbow and watched her closely. Though the shades concealed her eyes, he saw that she focused on the traffic. He suspected that she didn't care much about him and might have even forgotten that he was in the back seat.

Even so, he struggled to imagine what had just happened. And then tried rationalizing it.

She backed down the drive and told me get in the car. She said someone was watching us.

How the hell did she know someone was watching?

How did she know I was hiding in the rosebush?

And why would she care about keeping me safe?

That was what made him most skeptical. Why would she care about him after what he'd done? He'd followed her out of the Mall. He'd frightened her, freaked her out. And then she found him staking out her home.

And she saw the gun and silencer.

That last detail would be more than enough to scare anyone half to death.

Why not this girl?

Why should she even care about him?

Was there someone watching them?

Common sense told him not to sit up and take notice of the traffic around them.

"What the hell *is* all this?" he finally asked. "Why are we—"

"You know what this is all about," she snapped, and he could tell by her tone that she was definitely on the defensive. "So stop the crap and tell *me* what's going on."

Greer almost smiled. This babe was ballsy. She'd shown him compassion at the Mall after his mishap—which told him she was caring and sympathetic, and willing to lend someone a helping hand.

But this was different. This was courage and grit under fire. It made him feel much better for refusing to kill her.

However, her nerve and grit didn't begin to tell him anything else.

"How'd you know?" he asked.

"How'd I know what?"

"That I was hiding in the rosebush. And that deal earlier, when I was parked down the street, the binoculars in my hands and the gun on the seat beside me. And just a few minutes ago, what you said about someone watching me—"

"Someone *was* watching you."

"You *saw* someone out there?"

She paused. "Not exactly…"

"What exactly, then?"

"You first."

"How's that?"

"Start talking."

He hesitated.

She groaned. "Let me help. First, tell me what happened yesterday afternoon. Then that business at the Mall. Then the deal with the binoculars and the gun. Especially the gun. And even *more* especially, the silencer. And, of course, why you were hiding in my mother's rosebush." She turned slightly in his direction. "By the way, you're bleeding."

He suddenly noticed the cool wetness on his left cheek. The thorns from the rosebush, most likely. And there were several stickers he hadn't yet pulled out of his left forearm. "Thanks. I'll be okay. It's not bad, just a few—"

"I didn't mention it because I was worried. I just don't want you bleeding all over my upholstery."

He reached up to wipe his cheek. He could tell she was still watching him in her rearview mirror.

She tossed a small box of Puffs at him.

"Thanks." He grabbed it and used a couple to blot the blood.

"You're welcome. By the way, tell me why you were trying to hide in a rosebush."

"Your front yard didn't give me any other options."

"But…a *rosebush*?"

He shrugged. "Like I said…"

"Stupid, wouldn't you say? I mean, they're sharp, and you could easily lose an eye, or--"

"I get that, believe me."

"Okay, then. Start explaining yourself. Why were you there?"

He pulled himself into a sitting position and blotted the scrape on his jaw. This was going to be tough. Telling her about this would most likely endanger her life even more. But he had no choice. He'd come this far; it would only be a matter of time before they'd zap him with another blackout. This time, they'd know exactly where he and the girl were. But whatever happened, he didn't want them coming after her.

He wanted to keep all this from her but knew that she needed to be told what was going on. And she had to know quickly.

"I have to tell you some things that are not going to make any sense. They're going to scare you, but I want you to hear me out before—"

"Save it."

"What?"

"Someone's following us."

He jerked his head. "How can you be sure?"

"Just take my word for it."

"Really?"

"Positive."

He glanced at the heavy traffic behind them but could make out nothing out of the ordinary. However, he knew from experience how difficult it was to spot a tail in rush hour traffic. "Shit."

"I was gonna say the same thing. Hold on. I'm gonna try losing them."

Chapter 14

Her numb hands fixed firmly to the wheel, Erika weaved around a couple of slow-moving pickups and made a quick right at the intersection, taking her and her passenger north on South Orange Blossom Trail. The Hyundai was handling well so far, but it was no fancy sportscar, and had its limitations.

Even so, she was determined to gain as much distance as possible. Her latest feeling had been growing steadily during the last mile or so, edging her dangerously close to the panic mode, but she forced herself to concentrate on staying close to the heavy traffic while keeping a constant watch for quick turnoffs.

The man in the back seat no longer concerned her. The more he talked, the less she'd felt threatened. She'd been getting the strangest feeling that he might actually be a decent guy. But she still had to find out what was going on. She realized that, at least for right now, she had to concentrate on her driving. And, like it or not, she'd have to wait until they were relatively safe before attempting any further investigation.

After they'd gone two more blocks and the traffic around them had thinned, she gave herself a few moments to settle down and chill. Her nerves had finally stopped quivering. It now seemed like a really good time to ask him a very important question.

"Whoever's after us. Do you have any idea who it is?"

He didn't reply.

Great, she thought, a surge of anger taking over. *Now is not a good time to give me the silent treatment, buddy-boy.*

She decided right then that she'd have to stop being nice and just force the issue.

Gathering both courage and determination, she glanced at her rearview. In the next instant, she nearly lost her grip of the wheel.

Her passenger was lying on his back in the seat. His eyes were closed. He seemed to be out cold.

***

Fighting the panic, Erika pulled off the main stretch and eased the Hyundai into the parking lot of a busy shopping complex. She took the car to the end of the shopping center, where the paved road beyond the athletic shoe store disappeared behind the buildings. Only a dozen or so vehicles were parked in the area. Hopefully, they belonged to employees and wouldn't cause any unwanted distraction.

Erika parked beside a large gray SUV. She got out, opened the rear door and climbed in. Then pulled the door shut behind her and stared at the unconscious figure lying on the seat.

His face revealed no stress or trauma. She felt no darkness, no bad vibes. He was probably somewhere between thirty and thirty-five, with short, chestnut-brown hair and sharp features. She tried to regard him as just a guy with an obvious health problem. But as hard as she tried, she just couldn't get the binoculars, the gun, or the silencer out of her head. And she certainly couldn't forget the fact that this same man had been following her ever since they'd crossed paths on the sidewalk in front of Mr. Lohman's house.

As she gazed at him, she felt no hatred, no resentment. She also discovered that, for some strange reason she could not quite understand, she just couldn't hate him for what she'd caught him doing earlier.

If only she could find out why he was so interested in her... Or how he was connected to Mr. Lohman's strange death...

She had no answers, no theories. All she knew was this man had been following her since yesterday and was watching her folks' home with a pair of binoculars.

But that didn't explain anything. Not really.

Even if it did, it couldn't possibly ease her mind.

And it certainly couldn't explain why he was lying unconscious in her back seat.

Then, even before she realized it, she caught herself staring at his left ear. Something about it had caught her attention. What was it? And why was she suddenly so totally focused on it?

Curious, she bent closer.

There it was, in full view.

A flesh-colored earpiece.

Once again, her spy theory stampeded into her thoughts.

Had this been the source of the buzzing sound she'd heard at the Mall?

If so, what was it hooked up to?

Although she couldn't explain her sudden impulse, she felt an urgent need to pull it out.

Without hesitation, she reached down and, pressing the nail of her index finger delicately to its smooth surface, applied her thumb to the curved edge and carefully removed it.

She studied it closely. It was obviously some sort of listening device.

But it didn't explain why this man was wearing it.

After considerable thought, she found that she could come up with only two conclusions. The first, of course, was that whatever this man had been doing involved her family. And that whatever it was, it didn't make her feel any better.

But before she made any decision, she had to find out for sure. It was imperative to question the man. And this required waking him up.

Her limbs trembling, she reached out and delicately nudged his right shoulder. "Anyone in there?"

No response.

She nudged him again, this time harder.

"Wake up. Please?"

Still nothing.

She was just about to nudge him again when the earpiece buzzed.

104

Startled, she held her arm straight out—as if some sort of disgusting insect had been crawling around in her palm.

Her heart skipped a beat. Her limbs had become stiff. She couldn't move, could hardly breathe.

She had to do something. She couldn't just sit here like this, her arm held out like an idiot.

But what could she do? Toss the stupid thing? Flick it out the window and drive away? Stomp on it? Wedge it under one of the tires and crush it?

And what should she do with this man? Drag him out of the car and leave him lying on the pavement?

Heavens... She could *never* do something like that.

What *could* she do, then? Take him to the nearest hospital? Drop him off and tell the authorities she just found him lying on the sidewalk? How could she possibly live with herself if—

In the next moment, her thoughts were suddenly interrupted.

Her passenger began squirming.

***

Fighting the waves of warm dizziness, Greer opened his eyes.

The redhead was sitting on the edge of the seat, her left arm held out.

He was about to assess his situation when her right arm suddenly mashed firmly against his lips. He caught a faint whiff of vanilla—either from her hair or from her skin. Although the effect was

105

extremely pleasant, he reminded himself that he had to concentrate on more important matters. She shook her head and pulled her hand away. Then brought her left hand closer.

He gasped.

His earpiece. And it was buzzing quietly.

This was not good. Not good at all. They knew it was time for him to wake up. They always knew how long to wait before contacting him again. This last blackout was to teach him a lesson, remind him of what he was up against.

But something about all this didn't make sense. How in hell did she find it? The buzzing was always slight, designed this way so no one else would hear it. It had the same effect as a cell phone placed on vibrate. How could she have even noticed it? And, most important of all, how could she possibly know that the buzzing was a bad thing?

Although the large-framed shades concealed her eyes, he could tell by her body language that she was frightened. And she should be. After all, he'd been following her. But somehow, the tables had been reversed. He'd become careless, and she'd caught him. She'd also caught him before, in his car. But instead of having him arrested, as anyone else would have done, she seemed to be *helping* him.

This told him there was something extremely special about this young lady. And as a result, he had to keep her safe at all costs.

The earpiece continued buzzing. He motioned to her to give it to him. She hesitated but eventually complied, dropping it into his palm. Once again, he caught that same faint vanilla scent.

He sat up and pushed it firmly into his ear. "Yeah?"

"Are you fit to understand what has happened?"

He took a breath. Watching her closely, he said, "Yeah."

"Where are you?"

"I'm...not sure."

"You're not sure?"

He forced himself to ignore his growing anger. "I only just woke up. I haven't had much of a chance to explore my surroundings. You put me out again—or did you forget?"

A five-second pause. "And you have no idea where you are?"

"That's what I just said. Are you telling me you don't know where I am, either?"

Another brief pause. "Where's the girl?"

"I have no idea."

"You were spotted getting in her car."

His anger flared once again, this time more urgently. The redhead had been right. They were indeed within range, watching everything. He knew right then that he had to be extremely careful what he told them.

"She's not in the car right now. She might have gone into one of the stores across the street. I see several of them. There's a supermarket, a tee shirt shop, pizza place..." He winked at her. "There's

107

even a Subway a ways down, on the other side of the—"

"You're telling us you think the redhead is *shopping*?"

"I didn't say that at all. I'm telling you I have no idea where she is."

"Why are you in her car?"

"I haven't spoken to her yet. The blackout—remember?"

"It makes no sense to us why you are in her car."

He knew this would be tricky, so he decided to make it convincing. "I snuck into the car when she stopped in her driveway. She'd apparently dropped something, and when I saw her bent forward, I took a chance and jumped right in."

"You got in at gunpoint?"

"How else?"

Silence.

"I might have been able to do the job, but since you turned me off..."

A pause. "Did she take your gun?"

"Well, I don't see it anywhere. You did turn me off, did you not? And when I'm turned off, I kinda lose all control and perception."

More silence.

Still not moving, she watched him closely. Even with her sunglasses covering her eyes, he could tell her focus hadn't shifted.

After another pause, the voice said, "You can still end this assignment favorably for us."

"I know."

"You know what that means, of course."

"Of course."

"What is your plan?"

"Well, to tell you the truth, my head's still fuzzy. It always is after you turn me off. Otherwise—"

"We don't need to know the particulars. Just the working plan."

"Well, if she brings in the cops, I'll have to get away. If she comes back alone, I might be able to do the deed. I'll play possum until the time is right." He watched her closely, nodding slightly. To his amazement, she nodded back.

"We prefer you finish this before she gets onto a main highway. The least amount of people there are to become material witnesses, the better."

"I'll do it before we leave the parking lot."

"That sounds satisfactory."

"I'm really pleased and happy you agree."

As always, his attempt at sarcasm was ignored. "As usual, we'll need to know the moment the assignment has been carried out."

"I'd like to know if the girl's parents will remain unharmed."

"You know that we do not answer direct questions—"

"In this one particular case, I'd really like to know."

"And why would you have to know this?"

"There's a limit to certain things even a killer like me will accept. I won't do anything to her if

I'm not one hundred percent certain that her parents are safe and will remain unharmed."

Silence.

He sat back and waited. The redhead continued watching him. She did not move or even flinch. He could feel the terror coming from her. He wanted to reassure her but didn't know how to do it without giving them away.

About a minute later, the voice came back.

"No harm will come to the parents."

"You're telling me her parents will be safe? That they don't have to die? That they don't pose any sort of threat to you or—"

"I've just told you—"

"Then it's official?"

"Apparently the mother contacted the daughter. The supplied conversation suggests that there was no discussion of what has happened. In other words, they're not considered a threat."

"So then, no harm will come to them? None at all? At least, in this lifetime?"

"You are beginning to sound juvenile. We have made our decision. The girl's parents' lives are no longer a threat."

Click.

He took a deep breath and rubbed his eyes. When his vision cleared, he noticed that she still hadn't budged.

He removed the earpiece and clutched it in his hand. "Do you happen to have a washrag or anything like it?" he whispered.

110

She reached between the seats and opened the console. She removed a white washrag and handed it to him. He opened it, dropped the earpiece in it, and wrapped it into a tight ball. He held it in his fist. "Just in case they want to hear us."

"Don't they have to buzz you first?" she asked softly.

"I'm not sure. Needless to say, I don't want to take any chances."

She nodded.

"Your parents are no longer in any danger."

"Really?"

"Really."

"Whoever you were talking to... I take it you can't trust them at all, can you?"

"I never have, never will. But they are one hundred percent professional, and if they don't consider someone a threat, they'll find no logical reason to eliminate them. It's not that they're a virtuous bunch. They just don't like wasting time on people they don't consider threats."

She seemed to relax a little. Then she straightened. "Okay, then. Since we're alone right now and can obviously talk freely, if you don't mind too much, you can start telling me what this crap is all about."

Chapter 15

Erika left the parking lot and headed north on 441, until they approached another large group of vehicles waiting at the next light.

Her passenger sat beside her, staring straight ahead. She no longer felt any hatred or fear for him. She found that, for some strange reason, she was actually beginning to like him. Despite the dark nature of their past encounters, she sensed that he was an okay guy. Judging from what she'd heard him say in the back seat, she could tell that he was working for a group of horrible people who had been making him do dreadful things. Despite that, he seemed genuinely concerned for her safety and also for the safety of her parents.

But no matter how she felt, she had to get to the bottom of all this. Her gut told her that, if she wanted answers, she'd have to stop worrying about being nice. Although this man had managed to keep her parents out of this, it really didn't matter. She had the sinking feeling that she was somehow involved in something awful.

"So where are we going?" She was surprised that her voice was still working. "And why haven't you told me what this is all about?"

"I need to think."

"Just what *is* all this scary crap? You gonna tell me, or what?"

"I just have to figure out how."

"But you haven't lied to me, have you? I mean, my parents really *are* safe?"

"Yes."

"From who?"

He sighed.

She could tell he was uncomfortable. But this had to be done.

"The people who control me," he finally said.

"Control you? How?"

"It's a long story."

"Well, in case you haven't already noticed, I'm right here, listening to you. I have to be. I'm driving, and you're sitting right there, beside me. I can't go anywhere without you. At least, not now."

He didn't reply.

She wasn't in the mood for silence. Not at this point. "All right, then. My parents are safe. That leaves me with one obvious question." She took a breath. "What about me?"

"What about you?"

"Am I safe, too?"

He didn't reply. This told her she really did have reason to worry. It wasn't just his silence that frightened her; it was the image she'd just glimpsed in her head that told her she could be in serious jeopardy.

"Does this have anything to do with yesterday, when I nearly bumped into you on the sidewalk down the street from my house?"

He seemed to flinch. But said nothing.

"It does, doesn't it?"

After a short silence, he said, "Possibly."

"You're not sure?"

"I'm never sure about anything anymore."

"That guy talking to you in your earpiece. He doesn't tell you anything?"

"Not much."

"What *does* he tell you?"

"Where to go. When to be there. What to do when I'm there. When to disappear."

"That's it?"

"In a nutshell."

This sounded even more frightening. "Just who *is* this guy?"

"I...don't know."

"I don't understand."

"And you think I do?"

"Are you trying to tell me that guy's been keeping you in the dark all this time?"

"Now you've got it."

She stopped at the next light. This was beginning to sound like one of those spy flicks you couldn't possibly figure out because you never knew who the good guy was—or if there was even a good guy in the first place—until the very end.

He rubbed his temples. He seemed very tired. In spite of her confusion and the fear building up inside her, she began feeling sorry for him.

He looked down at his lap. "I was stationed in Iraq about six years ago. After a couple of really bad firefights, I was pretty banged up and goofy in the head, so they sent me to one of their hospitals in Germany to recover. And while I was there—"

114

"You were approached by someone in Military Intelligence?"

"H-How'd you know?"

She shrugged. "By watching tons of thrillers, undercover cop shows and spy movies." In normal circumstances, talking about this would have sounded ridiculous. But not so much right now. "Who approached you?"

"Army Intelligence."

"Did he tell you his name?"

"These guys never seem to have actual *names*."

"How about who he was working for?"

"They never tell you anything. They do their level best to sound vague—very cryptic—just in case you don't go for their shtick and tell them to bug off. They don't want to waste their time and energy worrying about you giving away any of their secrets. Otherwise, they'd have to kill you and anyone else you might have come in contact with."

"Is this anything like Black Ops?"

He sighed tiredly. "I guess just about everyone knows about Black Ops these days."

"Like I said before, spy thrillers, undercover cop shows..."

He nodded.

As she drove in the heavy traffic, she forced herself to stay focused. The panic threatened to take over again. So far, this man had managed to keep Mom and Dad out of this. She sincerely hoped he could keep her out of it as well. She was convinced that he was not going to hurt her. Although that made her feel a little better, she realized that it

115

might not be the end of her problems. If what he'd just told her turned out to be the truth, whoever he was working for would probably resort to other measures to have her eliminated. For some reason she just could not understand, these people considered her a threat.

"What's your name?" She suddenly realized that getting to know him better might make things slightly less frightening.

"You really don't need to know my—"

"I don't like talking to someone who won't tell me his name."

"It's less dangerous if you don't—"

"*Please* tell me…"

He said nothing.

"*Please*?"

"Oh, all right. It's Greer."

"Greer what?"

"That's my last name."

"You have a first one, don't you?"

"Justin."

"Your name is Justin Greer?"

"Yeah."

She wanted to smile. It was a nice, quiet name. It seemed to fit him. "Any of your friends call you Justin?"

"I don't have any friends."

Once again, she found herself feeling sorry for him. He was really a nice, likeable guy. It was a shame what these people had done to him. "If you did have friends, would they call you Justin?"

He shrugged. "It's been a long time…"

116

"Okay, then. Justin…"

After a short silence, he said, "What about you?"

"What about me?"

"You've got a name, too, right?"

She blinked. Was he serious? She'd been marked for elimination, and those monsters hadn't even told him her name? "You don't know my name?"

"Nope…"

"They really *don't* tell you anything—do they?"

He just shrugged.

"Erika Young."

He was quiet for a moment. Then: "That's a pretty name."

Slightly embarrassed, she turned back to watch the traffic ahead. It had been a very long time since anyone had used the word "pretty" when talking about her.

"Tell me something," he said.

"What's that?"

"What do you look like?"

Her heart sputtered. Luckily, the traffic had increased, and she was forced to focus on it. "Traffic's kinda heavy," she muttered.

"Why won't you tell me? Or just show me?"

"What's that?"

"Under that cap. And behind those shades. And that collar. I have no idea what you look like. It's just like you asking me my name—"

"I'm kinda…introverted," she said with some difficulty.

"You're awfully young for that."

"I've been that way for…well, all my life." She decided that now would be a good time to change the subject. "Maybe…maybe you can tell *me* something."

"I'll try."

"Why were you unconscious?"

Silence.

"You can tell me, you know. Like it or not, we're in this thing—whatever this thing is— together."

After another short pause, he said, "They made me that way."

"That little guy in your earpiece?"

He looked down at his lap, where he kept the washrag. "No one else would have the power."

This made no sense. She knew right then that if she wanted to find out what was going on, this unconscious thingy could be a major key to whatever this was. "How'd they do it?"

"Apparently they did stuff to me while I was in that hospital in Germany."

"What sort of stuff?"

He went silent.

By the sudden tension in the car, she sensed that he'd gone back to a very dark, cold, frightening place, one that had turned him into the neurotic mess he'd become. She hated to take him back there, but they had important issues to address. And she had to know what they were facing. "*Please* tell me. I have a right to know."

"Yeah. You do."

"Then tell me."

He hesitated.

She was beginning to get angry. After all, he'd pulled her into this. It obviously wasn't his fault, but he'd done it, nonetheless. The least he could do was tell her what this thing was.

Once again, he remained silent.

"You yanked me into this." It was time to let her anger take over. "Yesterday afternoon, I was walking down the street, minding my own business. I needed some fresh air. I'd been working on something for two solid hours and my eyes were clouding over. I couldn't even see the screen. I left the house and took my usual walk to clear my head and also to pump some fresh air into my lungs."

She gave him a quick glare. "Guess what happened next. Oh, that's right, you know all about it. You know because you were right there. In fact, if you hadn't stopped when you did, we would've bumped into one another. But we didn't. We didn't because you stopped just two feet short and let me go on ahead. I thought you were being a gentleman. But I was wrong, wasn't I? You actually stopped because you didn't want me to talk to you. That ass crawling around in your earpiece—the one who's been making you do all these awful things—he wouldn't want you talking to me. He'd find out, and that's why he'd want you to kill me, isn't it? You'd

119

have to kill me because I saw you coming out of Mr. Lohman's house. Isn't that right?"

***

Greer couldn't speak. He suspected that if he said anything, she'd know he was lying. He had the strangest feeling that it was impossible to lie to this girl. He believed she could somehow tell what came out of his mouth was the truth or a big fat lie. He feared that she might be one of those rare people who could look into someone's eyes and actually see what was going on inside.

But he *couldn't* tell her the truth. He *couldn't* tell her that his handlers wanted her dead simply because she'd seen him at the wrong time. To them, this meant that she'd figured out what was going on. Their plan would be in jeopardy. Their agenda would be disrupted. This could not be tolerated. Their plan could not be compromised. They needed to be able to work their evil without having to worry about any surprises or disasters. And to accomplish this, they wanted her dead.

But this time, they wouldn't get their wish. He was going to make sure she was safe. He was determined that she would be able to live the rest of her life without any further threats from them. He had no idea how he could do this, but he intended to make it happen. If it was the last thing he ever did.

"Well?" she asked. "Am I right or what?"

"You're actually wrong."

"Really? Seriously? Those bastards you work for don't want me dead?"

"I didn't say that…"

120

"Then you're saying they *do* want me dead?"

"More or less."

"I…don't understand. Are you supposed to kill me or what?"

"It doesn't matter."

"I still don't understand. Please help me out here, okay? I know I'm young and inexperienced and all, but I'm not stupid. And I can usually tell right off when something doesn't make any sense."

"In a nutshell, you're right. I *am* supposed to kill you."

"Then what are you talking about? Why did you just say—"

"I said, I'm *not* going to kill you."

He could tell by how she gripped the wheel that she was having trouble digesting all this. "I guess you're gonna have to tell me what's going on." Her voice had grown soft and unsteady. "I mean, tell me so…so I can understand."

"You know exactly what's going on. It's really very simple. My handlers want you dead."

"But why? What have I done?"

"You already know. You knew when you asked about your neighbor."

"They want me dead because—"

"They want you dead because you saw me coming out of the man's house."

"I didn't really see you coming out of his house. I just saw you walking down the—"

"It doesn't matter. Not to them. You were too close. You might have seen me come out. To them, that's more than enough to get their sphincters puckering."

"Whoever these people are, they're—"

"They're vicious. Yes. I know."

"And you can't tell me who they are?"

"All I know about them is that they're very highly connected, and their resources are limitless."

"This is really scary, ya know."

"Yeah. I know."

"How are you supposed to...how do they want you to...to do it?"

"Quietly."

"So no one else can see...or know...what you've done?"

"I don't want you thinking about that. I've already told you. This time, they're not going to get their wish."

She didn't reply. She seemed to be concentrating on her driving. But he could tell she was confused. And very frightened.

"You heard me. I mean it. I wouldn't say something like that if it wasn't true."

She slowed and stopped at the next red light. While three teens sharing a joint shuffled awkwardly across the street, she turned and looked him squarely in the face. "I heard you. I just don't understand what you're saying."

"Just slip this important tidbit into your head and keep it there. I'm not going to kill you."

"But if...if they want you to—"

"As I've already said, it doesn't matter what they want."

"What are you telling me, Justin? Are you trying to say that if you don't kill me, I'm gonna be safe? These powerful jerks who want me dead will just forget about me and move on?"

"I'm not going to kill you. And they're not going to send anyone else to kill you, either."

"But if...if they're as powerful and as well-connected as you just told me, how can you possibly get away with this?"

He sat back and stared at the traffic in front of them. He knew what he'd told her. He also knew what he'd just promised himself.

A minute later, she broke the silence. "You don't know, do you?"

He didn't reply.

"Justin?"

He took in a breath and suddenly felt smaller. "Well, actually...no."

"Then how can you promise me something like that?"

He stared at the glove box and wondered what he could possibly tell her.

"Justin, I know that you really believe what you're telling me. I just don't know how you're gonna do this. That is, without making them come after you."

He turned and stared at her, trying desperately to penetrate the dark shades. He imagined that her eyes were large and deep-blue and probably also soft and warm. He couldn't possibly imagine them closed forever. If that ever happened, he would never be able to live with himself.

He thought of the guys he'd gone back for during his stint in Iraq. The guys he'd risked his life for before being captured when the chopper was shot down. The guys he could never leave behind. Or forget.

Erika wasn't a guy. Nor was she a comrade. She was a sweet, innocent young victim who didn't deserve the hand she'd been dealt, and he promised himself that no matter what, she would not suffer for something he did.

"You can take this to the bank. I've never made a promise I couldn't keep. I'm just not made that way. I don't care who they are, who they know, or how much money they have. They're not going to get to you. Understand?"

Chapter 16

Just a few minutes later, Justin asked Erika to pull into the 7-Eleven at the corner of the hectic four-way intersection. "We need to fill up the tank and find something to eat."

Erika turned off and coaxed the car up to a vacant pump.

Justin opened the door. His expression was dark. "Call your folks."

She couldn't help sensing the darkness filling his spirit. Just moments ago, he'd given her some idea of what he thought they were facing. She could clearly tell that he was truly worried, and that she should comply with his wishes. "Okay..."

"Do it right now. Please?"

"No problem." She watched him as he pushed the door shut and went over to the pump. She pulled out her cell. It buzzed twice and was picked up. "Baby?" It was Mom.

"Hi, Mom."

"What's up? And where are ya? It's almost suppertime." She sounded worried.

"Something's come up." It was difficult to keep quiet about what was going on, but she knew she had no choice. Mom wasn't the most collected person on earth. Besides, Erika didn't think her mom would believe what she told her about this mess. "I'm afraid I'm not gonna be there."

"What's wrong, baby? Where are ya?"

She strongly sensed that she shouldn't give her mother any details. She had a feeling Justin's handlers had the capability of tapping into their phone. "I'm...with a friend."

A pause. "Really? Someone from Rollins?"

"No..."

"UCF?"

"Not exactly..." Erika knew what was coming next.

"One of your old girlfriends?"

"No..."

"A man?"

"Well..."

Her mother took in a breath. "Baby, why didn't you tell me you were seeing—"

"It's not like that, Mom."

"What's going on, dear? Are you in any trouble?"

"I'm involved in something complicated...right now." She didn't want them to worry. "I'll tell you all about it when I get home."

"When will that be, dear?"

"I won't be too late."

"Well, you *are* over twenty-one now, so we can't very well treat you like you're still in high school, can we?"

"I appreciate that, Mom."

"You've proven yourself a responsible adult. This means a lot—to both me and your dad."

"Thanks."

"This friend of yours, baby... Can't you tell me even a teensy bit about him?"

126

"I'll tell you all about him when I get home, okay?"

"This sounds, well, mysterious. But if that's the way you want it..."

"I really do."

"Well, you know we trust you, so whatever you wanna do is okay with us. But promise me you'll call us if you need us. For anything."

"Thanks, Mom. Like I said, I won't be that late."

"By the way...did ya hear what happened down the street yesterday afternoon?"

Her heart skipped a beat. "What happened?"

"You remember Mr. Lohman, don'tcha, dear? That older gentleman your father knows? Lives two streets down?"

Erika felt herself go tense. She knew right then that she needed to be very careful about what she said. "I remember him. He's a nice man, and he always smiled at me whenever I—"

"He's dead, baby."

She remained silent, thinking about what Justin had told her about his handlers. How vicious they were. And powerful. And highly-connected. And how they'd wanted to eliminate her parents.

"Did ya hear me, baby? Mr. Lohman—"

"That's just awful, Mom..." She waited for her heart to settle down before she spoke again. "What...what happened? Did he have...a heart attack or something? He was kind of overweight—"

"It was horrible, baby. He was cleaning his handgun and it accidentally went off. Killed him instantly."

"My God... That's *so* sad... He seemed like such a very nice man."

"Your dad's broken up over it. He and Mr. Lohman would get together occasionally in town and have lunch at that seafood restaurant on Church Street."

Her heart hammered. "That really is very, very sad."

"One thing I'll never understand, though."

"What's that?"

"Your dad said Mr. Lohman hated guns and once told him that he'd never have one in the house. Your dad never told him about that .357 he brought back from Saudi. He thought Mr. Lohman wouldn't want to spend time with him anymore. The man was definitely against having guns in the house. He was afraid one of his kids would find it and accidentally shoot someone."

"His kids are grown now, aren't they?"

"That's a fact. But it's still kinda strange— don't ya think? A man who hated guns? Accidentally killing himself while he was cleaning one?"

"That *is* strange, Mom."

Justin got back in the car just a minute or so after Erika had hung up.

"Everything okay?" he asked.

"Fine."

"Who'd you talk to?"

"My mom."

"And she sounded all right?"

"Just like always."

"You're sure?"

"I'm sure." She stared at the steering wheel. "Justin—"

"Yes?"

"Mom and Dad...they heard what happened to Mr. Lohman."

He didn't reply.

She turned and looked him right in the eye. And hoped he'd tell her the truth. "*You*...didn't kill him, did you? When you were leaving his house? You didn't...you weren't the one who--"

"I didn't kill him."

"Then why were you coming out of his house?"

"I was sent there to set things up."

She thought about that for a moment. The images popping up in her head made her nauseous. "You *staged* it?"

His slight nod told her the worst.

Her nausea grew.

"Erika—"

"Justin...how in heaven's name do you intend to keep me safe?"

"As I told you before, I have no idea."

More images filled her head. She closed her eyes and sat back, waiting for the nausea to go away. In just moments, the images darkened into nothingness and she began feeling slightly better. Perhaps it was Justin. Or the fact that he sounded so confident.

Or maybe it was the strong sense of relief she felt radiating from him. Whatever it was, she realized that if there was a way out of this, the two of them would find it.

"You believe me, don't you?" he asked. "That I'll keep you safe?"

"Yes. I do. I really do."

"I mean every word of it."

"I know you do."

He sat back in his seat. She could feel the darkness —and the tension—leaving him.

***

Just a few minutes later, they pulled up to a takeout window on the Trail and ordered cheeseburgers, fries, a vanilla shake for Erika, and a small black coffee for Greer.

He was relieved that Erika had been able to speak to her parents. And that everything, at least for now, was moving along fairly well. And, of course, that her folks were still alive and unharmed.

But just when he thought things might not be so bad, something came to him that he could not possibly ignore.

He couldn't stop wondering how he could keep professional killers away from Erika.

Despite his efforts, he found himself obsessing over this. He was still agonizing over it when Erika pulled the bags of food and drink from the skinny young guy at the takeout window and handed them over.

"You okay?" She was watching him closely.

130

He knew then that he'd been right about her—that keeping anything from her would be impossible. Forcing out a weak smile, he took the bags and placed them on the console between them.

"Just thinking," he told her.

She edged the Hyundai forward and began looking for a parking spot near the end of the busy lot facing the eatery. "This have anything to do with what we were talking about earlier?"

He didn't want to worry her, so he decided to be vague. "As I said, I'm just thinking."

She pulled into a vacant spot a few yards away from the side entrance of the building, put the Hyundai into park and killed the engine. She took the vanilla shake from him and shoved a straw into the hole in the plastic lid. "You're not a very good liar, you know." She sucked in some of the thick, cold liquid and let out a deep sigh.

He wanted to scold himself for thinking that he could downplay this. "I never have been." He pulled the burgers and fries out of the bag. "They say honest people are lousy liars. I don't know if I'm so honest, but I've always been a pretty piss-poor liar. If my parents were still alive, they'd tell you." He opened one of the warm wrappers.

"Oh, you're honest, all right." She slit open a ketchup pack and smeared it on her fries. Her eyes stayed on him as she picked up a fry and put it into her mouth. "I can tell."

He could tell she meant what she said. But it bothered him that she could read him so easily. "How?"

"I can just tell."

"You seem able to tell about a lot."

She nodded and sipped more of her shake.

"How?"

"Wish I knew."

He started to say something else, but she suddenly froze in her seat, and the parts of her face he could see beneath the shades turned pale. She held her shake in one hand, a ketchup-smeared fry in the other. She did not move.

"What's wrong?"

She didn't speak.

"Erika?"

No response.

He put down his burger and gently touched her hand. "What's going on?"

She shook herself, turned her head to the right, then her left. Then gazed at the rearview mirror.

"Erika?"

She dropped her fry into the paper wrap. "W-We…need to leave."

"Why?"

"Someone knows where we are."

"What? I mean, are you sure?"

"Positive."

"Any idea how much time we've got?"

"We need to go. *Now*." She jammed her shake into the dash cup holder and fired up the ignition.

Chapter 17

Erika had no idea where this latest premonition had come from. She only knew that the sensation had registered suddenly, causing an explosion of panic deep in her gut.

While Justin rewrapped and shoved their uneaten food back into their bags, she backed out of their space and hurried out of the lot. Heading north, she gained some advantage by sneaking through the yellow light half a block straight ahead. They reached the next intersection just as quickly, zipping through the moment the light turned red. However, their edge quickly evaporated halfway down the next stretch, as they approached three solid lanes of traffic slowing down at the red light.

"We were doing so well," she said softly, the fear coming right back, settling coldly at the base of her neck.

Justin didn't reply.

Behind them, traffic had slowed to a stop. Using her rearview, she watched the shiny gray Lexus creeping up behind them and tried hard to see into the front of the cab. Its visors were lowered, and with her sunglasses, she had limited view. But since she couldn't sense imminent danger, she decided they were still relatively safe.

"If I can just slip through the next light, we might be able to gain some distance..." She glanced at him. And cringed.

Justin had slumped forward in the seat, his chin resting on his chest. His eyes were closed. The seat harness kept him from collapsing into the dash.

***

The light changed.

Fighting the panic, Erika followed the metallic mess clogging the highway and hurried to the next turnoff. Ignoring the angry protests of blaring horns, she made a hairpin left in front of the three lanes of quick-moving traffic.

As she kept the Hyundai pointed west, she zipped through the next two traffic lights while keeping a close watch on her unconscious passenger. Halfway down the next block, she pulled into the deserted parking lot of a Protestant Church. Then, taking the Hyundai to the far end of the large block building, she slipped around the corner.

Her nerves snapped erratically as she brought the car to a quick stop in front of the recreation building on the other side of the church. Then, for the next ten minutes, she desperately tried to wake Justin. Her pulse raced as she slapped him smartly on both cheeks. No response. Holding in the rising panic, she swatted him again. Still nothing.

Growing frantic, she massaged his wrists—first gently, then much more vigorously. When these efforts failed, she grabbed his palms and slapped them sharply.

No response.

Desperate, she grabbed his left hand and pulled it toward her. It occurred to her that if she bit his fingers, he might respond. But the moment she brought his hand closer to her mouth, she sensed something emanating from his forearm.

It appeared to be some sort of tiny green glow.

It was coming from an area about halfway between his wrist and elbow, and looked like a tiny white crescent-shaped scar.

Just then, the phrase

(tracking device)

entered her mind.

Could it be true? Could she actually be *feeling* this weird image radiating from him?

She recalled the many similar instances that had happened during the last twenty-four hours. Feelings. Emotions. Sensations. Not to mention that frightening moment at the Mall, when she'd caused this man to trip merely by visualizing it.

The fact that she could somehow sense feelings and emotions—as well as visualize certain things—didn't necessarily imply that she could perceive something imbedded within the man's flesh.

Did it?

Believe it, her mind replied. *And use it.*

Keeping a firm grip on his hand, she opened the console and removed a pen from the assorted items she kept amongst the clutter. Working by feel, she made a tiny circle on the man's forearm around the area of the miniscule scar, where she'd sensed the green glow. She returned the pen to its niche, closed the console and searched the man's trouser pockets to see what she could find.

To her relief, she found a large penknife in his left front pocket. She opened it and instantly discovered that the blade was razor-sharp. Carefully she grabbed the plastic antiseptic bottle from the dash cupholder she used to sanitize her hands from time to time and squeezed a thick bubble onto the mark she'd made on the man's forearm.

After rubbing it in thoroughly, then carefully sanitizing the blade, she positioned the knife over his flesh and found herself trembling.

The shades. Should she take them off?

Don't be stupid. Of course you should take them off! It's not like he can see you right now…

And so what if he wakes up? He won't even know what's going on…

She removed them and placed them on top of the dash. Her nerves twitched as she pressed the blade firmly to the man's skin. A bubble of blood instantly appeared. Forcing herself not to succumb to the nausea, she applied a Kleenex to the dark bubble and sliced the area a little deeper. Justin still did not stir. The blood pooled thicker and darker, causing streaks. She reapplied the Kleenex and kept it pressed firmly to the wound. A moment later, she pulled it away and quickly sliced deeper into the opening.

More blood ran in thin rivulets down both sides of the man's forearm.

I've got to get this done.

She sliced even deeper, and after more feverish blotting, spotted something dark beneath the latest swash of blood. It looked like a plastic capsule about a quarter of an inch long.

136

Her spirits lifted as she used the point of the knife to gently coax the tiny object from the man's bloody flesh. Once it was free, she pressed a fresh wad of Kleenex firmly into the bloody opening and kept up the pressure with one hand while she searched the glove box for her first-aid kit. Using her free hand, she found gauze and a small spool of surgical white tape. She bathed the wound with antiseptic, covered it with gauze and wrapped it firmly with several feet of tape.

This done, she picked up the tiny capsule and studied it.

It was slightly larger than a grain of rice. Although she'd been using advanced technology most of her young life, it still frightened her that such a tiny, innocent-looking object could be responsible for enabling a group of dangerous individuals to keep tabs on Justin so easily.

At that same moment, the anger took over, and she realized what this little thing actually meant…and what it was designed to do…and what it had been doing to Justin. Scowling, she opened the window and flicked it out onto the pavement. She then picked up her shades and slipped them back on, put the car back into gear, eased out of the space and got back on the main road.

***

Ten minutes later, as Erika stopped on red at another four-way intersection, the earpiece, which had become visible when the washcloth in Justin's lap had slipped open, began buzzing.

Justin stirred. He opened his eyes and looked around, then noticed the bandage on his left forearm. Fidgeting, he squinted, gazing at it. Then cautiously touched the bandage with his right hand and moved his head closer. Finally, blinking furiously, he turned to her.

The earpiece buzzed again.

Groaning, he picked it up from his lap and used his free hand to push it into his left ear. Then he let his head fall back against the headrest. His eyes were closed. Erika could feel the anger and disgust emanating from him. "Yeah, I'm back," he said finally.

Silence.

He turned to her and pointed to the bandage. She nodded. He laid his head back and closed his eyes again. "I really don't know *where* the hell we are. I just woke up. You zapped me again—or don't you remember?"

Silence.

"I don't *know* where she is. As I told you before—"

Silence.

"Yeah, I know you don't like what happened. Sorry I can't control every situation you push me into."

A slight pause.

"No, I have no idea what she did. Or why she did it. Or when. Like I keep saying, I was unconscious."

Another pause.

138

"I guess maybe she did. There's a bandage on my forearm, so I imagine she did something to the damned thing. I'll ask her what happened when I see her again. Then—"

Another pause.

"No offense, but it's the best I can manage for now. Once my head clears, I'll try again. Who knows? Maybe we'll get lucky."

Another pause.

"Really?"

A few seconds of silence.

"Well, then, if that's the way you want to leave it..."

One last pause.

He sighed tiredly. "I guess this is it, then. I'd like to say it was nice dealing with you bastards, but I'm a really lousy liar."

Still using his right hand, he removed the earpiece and dropped it in his lap. He immediately pressed the button on the door that rolled down the window, grabbed the tiny object and flicked it through the gap.

"What did you do?" she asked, a little frightened.

He closed the window and sat back. "I tossed the damned thing."

"I saw that. I'd just like to know why."

"They found out what you did with their tracker and told me my contract with them was up."

She didn't like the sound of that. It sounded so final. So permanent. "Wh-What exactly...what does that mean?"

139

"It means they're gonna turn me off."

"Again?"

"This time, permanently."

"Permanently?"

He nodded.

"What…what did they say?"

"Their intentions weren't very clear. But it's really no wonder. They never say anything more than they have to. They don't want anyone to know what they're doing. They're obsessively secretive and like it that way. But when they tell you that they no longer have any use for you, you know what's next."

"W-What's next?"

"They can't have me walking around, knowing what I know. That's it in a nutshell."

"But you keep saying they only tell you certain things. Doesn't that mean you really don't know very much? And that you're not much of a threat?"

"I know about them. And since they don't want anyone to know they even exist…" He shrugged.

"Then they know how to turn you off? For good?"

"I've done some quiet research on the subject and discovered that these people have the capabilities of imbedding a certain chip inside their agents."

She was afraid to say it but knew they had to bring it all out in the open. "You mean like…like the one I took out?"

"This one's different."

"How different?"

140

"In simple terms, they've imbedded me with a chip that could cause either a brain aneurysm or blood clot."

She cringed. "My *God*... A *kill* chip?"

He nodded.

"Do you have any idea when...how...this could happen?"

He stared at the bandage on his arm. "All I know is, if they actually implanted me with one of those little bastards, they'll decide to use it to their best advantage."

"In other words?"

"They'll most likely switch me off at the most appropriate moment."

"Just what are you telling me, Justin?"

"When they feel that my demise will best suit their needs. They're intensely fond of that "killing-two-birds-with-one-stone" idiom. It's kind of a credo with them. Their very own made-up Commandment. Efficiency is what they live for. They find that it's safer, cheaper and more reasonable in the long run. Done this way, they don't have to worry about tapping more of their resources to keep themselves out of the headlines."

"This doesn't tell us much, does it?"

"Since you removed my tracking chip, this tells me that they might go back to targeting your folks. This way, all they have to do is send someone over there to wait."

"Wait? For what?"

"For you to go back home. They'll figure that when you go back, I'll probably be with you."

"You mean they already know we're—"

"They've probably figured out that I have no intention of killing you. Which also tells them that we're now on the same team. And to them, we're now both enemies of the state."

"But...how do they know for sure?"

"When they decide something, they figure it's written in stone. Anyway, this'll turn out well for them—especially if they're right. They'll assume I'll be with you when you get home. Then they can get us both—as well as your parents—and have someone tell the press something that'll take the heat away from them and keep the public jumping at shadows for weeks, maybe months."

Oh no, she thought. *This can't be happening...*

"Then what do we...how can we...how can I possibly—"

"The only thing I know for sure is that they might seriously consider using your folks to set up some sort of trap for us."

She found it difficult to keep control of the Hyundai. The only thing that mattered right now was that she'd inadvertently signed her parents' death warrant. "I don't believe this. I can't. It's so...so *crazy*. In saving you from them—"

"Believe it or not, you just set up your parents for a contract hit."

142

Chapter 18

Trembling as she drove, Erika couldn't shake the rage or the panic that had taken over. By removing the tracking device from Justin's forearm, she'd condemned her parents to death.

What have I done? she kept asking herself. *How could I have been so stupid? So reckless?*

Why in heaven's name didn't I stop for just a moment to consider the consequences before I grabbed Justin's knife and cut out that stupid thing?

She couldn't help feeling like such a moron. She did what she thought was right to keep those horrible people away. But because of her thoughtlessness, someone else would most likely be sent to murder her parents.

Maybe not, came a thought out of the darkness.

Now what were her senses telling her? Was this her imagination stepping in again? Or had she suddenly become delusional?

Use your new gifts. That special clear-sightedness that has been guiding you the last several hours.

But how can I possibly do this on my own? she asked herself, not expecting any sort of answer.

An answer came, nonetheless:

You don't have to...

Justin shifted in his seat, and the message quickly became quite clear.

The man sitting beside her would know what to do, how to deal with this. A brief image of the binoculars, the gun and silencer blipped brightly in her head. He most certainly knew how to use them. This was why his controllers used him in the first place. The time he'd spent in Iraq had no doubt taught him to deal with some horrible scenarios. And everyone knew that the soldiers sent over there were forced very quickly to learn how to handle themselves.

If he could handle deadly situations for the Government, he could certainly use his frightening talents to help save them, couldn't he?

"Tell me something," Justin said suddenly, breaking her concentration.

"What's that?"

"How'd you know?"

"Know?"

He pointed to his bandage.

She knew what he meant. But she wasn't quite ready to tell him what had been going on. She'd have to tell him the other stuff, too. And that meant telling him what had happened at the Mall.

But this wasn't why she was hesitant about revealing anything. Despite her strange new perceptiveness, as well as those other unexplained emotions that made no sense whatsoever, she still had no idea what had happened.

"How'd you know where to look?" he asked. "Or if I even had one? Or, most important, what the damned thing was?"

Her thoughts spinning wildly, she stared straight ahead at the traffic slowing down at the light. And struggled to decide what she could tell him.

"Like it or not," he said, "we're in this together—which makes us partners. From now on, it's five-oh, five-oh, all the way down the wire. And whether you know it or not, you can trust me. I may not be the sort of guy any girl in her right mind would want to introduce to her parents, but I'm honest, and as faithful as anyone you'll find these days. I've already told you what I'll do to make sure you and your parents stay safe. And even though the people controlling me just upped their game plan, I still mean exactly what I told you before. In fact—"

"I saw it." She hadn't meant to blurt it out, but what he'd just said had touched her so deeply, she knew she'd hate herself if she didn't share everything with him.

"You what?"

"I know how this must sound, but—"

"You *saw* the chip?"

She nodded.

"But how could you possibly have seen something that was imbedded in my flesh?" He paused for a moment. "It was buried, wasn't it? It wasn't poking out of the skin, was it?"

"It was about three-quarters of an inch inside, wedged between the muscles."

"Then how—how could you possibly...?" He sat forward, gawking at the dash—as if it held the answer he was looking for.

She decided that since she'd already told him the unbelievable part, she needed to tell him as much of the truth as she dared. "I don't know how I saw it. But I did. It was like a tiny green glow—as if a miniature fluorescent light was shining on your skin."

"A glow?"

"Yes."

He was silent for a few moments. "A glow? Shining on my forearm? Telling you it was a chip?"

"It didn't actually *tell* me."

"Then how could you have possibly known what it was?"

She joined the solid three-lane pack straight ahead and pulled off the side of the road halfway down the next block. She slowed, then stopped in the front lot of a small strip mall and parked. Her hands were shaking; she let them drop to her lap. Then she took a couple of deep breaths to calm down. "I have no idea. I just knew."

"You saw a strange green glow appearing just above my skin and knew that it was actually a *tracking device*?"

"As I just said, I didn't know *what* it was. I only knew that something was there. It's kind of like when…well, when something doesn't feel right with your foot, so you take off your shoe and find something—a briar, or pebble—wedged into the side, in the stitching."

The way he stared at her made her wonder if he thought she was crazy. "Like something was off?" he asked.

146

She nodded.

"Something you could tell was wrong?"

She didn't speak right off. This was getting out of hand. If she didn't explain this better, he'd think she was mental. "A lot of weird things have been happening to me lately."

"Like what?"

Despite what she'd originally decided, she realized that she had to toss caution to the wind and tell him what was going on. She hoped that if she phrased it just right, he might not consider jumping out of the car and running away, screaming. "Remember when you were following me at the Mall on Colonial?"

"Vividly."

"Remember when you tripped?"

"I happened to be right there at the time, yeah."

"The instant before that, I…well, I…visualized it."

"Visualized what?"

"Your tripping. Falling down."

He went silent again. She could practically hear his thoughts bouncing around in his head as though helplessly trapped in a pinball machine. She expected him to laugh. Or shake his head in disbelief. Or stare at her to see if she was having fun with him.

He just sat there, watching her. She didn't want to stare back at him for fear of sensing his mood. She didn't have to. His emotions radiated just as strongly as when she'd come out of the drugstore at the Mall. But these emotions weren't dripping with

147

rage, hatred, or contempt. They centered on confusion and disbelief. However, the disbelief felt much weaker than the confusion—which made her feel a little better.

"You're serious, aren't you?" he finally asked.

"I honestly wouldn't make up something as weird as all that."

More silence. She could tell that the confusion remained, but the disbelief had all but disappeared. Then he said, "Tell me about the drugstore."

"What about it?"

"Your expression when you first looked at me. I remember it very well."

"My expression?"

"The moment your eyes fixed on me, you looked frightened."

She nodded.

"Why were you frightened?"

"I felt things coming from you the moment I saw you sitting on that bench."

"Like what?"

"Hatred. Fear. Confusion. Rage."

He went silent again. She tried once again to pick up on the disbelief, but felt nothing.

"Is this how you tracked me down when I was staking out your house?"

She nodded.

"And you have no idea how you did this?"

"Not even the slightest."

He turned and watched the traffic passing in front of them. "I hope you realize how weird and screwy this all sounds."

"Ya think?"

"And how incredible it was that you actually *saw* the tracking device in my arm."

"I'm still trying to process that."

"And you have no idea why or how you've acquired these strange abilities?"

"None whatsoever." Just then, a flash of something dark and cold stabbed her in the pit of her stomach. The image of her folks having supper blipped for a moment, then vanished. A dark figure lurking nearby made her tremble.

"What's wrong?" he asked.

She couldn't speak. The cold lump in her throat prevented it.

"Erika?"

She forced the lump down her throat with a cough. Once she'd collected herself, she said, "Something's happening. Something really bad."

"Talk to me."

Her heart climbed halfway up her throat. "I'm getting this horrible premonition. Someone's sitting in a car...down the street...from my parents' house!"

Chapter 19

After making several quick turns, Erika began backtracking, heading southeast and working her way onto the roads that would take them back to the Lake Underhill area.

Greer sat tensely in the passenger seat, concerned about what would happen if they got to her folks' home too late. If his predecessor had already done the ghastly deed.

He had to take care of this. He had no choice. Erika didn't deserve to be trapped in the middle of this mess. He'd done in innocent people before. His first victim was a middle-aged guy who'd accidentally crossed one of Greer's handlers. Greer had learned later on in the news that the man he'd eliminated was actually a convicted child molester. Greer hated molesters of any kind. But even so, the incident had raked on him.

This was entirely different. Although he hadn't known Erika for more than just a few hours, he knew she was a good person. He had no idea why she insisted on hiding her face, but he'd seen a lot of people during his stint in the Military, and what he'd learned was that everyone lugged around his own personal nightmare. He didn't know what sort of private horror a girl Erika's age could possibly be hauling around, but that didn't matter—not in this case. And it certainly had no bearing on what was going on here.

He'd grown very fond of Erika. And he knew that there was no way he could live with himself if he didn't do what was necessary to prevent her parents from being murdered.

If only we could get there faster...

If only we could get there before—

A flurry of images filled his head, perking him right up.

Erika's strange gift. So far, it had served both of them well. Because of it, he no longer carried around the tracking device that had kept him enslaved to his handlers the last five years. In his view, her "seeing" the damned thing in his arm was proof enough that her gift could possibly help them through this.

He'd never been sure where the device was. Or if he even had one. He'd always suspected that they'd implanted him with something that would cause the blackouts, but had no way of knowing if the chip itself had been responsible, or if there had been more than one implant. All he knew for sure was that his handlers had done things to him during his convalescence in Germany. He had no idea what was done, but he did know that it was obviously approved by the Government, as well as the Military.

But Erika had somehow located the chip and removed it, and without causing him serious injury. In his view, this was a miracle in itself.

He knew he could never repay her for what she'd done, but he intended to try. And the first thing he had to do was to somehow keep her parents out of this mess. To do this, he'd have to rely on her special gifts.

"That feeling you got just a few minutes ago?" he asked.

She zipped through a yellow light. "You mean about someone watching my parents' house?"

"That's what I mean."

"What about it?"

"And you experienced this same feeling earlier, when I was watching your place?"

"I've already told you that…"

He went silent.

"Justin…what are you trying to say?"

"Do you think you'd sense it if this man had already done the deed?"

"Judging by how my mind has been working lately, I'd say yes. Probably."

"Then I think it's safe to say that we still have time to get there."

"I hope you're right…"

"But you wouldn't be able to feel anything else, would you?"

"Like what?"

"Would you be able to tell if your parents were actually being harmed? Right this instant?"

"I really don't know. Maybe, maybe not. I hope I could. But all I really know is that we've got to get there quickly."

"How long before we're in the area?"

She glanced at the dash clock. It said 7:09. "With this traffic? I'd say at least fifteen minutes."

He sat back and thought about what they were going to do when they got there. And then he thought about the firepower he'd need to handle the operative assigned to target Erika's parents.

"You're not carrying, are you?" she asked.

He gawked at her. "You don't read minds, too, do you?"

"I don't *think* so… At least, I *hope* not." She smiled tiredly. "I have more than enough crap going on in my head right now. Why do you ask?"

"I was thinking that very same thing the moment you asked."

"Just when I thought I had more than enough on my plate…"

"It was probably just a coincidence."

"Hopefully, you're right. But it doesn't answer my question. You had a gun and silencer when I caught you spying on us in the Challenger."

He sighed.

"Well? What happened with them? I can't help noticing that you don't have them with you. Unless, of course, you've got a really dynamite hiding place for them."

"I don't."

"Terrific." She turned back to the traffic moving ahead of them.

"They always use a good cleanup crew whenever a job goes south. Once they switched me off, the first thing they did was grab the gun, silencer, and binoculars before taking me out of the rental."

"Then what?"

153

"Who knows? I woke up in my apartment. They no doubt returned the Challenger to the rental place while someone else brought me home."

"Do you have *any* weapons? Other than your pocket knife?"

Instinctively he felt for the knife in his pocket. He wanted to smile when he thought of her searching him while he was out. "You used my knife to pull out the tracker, didn't you?"

"It was either that, or my nail file."

He grimaced. "Sounds painful."

She smiled.

"Can you really see very well with those shades?"

"I...manage."

He could tell by the abrupt change in her tone that he'd stumbled into forbidden territory once again.

"I seem to be doing all right, wouldn't you say?"

"I'd say you're doing quite well, actually."

"So then, what are we gonna do when we get there? That guy's bound to be equipped with what they gave you, right?"

"That would be a safe bet."

"Then what can we do to put him down?"

"I told you I was in Iraq, didn't I?"

"Uh-huh..."

"I have other skills."

"For instance?"

He didn't want to frighten her. Besides, there were too many other things to think about right

154

now. "Let's just say that I don't need a gun to disable an armed man."

"That sounds, well, scary."

"It is. Especially for the armed guy."

"You'll probably have to sneak up on him...won't you?"

"When you're facing someone with a gun or knife, you look for any and all possible advantages to shift the odds in your favor."

A few minutes later, they got onto South Conway and gained some advantage in the thinning traffic. The moment they drew closer to Lake Underhill, Erika tensed up and drove stiffly, staring straight ahead.

Greer could feel the tension emanating from her. He began to wonder if portions of her special gift were rubbing off. But he knew it wasn't the time to be thinking such thoughts. He needed to focus on the main issue.

Just then, Erika groaned softly.

"What's wrong?" he asked.

"The man watching our house."

"What about him?"

"I just had a very strong feeling that he's getting ready."

"For what?"

She didn't reply.

"That's it?"

She turned sharply toward him. He felt the fear—as well as the anger—emanating through the dark shades hiding her eyes. "Isn't that enough?"

He nodded.

She turned back to her driving. Decelerating, she turned onto a secondary road. She pulled onto Wayfarer, and they eased down the street, passing palmettos, rows of mailboxes and trimmed bushes while inching past condos and then the private homes lining the street. When they approached the end of the block, Erika pulled off the side of the road, where a large palmetto bush hid them from view of the street to their left, separating Wayfarer from Rockledge, where her parents lived.

She put the car into park and sat in tense silence, gazing at the dark windshield.

"What's going on?"

"I'm getting another...wow...this isn't good..."

"Talk to me."

"He's sitting in that car, doing something," she said softly, still gazing into the approaching darkness. "On Adirondack. I'm afraid we don't have much time."

***

Greer slipped out of the Hyundai and inched the door shut. Keeping low, he crept over to the palmetto bush at the corner of the property. It was now well past 7:30 and already fairly dark. The streetlights had already blipped to life. Only a few other lights came from windows, with nightlamps highlighting driveways and front porches.

The element of surprise remained in his favor.

If Erika's senses were accurate, the figure in the black Lexus at the end of the block was watching the Young residence through a pair of infrared

156

binoculars and would make his move when he decided the time was right.

Greer figured the hitter would wait until the two went to bed. They'd be tired from a hard day and ready for a night of rest. They might have had a drink or two. They would be most vulnerable and wouldn't expect an intruder. And once they were eliminated, he'd wait in the dark house for Erika and Greer to come inside, and then eliminate them and stage the whole thing to implicate Greer.

However, something just didn't feel right.

Why had the hitter parked the Lexus in such a conspicuous place? This was a quiet, respectable neighborhood. The bushes were trimmed, the palmettos tended to, the lawns mowed. No other vehicles were parked along the curb. The Lexus was bound to be seen by the neighbors and would surely attract attention.

A call to the police would most certainly be made if a strange vehicle was spotted in front of someone's property.

Greer reached into his side pocket and removed the penknife. He didn't know if he'd be able to bring it into play, but it was reassuring to have it. He had no idea what he'd be facing. All he did know was that these people used only capable killers.

His trained senses on full alert, he kept his eyes on the Lexus. It was time to approach the vehicle to check it out. He waited another minute before slipping away from the palmetto. His penknife ready, he hurried across the street, stopping the moment he reached the thick rosebush at the front of the property just twenty feet or so behind the Lexus.

His pulse racing, he rested only long enough to catch his breath. Then he peered around the edge of the rosebush.

The taillights of the Lexus abruptly came on.

A moment later, the engine fired up.

The Lexus eased away from the curb. It crept up to the end of the block and turned left.

Greer rushed back to the Hyundai, pulled open the passenger door and jumped in.

"What happened?" Erika asked.

"I have no idea, but my gut tells me that we need to follow that Lexus."

Chapter 20

The Lexus should not have pulled out when it did.

To add to their suspicions, the driver immediately proved ridiculously easy to follow. Keeping just slightly over the speed limit, the car pulled onto Semoran and stayed in the slow lane, yielding to traffic and stopping at the intersection the moment the light turned yellow.

"Why's he making this so easy?" Erika asked. "If I didn't know better, I'd think they contacted him and called off this stupid thing."

"Unlikely." Greer knew how they worked. There was definitely something else going on. "Once the job's been set into motion, it's never cancelled."

"Then what's happening? I'm certain he never even went into the house."

"Are you sure?"

She thought about that for a moment. "Think I should call them?"

"It might ease our minds."

She remained silent.

"I trust your gut completely," he said. "But if you're not totally convinced... If you have even the slightest doubt..."

Erika got out her cell and punched in the number. A moment later, she nodded to him. "Hi, Mom. No, everything's fine. Did supper go okay?"

A pause. "Good. Great." Another pause. "Nope, I'm just calling to check in. I'll be a little while. Tell Dad I love him." Another pause. "Tell ya later, okay?" A pause. "Can't really talk now." She pocketed the cell.

"I take it everything's fine?"

"She sounded the same as always…"

"You'd be able to tell if she was under duress, right?"

"Of course. By the way, she wanted me to tell her all about you."

"She *knows* about me?"

"Just that you're a guy…"

He sighed in relief. "Well, at least we know they're safe."

Erika was silent for a moment. "You don't think…you don't think he's just…just a *decoy*, do you?"

That thought had crossed his mind. They'd know he and Erika would be anticipating their next move and would guess they'd target Erika's parents. They would figure he and Erika would come back to the house to complicate things. Then it would be relatively simple to get them both.

So why was he leading them *away* from the house?

"I'm beginning to think it might be," he told her.

"I'm gonna turn around and—"

"I wouldn't do that right now if I were you."

"Got something in mind?"

Another thought came to him. "Something about all this makes no sense."

"For instance?"

"Why would they use one of their hitters as a decoy? They never used me as a decoy. Whenever they needed a distraction, they'd most definitely work the job some other way. This is way too damned obvious."

"Well, they probably know we're on to them by now..."

"That still doesn't explain what's happening."

"You said when they take you down, it'll be to their best advantage, right?"

"Right."

"Then wouldn't they send a decoy to get us away from my house? We'd no doubt make things much more complicated for them if we show up there. It could turn sloppy and violent. The neighbors might even get involved, and they'd have the police—maybe even the local media—to deal with. With just Mom and Dad, things would be simple. Mom's not what you'd call a fighter, and Dad's put on a lot of weight since he came back from Saudi, so he wouldn't be much of a problem, either. These people could do them in easily and send someone else for us."

He nearly smiled. "You're beginning to sound like you actually know how these bastards operate."

She laughed. "It's just my panic button tripping off to let in whatever logical thoughts I'm still holding onto. This way, I can at least try and make some sense out of all this."

161

"Well, whatever's going on inside your head, just keep it there. We need to use as much of it as possible. Let's turn around and head back."

She stopped at the next red light. The Lexus had gone right on through just moments earlier. She watched as it went down the block, pulled into the turning lane and stopped there.

"I don't think so," she said softly.

The Lexus just sat there at the curb. It didn't move.

"He obviously wants us to follow him. It reeks strongly of a trap."

"Maybe…"

He could tell she was considering the odds. "What's going on?"

"I can't really explain what I'm feeling, but I kinda think we should keep following him."

"Like I just said, this is too damned obvious. He's probably been told about me and knows I wouldn't fall for such a stupid trick."

"Then why's he doing this? He's clearly leading us farther away from my place."

Greer thought about that for a moment. "In this case, we might not have much of an option."

"We don't know if he's alone. This is what's bothering me."

"Are you picking up anything else from your folks?"

"Nothing."

"In other words, they're still okay?"

"As far as I can tell…"

"I have the strong feeling that the guy in the Lexus is alone."

"And he wants us to follow him."

"But we have no idea why."

"Exactly."

Greer considered the odds. They didn't seem favorable, no matter which way he looked at it. "You still want to go through this?"

"I honestly think we should call their bluff."

The light turned green.

He decided to go along with her instinct. So far, it had been too damned accurate to dismiss. "Let's go, then. We've got to see what's on this dirtbag's mind."

***

The Lexus turned off into the front lot of a Jiffy Lube just north of Casselberry. Then, easing past the dark building, it went down a narrow road that led to a private lot behind a chain-link fence. Once it reached the end, it turned left and disappeared around the corner.

Erika brought the Hyundai to a stop at the store entrance. Once the Lexus' taillights dimmed at the corner, she hurried down the straight path.

Just as she approached the end of the building, Justin said, "Stop here. I have to get out and see what's going on. It's just too dark. We can't see any taillights. I don't like that at all."

Erika could tell he was trying to protect her. But she didn't want him walking into such an obvious trap. Justin was good at what he did, but she suspected that the man in the Lexus was equally good. Even if he wasn't, the fact that he knew they were following him told her he had a definite advantage.

"He might've gone down a few yards, parked, then got out of the car. He could be waiting for us just beyond the corner." She couldn't ignore the fear sliding down her back.

"I have to find out, don't I?"

"That would be the hard way of doing it, wouldn't you say?"

"Whoever told you this would be easy?" he asked.

He had a point. It was vital that he checked to see if their enemy had backtracked.

She wanted this business over and done with. Her nerves were shot, her imagination kept going berserk, and she found her anger taking over. She found it incredibly horrible that anyone would send a killer to murder her parents. Especially since they hadn't done anything wrong.

Most of all, she found it despicable that anyone could turn someone like Justin into a killing machine, then switch him off whenever he didn't dance to their instructions.

She flicked off her lights and put the car into park. "How long should I give you?"

"If I don't come right back, turn around and hurry back home."

She couldn't believe he'd said such a thing. "I can't possibly do that!"

"I don't want you here if—"

"If what? If this really *is* an ambush?"

164

He didn't reply.

"Tell me what good it would do if I drove back home. They're just gonna come after me again. If I'm at the house, they can just do me in right after they've done in my parents. No, dammit. I'm much better off right here. With you."

"But what if they get me the moment I—"

"Then they'll have to get me too, because I'm *not* gonna finish this without you."

"Erika, you don't have to—"

"I most definitely have to. You put me in this— don'tcha remember?"

He sighed.

"Well?"

"I've already told you why they sent me to—"

"I know why they sent you. No one but an idiot could forget something like that. And I understand, believe me. I've also forgiven you for that. Let's not get into that again, okay? Just go check it out. I'll be here, no matter what happens."

Sighing tiredly, he opened his door and slipped out into the darkness.

***

Greer pressed his back against the chain-link fence. He stood as still as a statue, his heart racing as he listened to the darkness.

The alley revealed nothing. The square black shape of the Lexus sitting in the middle of the alley thirty yards straight ahead had become just another part of the stillness of his surroundings. As far as he could see, nothing moved around it.

Although his vision was limited, he guessed that the buildings farther down could be storage units. But he knew that unless he took a closer look, he couldn't really be sure.

What concerned him most of all was the Lexus itself. If the driver was still inside. If he was cradling a gun and silencer. If he was listening to his earpiece. Waiting for further instructions.

What would the man do once Greer got closer? Would he kick open the door? Pump a couple of rounds into his chest, then sneak back to the Hyundai and calmly take out Erika?

He knew how these people worked. They knew what they wanted and acted on it. Popular opinion would consider them successful, well-adjusted executive types who went about, accomplishing their goals regardless of the consequences.

But he knew better. They were monsters. Psychopaths with more blood on their hands than society's most vicious serial killers. Sociopaths with more than enough money to buy and sell human lives.

They're not gonna get her, he promised himself as he moved away from the fence. *They won't be able to kill her or her family. They're not going to get near her again.*

He'd only taken half a dozen silent steps when he heard the faintest sound of something tapping the hard pavement just a few feet behind him. Before he could react, something hard slapped him sharply just behind his right ear.

The resulting blackness was strangely comforting.

PART 2—OUT OF THE DARK

Chapter 21

Erika sensed something dark and very wrong.

The dash clock said 8:27. It was 8:15 when Justin had gotten out of the car. Twelve minutes since he'd disappeared into the darkness. Entirely too much time just to check out the premises and come right back.

What had he said before he'd left?

"If I don't come right back, turn around and hurry back home."

Abandoning him was not even part of the equation. As she'd told him, it made no sense to return home and just sit there like an idiot, waiting for someone to show up and kill them all.

Besides, what could she do once she was back home? Tell Mom and Dad about the whole mess? That she'd been targeted by an evil group operating within the Government? That she'd seen something she shouldn't have? Had been in the wrong place at the wrong time? And because of this, they wanted her dead? And since they thought she'd told her parents what was going on, they also had to die?

Dad had never been conspiracy minded. Neither had Mom. They trusted the Government, showed up for jury duty whenever they were called, and voted dutifully. They paid their taxes and didn't do anything they thought was wrong, or illegal.

They'd think that after her trauma, something had gone very wrong in her head.

However, none of that was relevant right now. She and Justin had come here together. She was determined that they left together as well.

A little shaky, Erika groped for the penlight she kept in the console. The sunglasses made this simple task nearly impossible in the dark cab, so she pulled them off and placed them on the dash. Working by feel, she pulled it out and flicked it on to see if the batteries were still good. The white sliver of light came right on.

She eased open her door, got out and closed it quietly. After waiting for her nerves to settle, she made her way silently to the corner, where Justin had gone. She truly hoped she'd see him coming back.

But the moment she eased around the corner, her heart sank. The darkness filling the alley revealed no sign of him. However, a dim sliver of yellow light about a hundred feet farther down, just past the parked Lexus, gave her a glimmer of hope.

Her penlight gripped tightly in her hand, she moved cautiously toward the car. It didn't take her long to realize that the buildings extending beyond the parking lot were storage units. As she passed the Lexus, she focused on the slender yellow beam three units straight ahead. As she drew closer, the beam thickened. It seemed to be coming from inside a unit. A few more steps convinced her that the rollup door wasn't totally closed. Two more steps revealed that the bottom of the door hung about six inches shy of the concrete floor, permitting the light inside to escape and project a hazy glow into the alley.

As she moved closer to the door, she heard voices coming from inside. One belonged to Justin. The other was unfamiliar. The tension in Justin's voice alarmed her, telling her that her initial sense of danger had been accurate.

She lowered herself to her knees. Then bent over and lay down on her stomach to peer inside.

The six-inch gap permitted her to see the interior of the unit. The area was filled with boxes stacked almost to the rafters. Furniture cluttered much of the area in front of the boxes. Couches. A bed. Several mattresses sheathed in plastic. A dining room table and six chairs. A large wooden ottoman.

The center area was clear, except for a metal folding chair and two figures. One figure sat in the chair. The other was Justin. He lay on his back on the concrete floor, his arms pulled behind him. The figure in the chair sat less than two feet from Justin's left side. He wore dark clothing and a black hood, and sat forward, his elbows on his knees as he spoke to Justin.

But what alarmed her had nothing to do with the man's voice, or the hood covering his face. What frightened her was the stiletto in the man's hands.

The long, gleaming blade was pointed directly at Justin.

**

"It sure was easy, gettin' you here, buddy-boy."

170

However, the fact that Greer wasn't already dead suggested that he and Erika had probably been right. His handlers had no doubt ordered them to be taken out together.

Just then, he felt the notch at the end of the blade. Keeping his back arched, he shoved his thumbnail into it and began sliding it out of its tiny niche.

"The girl's still out there, right?"

"I told her to drive back home."

"It won't take them long at all to find out where she is. Then I'll—"

Just then, he stopped.

Greer heard the familiar buzzing.

The man tilted his head. "Yeah, I got him."

Silence.

"No, not yet."

Silence.

"All right. I'll put them in the car, then head back to Lake Underhill and finish up."

Silence.

"Copy that." He turned back to Greer. "That was—"

"I know who it was."

"Then you know what that was all about."

"I couldn't exactly hear what they were telling you."

"Wanna know what's gonna happen?"

"Go right ahead. I've got a little time."

The killer chuckled. "You got sense of humor, pal—for a hitter."

"I've never been told that before. But to repeat myself, I'm not your pal."

"Anyway, just to make sure you know the plan… I've got to collect the girl first. After I do her, I do you and make it look like you did her. But I've also got to take the two of you back to her place and make it look like you did in her folks. Sounds like a lot of busywork, but I'm pretty sure I can handle it."

"That's cold, even for a shitload of demented assholes."

"Temper, temper…"

"You really expect me to have a warm feeling about all this?"

"How long have you been at this?"

"Too long."

"Sounds like it. Look on the bright side. You'll be out of it shortly."

"That makes me feel *so* much better."

"By the way, they did a perimeter scan about a minute ago. This facility has cameras at each corner. Her car's right where it was. Tell you anything?"

"It tells me she didn't listen to me."

"That's right. You told her to--"

"I told her to get out of here before you or any other of their psychos could lay a hand on her."

He tilted his head. "Think I'm a psycho?"

"I *know* you are."

He shrugged. "I'm no different from you, asshole. I do what they tell me. They pay me and tell me what to do next. *Quid pro quo*—know what I mean?"

"Only too well."

He stood up. Still watching Greer, he reached into his jacket pocket and removed another zip-tie. Then, moving around Greer, he dropped to his knees and quickly secured Greer's ankles together. He straightened and looked down at Greer. "Can't risk you going anywhere while I collect the girl."

Greer didn't reply. He was too busy keeping his wrists out of sight while using the tiny blade to finish slicing through the ties.

"Don't worry. I'll be right back. And by the way, don't go anywhere." He crept over to the door, bent and, grabbing the handle, very slowly raised it. When the top of it had stopped just a few inches lower than the level of his head, he suddenly let go of the handle. And stood stock-still.

A slim, dark figure stood on the other side of the door, staring at him.

***

Trembling, Erika boldly faced the rollup door. The penlight, held tightly in her right hand at belt level, was pointed directly at her face.

Her trembling increased as the door pulled open, but she forced herself to stay strong. Her knees shook, ready to cave in. She took a deep breath and told herself she could do this. She *had* to. The lives of her parents—as well as her own, and Justin's—depended on what she did right this very second.

175

The door continued to roll up. Several long, agonizing seconds later, it stopped just short of the top of the doorway. The tall, hooded figure in the wide doorway did not move. The man's eyes, revealed clearly behind the two slits in the dark cloth, focused on her.

Erika flicked on the penlight.

The man remained perfectly still, his gaze fixed helplessly on her.

Erika kept the beam focused on her face. Hundreds of hurtful, unpleasant memories rushed by, but she struggled to keep them from taking over. It was vital that she use her own personal nightmare to help both her and Justin. To use whatever resources she needed to bring this horrible man down. This same man who would not only kill both her and Justin, but also her parents. So instead of turning away, as she'd done so many times in the past, she stood her ground, staring right back at the two shocked, unblinking eyes gawking at her from inside the black hood.

Then, after deciding the time was right, she realized she had to make her move. With a causal flick of her wrist, she tilted the penlight toward him, directing the harsh beam of white light into his wide-open eyes.

The result was startling.

Gasping, the man dropped the knife in his hand. It clattered on the concrete. Reaching up, he covered both eyes and spun around.

This was when she first noticed Justin rushing over.

176

In less than an instant, Justin had wrapped one arm around the man's forehead, reached underneath the hood and applied something to the man's neck, then spun him around and forced him face-down onto the concrete.

Blood spurted freely from the area around the man's neck, splashing everywhere. His body bucked and jerked, the blood spewing in long, thick spurts, gathering in heavy pools on the floor.

Seconds later, he stopped moving.

Justin bent over him. Since his back was to Erika, she couldn't see what he was doing. Before she could even guess what had happened, he'd already straightened and turned. "We need to get the hell out of here."

She forced her body to start functioning again. It took her much longer than she imagined. Her knees were locked, and her moist hand still held the penlight in a death grip. After what seemed a very long time, she forced her legs to resume working. Then she turned and ran back down the alley. By the time she got back to the Hyundai and slipped behind the wheel, Justin had circled the front of the car, opened the passenger door and jumped in.

A strong sense of warm relief filled her at that same moment, but she knew this wasn't the time to rejoice. They might have done in their killer, but that didn't mean there weren't others out there, waiting for the word to swoop in for the kill.

"Where to?" she asked uneasily as she fired up the ignition.

"Anywhere! Just go! Now!"

Her pulse racing, Erika put the Hyundai into reverse, backed up all the way to the main highway, turned the car around and swiftly joined the pack of fast-moving, northbound evening traffic.

Chapter 22

Erika didn't notice the gun and silencer in Justin's lap until she'd stopped at the first red light. Since she hadn't seen him grab the firearm in the storage locker, viewing it right now gave her a renewed respect for him. It also made her feel more confident about their situation.

She turned back to the windshield. And cringed.

Her sunglasses. They lay on the dash where she'd left them.

Trying not to show panic, she reached for them.

"Can't you see better without them?" Justin asked. "It's kind of dark out there. It usually is at this time of night."

Her heart fluttered as she picked them up, but instead of slipping them on, she held them in her trembling hand.

What should she do? It was dark in the cab. Maybe he wouldn't notice her face if she didn't look at him so much. She could just subtly nudge her collar up a few inches, then slip the sunglasses back on once they got out of the car.

"I've seen your face," he said.

She slumped in her seat. *Damn.* Of *course* he'd seen her face. She'd lit it up kind of spectacularly back at the storage place, hadn't she? That had been her intent, hadn't it? To shock their assassin? Gross him out? Distract him? Break his concentration?

Stop him in his tracks? Do whatever it took to gain an advantage?

You didn't think you could hide your face from Justin while you were flashing it at the other guy, did you?

She hadn't thought of that at the time. She'd been too busy wondering what she could do once she'd temporarily stunned their killer. She hadn't worried at all about Justin seeing her simply because their killer had been standing so close.

But now that it was all over, she realized what she'd actually done. She'd made it possible for Justin to get free and kill the assassin. But in the process, she'd done something she hadn't done since her accident. She'd deliberately shown her face to someone other than her parents.

It had been necessary. Something drastic had to be done to put the other guy out of action.

However, something was bothering her now, and it had nothing to do with her horrid fear of being seen. It was something she hadn't expected. Something she'd never dreamed would ever happen.

Justin hadn't shown any repulsion. Of any kind. There had been no shock. No lingering curiosity. He wasn't even gawking at her.

The light turned green. She snapped herself out of the fog and told herself that if she wanted to get the car moving again, she had to press down on the gas pedal.

After a few awkward moments, her foot finally obeyed her command.

"Did you hear me?" he asked softly.

It took her a few moments to respond. At first, she didn't know how to. Then she decided that since the damage had already been done, what harm would it do to reply?

Finally, she nodded.

"You're a very pretty girl," he said. "You have beautiful eyes. You shouldn't hide your face from anyone. Especially me."

She couldn't reply. Had he said what she thought he'd said? Or was her imagination trying to hide her fears by having her fabricate a make-believe deception about this man? After all, he was a hired killer. He'd just killed a man not ten minutes earlier. Since it had taken him only a split second to do it, it obviously hadn't been difficult for him. The other guy had a switchblade and a gun, yet Justin had still managed to kill him. She hadn't seen what he'd used to do it. All she had seen was that in just a couple of seconds, he'd put the man down, snatched the gun and told her to get back to the car.

How could a man who was able to act so viciously have the capacity to say such a lovely, beautiful thing?

The answer was simple. He *hadn't* said it. In reality, he'd said something different, and in all the excitement and confusion, she'd heard it all wrong.

It *had* to have happened that way, right?

There was one sure way to find out, wasn't there?

Even though she didn't want to make the situation worse by asking questions, she really and truly needed to know.

"Wh-What did you just say?" she finally asked, in a soft, unsteady whisper.

"You heard me."

She struggled to recover from this very unexpected but extremely pleasant surprise. "I just…just wanted to hear it again…but if you don't…if you don't really want to—"

"Erika, you're a very pretty girl. And you're also very bright. And by the way, just in case you forgot, you saved my life back there. Thank you."

She still couldn't believe what she'd just heard. It suddenly seemed as if the last two years had somehow come undone and, in doing so, corrected much of itself.

"Nothing to say?" he asked.

"It's just that…well…I just can't believe what you said…"

"I meant every word. You shouldn't hide your face from anyone."

She felt the warm tears gathering and knew right then that the sunglasses definitely needed to stay off. The shades couldn't possibly hide the tears drifting down her cheeks.

So, for the first time in two years, she shoved the cursed things down the front pocket of her lightweight jacket. And, with a sigh, pushed down her collar. And, strangely, felt freer than she'd felt in a very long time.

"Lots of people have battle scars," he said. "I saw more of them in just a few years in Iraq than you'll ever see in your entire life. If you're lucky."

That made sense. He'd been in combat and had surely seen horrible things. This was probably why her scars didn't have much of an effect on him.

Nonetheless, her accident had nearly destroyed her life. The last two years had changed her immeasurably. Her hospital stay was bad enough, but even after the months of skin grafts, she knew she'd never ever be able to live a normal, happy life. She'd been told that in this day and age, people accepted deformities and disfigurements much easier, but it still didn't prevent her from wanting to disappear each time she had to deal with someone face to face.

She just couldn't shake the fear that whenever she showed her face in public, she would be gawked at. She felt that she could never find a job where she had to deal with people without wondering what they were thinking when they were talking to her. She was afraid she'd never be accepted, and would always be looked upon as some oddity. She couldn't even see herself finding someone who would actually care for her. And love her for who she was. And not give a damn about her scars.

Society showed no patience for imperfection. TV abounded with perfection, beauty, and glamor. Gorgeous models and actors graced the screen. Perfect, abundant hair proved the norm. Flawless makeup was mandatory. Custom-tailored outfits and toned, buffed bodies decorated the flawless, sanitized locations. There was no room for ordinary-looking actors on the screen, and anything but beauty and sex appeal would be rejected.

Erika found it very difficult to process Justin's reaction. It was baffling, to say the least. Here was a man who killed people for a living. A man who had been hired to kill her. However, fate had intervened, and now this same man had become not only her partner, but also her ally.

This was utterly incredible.

"Thank you," she whispered, not knowing what else she could possibly say.

"For what?" he asked.

She wondered if she should tell him what she really wanted to say. If what she said would sound silly. Or ridiculous. But then she realized how very rare this man was. He'd said something that could quite possibly change her outlook about everything that had gone wrong in her life. She wanted to tell him what was on her mind. She somehow sensed that he wouldn't consider what she said silly or ridiculous.

"For saying what you just did. And for not…not looking like you wanted to throw up when…when—"

"I said you were a very pretty girl." He sounded angry. "I meant it."

"I know…"

"So then, what's next?" he asked, and when she glanced in his direction, she saw him quietly stripping the pistol in his lap, checking the magazine and unscrewing the silencer. "I've got four bullets here. That figures. Two for us, two for your parents. Ordinarily, four would be enough. But

184

since we have no idea what we're actually facing…" He went silent.

She was happy he'd changed the subject. As much as she'd wanted to tell him about her accident, she had to come to grips with their present situation. And so, after forcing her attention on this most important issue, she decided to start working on some strategy they could use. And this meant finding out all there was about Justin. And his predicament. And the monsters that had been forcing him to kill people.

"You're right," she said.

He didn't reply. He merely slammed the magazine back into the pistol, clicked it on safety, and sat back.

"There *is* a strategy that just might help us, though," she said after a short silence.

"I'm all ears."

"It's very simple. Just tell me everything you know about your handlers."

***

Greer couldn't help being totally baffled by what Erika had just suggested.

Here she was, a girl barely out of her teens who had been through hell, and hiding from the world ever since. But not only had she risked her own life by facing an armed killer, she'd also managed to save Greer's life in the process. And even though Greer's handlers were after her and her parents, instead of abandoning all evidence of coherent thought—as most others would have done—she appeared to be in total control. She knew exactly

185

what was going on, accepted it, and was asking questions. And by her tone, he could tell that she was more than capable of dealing with this.

"What would you like to know?"

She gave a slight shrug as she drove in the steady-moving stream. "Everything."

"Why?"

"Does the phrase, "Know thy enemy," tell you anything?"

"*Touché*." He wanted to smile. He was right about her. She really *was* in total control.

"So…now that we've got that out of the way… Please tell me everything you know about these people."

"I honestly don't know where to start. What would you like me to tell you?"

"I'll let you know once I have a clear picture."

He felt it necessary to warn her about their situation. Erika was very bright, but they were dealing with something she most likely had never come across before. These people were vicious. They took no prisoners. And the last thing he wanted was to see Erika and her family reduced to just another statistic covered briefly on the evening news.

"I know you want to help, but these people have unlimited resources. They've got money—lots of it. And contacts. And, most of all, total access to any and all information and assets they could possibly—"

"Do you have any idea what I do for a living?"

186

He couldn't help wondering what she meant. "You live with your folks."

"What else?"

"You're very isolated. Private. A classic introvert."

"Anything else?"

"No offense, but from what I've seen, I don't believe you have many friends."

"I *don't* have any. But that's not relevant."

"Then tell me what's on your mind."

"I operate a home business. I edit and sometimes ghostwrite term papers for college students. I've been doing this for the last two years, and I'm very good at it."

"Okay..."

"To be blunt, I'm extremely good with a computer."

"How does this help us?"

"Know anything about computer people?"

"They're weird."

She nearly smiled. "Besides that."

"They don't read. Unless, of course, it's a graphic novel—with lots and lots of pictures. They're always talking on their cellphones. They take them everywhere, sleep with them, too. And they like to play video games."

"Anything else?"

"They really don't care much about what's going on around them."

"Most of them are like that, but there are a few exceptions."

"They don't care much for people who don't center their entire existence around computers."

"You're definitely right about that."

"They don't pay much attention to reality. Life is just a video game to them. They don't seem to understand real life at all."

"Right about that, too."

"I'm running out of explanations."

"You're obviously not getting it, are you?"

He shrugged. "That's probably because I'm not a computer guy."

"Really?"

"What's your point?"

"My point is, I know who I should get in touch with when I have a major problem."

"I still don't understand what you're trying to say."

"A problem. And in this case, a *big* problem. A *ginormous* problem."

He still couldn't get her point. "I'm listening. And still very much in the dark about what you're—"

"How about this? A problem that involves the Government. And conspiracies. And shadow cells."

"How do you know about all that?"

"Ever hear of TV? Netflix? Google? The Net? YouTube? Everything's out there. That is, if you know where to look. And believe me, I know where to look."

He didn't reply.

"Let me put it this way. Forget all your questions about me and what I'm up to and just tell me everything you know about your handlers."

"And then?"

She shrugged. "Then I'll do what needs to be done to find the bastards."

Chapter 23

Erika took the Hyundai south on 441, to downtown Orlando. She made a right on West Michigan and headed west, until they came to South Nashville. After making another right, they turned west on 24th Street, made a left onto Rio Grande and went a few blocks south. She then turned right, where the next block brought them onto a street of older one-story homes.

It was nearly 10:00. Traffic had thinned considerably.

Greer had been extremely uneasy about this trip. Telling Erika what he knew about his handlers had not only made him more nervous, it had made him feel like a moron. Surrendering your life to people you didn't even know proved dangerous, as well as stupid. And after evaluating the last five years, he reached the abysmal conclusion that he'd totally given up on himself. He'd placed his future in the hands of people who didn't care about him and exploited his talents to bully him into carrying out their own personal agenda.

But now it was time to turn the tables. He had finally found someone who did actually care about him. Someone brave. And just as desperate as he was. Someone who obviously knew what she was doing. Someone possessing the knowledge and the training that could easily cause his handlers major problems.

"I'll do what needs to be done to find the bastards."

As bizarre as that sounded, he knew damned well that Erika had meant it with all her heart. And judging by how she'd stood up to their killer in the storage locker, he found that he had more confidence in this girl than anyone else he'd ever known.

Erika took the car down the street and pulled over to the curb about halfway down the block, just a few feet short of a paved drive.

"What exactly are we doing here?" he asked, more than a little nervous.

She killed the engine and the lights, sat back and stared at the house. "The only thing I know that makes any sense."

He peered down the hazily lit driveway that led to the one-and-a-half-story brick house sitting behind a row of thick, untrimmed shrubbery and a couple of overgrown palmetto bushes. Two large windows faced the street. The one on the right was dark. The one on the left, lit.

"Who lives here?" he asked.

"Someone I know. Well, sort of…"

"*Sort* of?"

She just shrugged.

Her sudden evasiveness made him even more edgy. "Just who the hell is this person? And, once again, why are we here?"

"Do me a favor?" Her eyes showed clearly in the darkness of the cab as she stared directly at him.

"If I can…"

"Don't ask any more questions. Not yet, anyway. Please?"

He wanted to ask her something else but thought better of it. This girl had saved his life. The least he could do was honor her wishes. "No problem," he said.

"Thank you."

"By the way," he said, "I took this off our friend back there. You just might want to have it. Just in case."

He held out his hand. The earpiece rested in his palm.

"His?"

He shrugged. "He won't be needing it anymore."

She took it, opened her door and got out.

Greer followed her up the paved walk leading to the house.

***

The thickset woman answering the door was close to six feet tall and weighed in at well over two hundred and fifty pounds. Her dark hair was pulled back and tied in a bun. She had a puffy face with large round cheekbones and small crinkly eyes blinking at them behind a pair of silver horn-rimmed glasses. A long silver chain attached to the glasses dangled down, rubbing the front of her dark-blue housecoat. A pair of fuzzy red slippers covered her unusually large feet.

She glanced at Greer, then at Erika. Then, frowning at Erika, she said, "Help ya?"

"Yes, Ma'am. Would it be possible for us to see Greg for a few minutes?"

She tilted her head. "This business?"

Erika nodded.

The woman shrugged. "He's out in the back, as usual."

"The back?"

She jabbed a large thumb toward the rear of the house. "The garage. It's where he lives." She tilted her head again. "Know my son?"

"Actually, not very well…"

The woman nodded. "Just about everyone knows he took over the garage five, maybe six years ago. Got all his toys and games in there. His dad and me? We ain't allowed in there." She snorted. "Hell, we gotta park the cars outside, in the elements. Fancy that."

"I think I understand," Erika said.

The woman stared hard at Erika again and moved a little closer, letting the overhead porchlight focus on Erika's face. "You that young lady? The one that, well—"

"Yes, Ma'am."

The woman squinted and shook her head. "Doin' okay, sweetie?"

"I'm all right, thanks. We really would like to see Greg—if you don't mind."

"You go right on ahead, then. Need anything? Just walk right up those steps in back. It'll bring ya into the kitchen. Just c'mon in and yell. I'm usually in the livin' room, watchin' Netflix. House ain't that big. I'll hear ya."

"Thank you."

Greer followed Erika down the dark path that went along the side of the house. A large concrete slab covered with lawn furniture and a barbecue grill filled the area.

Three cars were parked in a row in the driveway—a dark-colored Lexus, a black SUV, and a fairly-new VW. A two-car garage sat at the end of the property, about fifty feet from the slab. Both doors were closed. Hazy light showed through the long row of small square windows.

"Greg?" Greer asked as they approached the building.

"His name's Greg Hillsman. He doesn't go by that. Just his parents call him Greg. Everyone I know calls him Gus."

"Why Gus?"

"Short for Gusano. It means worm in Spanish."

"*Worm*?"

"Gus is probably the best hacker in Central Florida."

Greer didn't reply.

"That's what he's been doing ever since he graduated from high school. I think I heard that he was even doing it in college."

Greer found himself even more confused. "A *hacker*? Seriously?"

Erika shrugged. "I think he just might be our best shot at this."

Greer smiled. He was absolutely right about this girl. She knew exactly what she was doing.

His eyes stayed on her as he followed her to the left side of the block building and waited a couple of feet behind her as she knocked on the door.

***

The door creaked open.

A huge man about twenty-seven years old filled the doorway. At least six-four, he wore a bulky white sweatshirt and gray sweat pants over a massive three-hundred-pound frame. His tennies were enormous. His dark greasy hair reached his shoulder blades, and his heavy dark beard was wild and unkempt.

He scowled at Erika, whose face was illuminated by the hazy glow of the nightlight attached to the underside of the sloped roof. After about fifteen seconds of tense silence, he reached up with a large paw and shoved a thick lock of hair away from his face. "Yeah?"

Erika faced him boldly. "Sorry to bother you this late, but we really need your help."

He tilted his head and squinted. He seemed to be studying her again. "Heard ya got roasted a year or so ago, in that T-bone cluster—"

"You heard right."

He continued studying her face. "Bummer. Also heard ya holed up with your folks and keep yourself mummied-up most of the time."

"I changed my mind very recently."

"Ya don't say?"

"I started getting claustrophobia."

"No shit?"

"I wouldn't shit ya."

Greer wanted to smile.

The big man shrugged a beefy shoulder. "Whatever turns your crank. Haven't heard much about ya in a while. Thought maybe ya moved away or something."

"I haven't moved away or anything. And just in case you forgot why we're here…we need your help."

Greer really admired how she stood up to this gorilla of a guy.

Gusano suddenly noticed Greer standing behind her. "I can't help noticing that dude with ya," he said suspiciously.

"I'm the reason we need help," Greer said.

Gusano continued staring at Greer, then at Erika. He finally glared at Erika. "He looks Fed to me. Ya shittin' me, Young? Ya brought along a *Fed* with ya?"

Greer took a step closer and glared right back. "I'm *not* a goddamned Fed. I'm ex-military. *Very* ex-military. In fact, I'd rather have a lobotomy and even maybe a couple of root canals than be military again."

Gusano seemed surprised by Greer's heated reaction. He stood there in silence, gazing at Greer, then Erika. Then, focusing on Erika, he said, "And just what do you and Mr. Very Ex-Military want with me?"

"He's a hired drone. And he just went dark."

Gusano stiffened. He went back to staring at Greer, but his expression changed. The suspicion disappeared. "This for real? A hired drone?"

"Former."

"Why former?"

Greer hesitated.

"Tell him," Erika coaxed. "Otherwise, he won't want to help us. He's not exactly what anyone would call generous."

"I resent that remark," Gusano snapped.

"Why? 'Cause it's true?"

"Everything about me is generous, dammit."

Erika lowered her gaze to the man's ample gut. "I can see that."

"You don't have to get personal, now…"

"Why not? *You* are."

"That's beside the point." Gusano turned to Greer. "Why former?"

Greer sighed. "I've been a Government assassin for the last five years. The bastards handling me wanted me to kill Erika. They got pissed when I informed them that I didn't want to. And they've been trying to kill both of us ever since."

"And now they want to kill my parents," Erika said.

"This on the level?"

Greer was getting impatient. "Would anyone in his right mind make up such a ridiculous story? It's right out of Ludlum, for God's sake!"

Gusano grinned at the name. "C'mon in. Let's rap."

Chapter 24

Half a dozen fluorescents hissed and popped from the rafters.

The large area smelled of burnt coffee and marijuana and looked like it had been taken over by a hoarder. Boxes of different shapes and sizes had been stacked and shoved against two walls of the building. Computer equipment took up a third wall, as well as the center of the room, where two folding tables placed end-to-end were covered with computers, hard drives, laptops, and boxes overflowing with cellphones. A widescreen fastened to the west wall displayed a split screen, shared by the latest DOW stats as well as what appeared to be a Bourne movie with the sound turned way down. A metal table placed near the opened door of a small dimly-lit bathroom was topped with a coffeepot, microwave, and plastic jars stuffed with sugar packets, small bags of chips, cheese puffs and pretzels. Next to it, a cold drink machine hummed and clicked.

An old couch, its stuffing held in by long strips of silver duct tape, sat in the center of the room. Two feet in front of it, an ancient mahogany coffee table covered with graphic comics provided light reading and entertainment. A faded, well-used recliner sat next to one end of the couch, with two dining room chairs positioned at the opposite end. A worn, oval-shaped Turkish rug covered most of the central area.

Gusano jabbed a thumb toward the couch. "Take a load off. That couch may not be pretty, but it's comfortable. I sleep on it all the time."

Erika frowned.

"Don't worry," he said, chuckling. "I never crash in the buff."

She blinked. "*Real* good to know."

"She's always been the sassy type," Gusano said to Greer.

"Tell me about it." Greer sat down beside her.

Gusano lowered his large butt into the seat of the recliner. Ignoring its squeaky protests, he heaved it into its most extreme position.

"We need to find out who his handlers are as quickly as possible," Erika said. "The lives of my folks are at stake here. As well as our own."

Gusano pulled a crumpled joint from his shirt pocket. "You're--?" He raised his thick black brows at Greer.

"Greer. Justin Greer."

Gusano lit up and sucked in a heavy gray cloud. He held in the potent vapors for about ten seconds and let it out slowly, with a loud hissing noise. He held out the burning joint in their direction. "Good Colombian. Got a small grow behind the garage in a shitload of weeds neighboring the vacant lot. Plants are hidden pretty well." He chuckled. "I made sure no one can see 'em by strategically disguising the area with beat-up garbage cans, sheets of moldy particleboard, and weathered lumber covered with rusty nails. You leave that kinda shit out in full view? You can damned well put all sorts of valuables around it. People don't wanna get close to garbage. Or anything else that might hurt 'em if they get curious."

Erika sat up and glared. "How're you gonna help us if you're stoned?"

Gusano grinned stupidly. "Takes more than one of these little brown babies to turn the old gray computer into mush, girl. I usually go through ten of these guys a day."

"You'd better not be lying to us," she said softly. "We came here because we really need your help."

Gusano screwed up his puffy features. "I thought you got high."

"I do. Once in a while. But you kinda need a seriously clear head when a bunch of government killers have decided to come after you and your family."

Gusano had a much smaller hit and let it right back out. "Gotcha," he said in a low-pitched croak. "All righty, then. Go 'head, tell me what's going down."

Erika told him everything that had happened from the time she and Greer had first crossed paths on Rockledge Road until their close call at the storage facility just hours earlier.

Greer sat and listened, feeling even worse about all this and hating himself for bringing her into it in the first place. He couldn't help wondering how this huge pothead would help them. Gusano sat in his

200

recliner, his smoldering joint sending slithering wisps of gray smoke up into the small fan bolted to the rafters.

When Erika had finished, Gusano mashed what was left of his joint in a small tin ashtray on the coffee table. He looked at Greer. "You're up, dude."

"How's that?"

"She just told me what happened with her. Now *you* can tell me what happened with *you*."

Greer blinked. "Erika just told you—"

"I know what the chick just told me. I've been right here. Don'tcha think I was listening?"

Greer stared at the dead black stub smoldering in the ashtray. "I'm not totally sure."

"Every damn word she said is right up here. It's, like, programmed permanently into the computer." He tapped his right temple.

"Then why do you want me to—"

"If ya want me to help, I need to know everything. Know what that word means, dude?"

"Yeah..."

"What's it mean?"

Greer sighed. "It means, well, everything."

"Dude, there are two sides to everything. Sort of like that yin/yang bullshit, only totally different. Get what I'm saying?"

"No..."

"Good. Glad we're on the same page. To make it simple, I'll toss it to ya this way. Something happened to her, and she wants me to help her fix it. Right, girl?"

Erika nodded.

"But what happened to her," Greer said, "involves me."

"Rightomundo. Here's the wrinkle, dude. The way I see it, the same thing that happened to her also happened to you. But since you two are on opposite ends of all this, so to speak, what happened to you involves a ton of shit she couldn't possibly even know about. Am I right?"

Greer had to admit that the big guy knew what he was talking about. "Well, yeah..."

"Then quit yanking my chain and start revving up. I'll even help out your ass, just to make it simpler. You can start off by telling me what was going down, say, an hour or so before you two bumped heads on Rockledge."

Greer began his tale with his trip to Rockledge Road, where he left the pistol in the home of Ernest Lohman.

"You *planted* the gun?" Gusano asked. "Nothing else to it?"

"That was the extent of it."

"Then I guess the suicide story was just for shits and giggles? And for the media to get their jollies off on it?"

"All I can figure is that Lohman somehow pissed off someone important. In this case, I'm almost positive that it was all about the money."

"He was a developer," Erika said. "According to the *Sentinel*, there wasn't much of an investigation."

Gusano was silent for only a moment. "Slick. Someone plants the gun. Then someone else sneaks

202

in to finish the job. But he would've had to put the guy out first. There were no signs of a struggle?"

"These people generally use chloroform and other knockout drugs for jobs like this," Greer said.

"And they also put a lid on an investigation."

"They definitely have the resources for that."

"I take it you never saw the other guy? The one who finished the job?"

"I've never seen or have ever been contacted by anyone else since my recruitment. These people don't want us socializing."

"That would definitely be *such* a ginormous bummer," Gusano said.

"They let me know only what they think I have to know about the job. They don't answer questions and they don't tolerate foul-ups. And they take great pains not to reveal anything that could be used later on."

"I think I get the picture. Keep it rolling."

Greer told him about the incident at Fashion Square Mall. He mentioned his mishap out in the parking lot but did not include Erika's explanation of the incident. He didn't know this guy and had the feeling Erika didn't know him very well, either. Even if they did know one another, he didn't think Gusano would accept Erika's strange abilities.

Gusano tore open a Doritos bag and stuffed one into his mouth. He then picked up a large white mug from the table and took a sip. "So now this chick's a liability just because she saw you leaving the dead dude's house?"

"Exactly."

Gusano picked up another chip. "I daresay this is setting pretty solid with my conspiracy theory gene."

"Any ideas yet?"

"A few. But keep up the rap. I'll letcha know when to push the pause button." He shoved the chip into his mouth and munched loudly.

Greer continued with his instructions to stake out Erika's home. He told them that his handlers ordered him to eliminate her parents and ended by telling them how he'd talked them out of it.

Erika turned to him and glared. "*That's* why they wanted you to kill my folks? Because they thought I *might* have told them I saw you leaving Mr. Lohman's house?"

"I told them to check out your phone records. Which they did, of course. They got right back to me and told me they hadn't heard any such activity in your conversation with your mother, so there was no need for me to eliminate them."

"They actually *tapped into* our conversation?"

Greer nodded.

"Bastards..." She sat back, crossed her arms over her chest and trembled.

"How long did it take?" Gusano asked.

"How long did what take?"

"How long did it take them to do the tap?"

"Just a few minutes."

Gusano frowned. "If these boys can pull phone records and work up a tap that fast, we're talking *serious* 'nads."

"I could've told you that. They deal with me through an earpiece. If there are any cameras or monitors in the area, they tap into them as well and guide me step-by-step so I can complete the assignment."

Gusano nodded thoughtfully. "So now we're talking phone and camera surveillance." He got up heavily and plodded over to his worktable. "Now I know why I got a major whiff of Fed when I first saw ya outside."

"Oh, they're Fed, all right," Greer said. "I just don't know high up they go."

Gusano demolished another tortilla chip. "On second thought, this reeks more of Black Ops or Black Ops Rogue shit."

"Well, as you probably already know, no matter what it is or where it goes, this could possibly suggest an existing shadow Government."

"It'd have to be—especially when they start targeting private citizens. Which, as anyone with a working brain cell already knows, is a super ixnay in this country." Munching on a chip, Gusano logged onto his system and began punching keys.

In just a few moments, Gusano had already hacked into several FBI databanks. The screen filled up with pages of overlapping data and codes.

"How deep can you go?" Greer asked, standing over him.

Gusano chuckled. "How the hell d'ya think I earned my nickname?"

"That doesn't answer my question."

Gusano's fingers continued punching keys. "Once I set up my jamming system, I can pretty much go where no human mortal has ever gone before."

"Is that what you're doing now?"

"I've already sent opposing signals directly to my own station, which my buds and I set up a couple of years ago. Once it starts mixing up the frequencies, it disrupts the original feed, and I'm good to go anywhere I choose without being buttfucked with an interception."

"Sounds dangerous."

"The Government does whatever it wants and doesn't give a crap. But they always pitch a ginormous fit when a private dude does anything even remotely similar without Federal approval. To me, it looks that they want to pull their famous CYA tango by putting someone else on the spit. Whaddya think the FBI and CIA do when they need super sensitive information?"

"You've got a point there."

"By the way, just in case you're wondering… There are two types of hackers. The first type—me, actually—slithers his way into forbidden sites to get information, legal or otherwise, that can actually help someone—as I'm doing right now. The other type, the saboteur, digs into banks and other security systems to steal money or bank account numbers, then piles the stash into a fictitious account—or resells personal and private accounts to the highest bidder."

"If they catch you, they most likely won't care which kind you are."

Gusano grinned. "I've got this dynamite jammer system. It's orbital, of course, and highly sophisticated. If I spot any strange activity working its way in, I'll automatically shift my satellite closer to the doorstep of one of those saboteurs I just mentioned. This makes it literally impossible for anyone to leech anything that comes out of it."

"I take it you're friends with other hackers," Greer said.

Erika said, "There are three really great hackers in this area. I've heard that this guy's been working with all of them."

"Actually, those dudes are working with *me*." Gusano continued his assault on the keyboard. Just seconds later, he stopped abruptly and sat in silence for nearly half a minute, his gaze on the computer screen. He gave a deep sigh. "Shitfire."

"What's wrong?" Erika asked.

"I'm already scoping out some seriously scary shit here."

She bent over his shoulder and stared at the screen. "Damn. This *is* serious."

Greer moved closer to Erika. He was staring at the screen but couldn't make out what he was actually looking at.

"I was hoping I might be wrong," Gusano said.

"Does that look like Agenda 21 you?" Erika asked softly.

"You're not serious." Greer felt the hair stand up on the back of his neck.

Gusano sat back and ran both hands through his hair. He shook his head. "This actually looks like your handler dudes might have a direct connection."

"Seriously? Agenda 21?"

Gusano sighed tiredly and nodded.

Chapter 25

A chill trickled down Greer's back.

Like most servicemen, he'd heard of Agenda 21, but had never thought too much about it. The whole concept sounded too outlandish and very sci-fi, its scope staggering the imagination. A collective plot to wipe out 95% of the world's population, especially a plan that involved the leaders of major countries, sounded more farfetched than any James Bond novel.

"Are you absolutely sure about this?" he asked uneasily.

Gusano nodded. "I'm afraid so, dude."

"That scare has been going around for years," Erika said. "Anyone with a couple of active brain cells to rub together could tell it was some sort of hoax."

"I could never decide if it actually was a hoax or something a brickload of mega-rich psychos cooked up," Gusano said. "I've done boocoo research on it, but as you both already know, something this huge tends to run its course really fast. Technology doesn't help at all. I'd say at least seventy-five percent of all Net searches bring up every conceivable form of bullshit, gossip, hoaxes, myths, and total misinformation. There are just way too many blogs out there, and every single one of them turns out to be a total waste of time. They're nothing more than some fruitcake's biased opinion.

There are just too damned many fruitcakes out there, making everything even more of a cluster fuck."

"You get pissed and eventually give up trying," Greer said.

Gusano nodded. "So here's what I found out. As its history goes, the plan was first offered as official UN policy in 1992, in a document called UN Sustainable Development Agenda 21, issued at the UN's Earth Summit. Today, it's referred to simply as Agenda 21. Nearly two hundred nations adopted it as official policy during a signing ceremony at the Earth Summit."

"For obvious reasons," Greer said, "it didn't receive the coverage something of that scale should easily have generated."

Gusano munched on a tortilla chip. "I kept finding a boatload of sites about the Feds bringing in hundreds of thousands of body bags and storing them in abandoned fields, storage facilities, silos, and deserted barns in the Midwest."

"As I remember it," Erika said, "this was the UN's plan. They wanted it completed by the year 2030."

"I'm pretty sure that was debunked," Greer said. "It took quite a while before they could get the right brains working along the same lines, but my guess is that those idiots eventually figured out that a scheme like that was entirely too problematic. They no doubt decided that they wouldn't be able to actually finish it in their allotted timeframe."

"In my humble opinion," Gusano said, "I think those arrogant fucks actually tried doing it, but when they found out that it had been trickling all over the Internet, they got working on a quick plan to nip it in the bud. That's when all the hoax reports started coming in, and people got so tired of going online and finding every conceivable form of conflicting shit, they just gave up and decided the whole thing was nothing more than someone's wet dream gone totally bad. It didn't help at all that many of those sites contained Trojans, or other equally destructive malware. If you want people to stop doing research on anything, just slip in some malware. Works every time."

"But what about all the money they actually spent on body bags, storage fees, and everything else?" Erika asked.

"Ever heard of Agenda 2030?" Gusano asked.

"I believe I heard something about that being their replacement plan," Greer said. "It sounded less grim."

"And it sounds nothing like its predecessor," Gusano said. "I believe the word "prosperity" was their brainstorm for a theme for this bad boy." He chuckled. "Prosperity. Definitely positive—especially if you keep slipping the word in at every given opportunity. That would attract serious attention. You gotta give those bastards credit. They know how to throw curve balls."

"This happened just a couple of years ago, I believe," Greer said.

"Adopted at the United Nations Sustainable Development Summit on 25 September 2015," Gusano said. "This one was a plan of action for people, planet and prosperity." He laughed. "That just tears my ass up. Prosperity again. Cool concept. This brainstorm was most likely thought out by the same idiots that want to take guns away from law-biding people to eradicate every conceivable form of gun violence even though they don't give one wet fart about taking illegal guns off the streets." He turned back to the screen. "Officially dubbed "Agenda 2030," the UN plot, as its full title suggests, is aimed at transforming the world."

"No matter what they call it," Greer said, "it's just as ridiculous as Agenda 21."

"But they say this one is more efficient." Gusano let loose with a smirk. "It's a follow-up to their last fifteen-year plan, the defunct "Millennium Development Goals," or MDGs. It also dovetails nicely with Agenda 21, and even includes much of the same rhetorical bullshit. The combined Agenda 2030 goals for achieving what is euphemistically called "sustainable development" represent previous UN plans—deeper, more radical, more draconian, and astronomically more expensive."

"The Orwellian theme on steroids," Erika muttered.

Gusano punched more keys. "These plans include microchipping everyone. One of their brainstorms was a twenty-year plan which grew directly from Agenda 21. They apparently kept the most unpleasant and inhumane methods of their strategy in its original form. And now, hidden beneath such adjectives as prosperity, human welfare, and happiness for one and all, they stuck them in there so no one could find them amongst the hundreds of thousands of pages of their manifesto." He stopped typing. "Shitfire. I just found something. A shitload of other programs cropping up. They seem to be piggy-backed from both Agendas."

"What type of programs?" Greer asked.

"From the codes I'm getting, many of these are government clone-types—damnation. Hold it." He opened another window. "Looks like at least half a dozen military operations here, half of them obsolete."

"What about the others?" Greer asked.

"Seems like they've been used as terrorist-seeking operations presently being deployed by the Navy and the Marines. Here's one the Army's been using since 2016." Gusano punched another key. Several more windows quickly covered the screen. "Nope. Not that one." He punched yet another key. A window disappeared, and another opened, this one with *FORBIDDEN* covering most of the data. "Shitfire..."

"Dead end?" Greer asked.

"Methinks I've just been firewalled." Gusano turned to one of the small black boxes sitting on the desk to his left and pressed a sequence of keys. "Looks like we'll need the big guns after all."

"What's that?" Greer asked.

"Don't ask," Erika said.

Gusano went right back to his keyboard, deleted the *FORBIDDEN* window, then clicked on it again. This time it came right up. And without the *FORBIDDEN* block.

"I just broke through. Here goes. Now we can see what in holy hell this is."

"Military?" Greer asked.

"Judging by the long stack of numbers and letters preceding it, definitely military. And by the code stamp, it was officially cancelled months ago. This looks like something that most likely got hit due to Government cost-cutting and all that other shit the CIA was going through at the time. The Benghazi fiasco didn't help much, either. And when the Presidency switched hands, many of these undercover operations got zapped."

"Then it can't be the program that's been working me ragged the last five years," Greer said.

"When they recruited you, did they tell you *anything* about who the hell they were?" Gusano asked.

"Just the job itself."

"When exactly did they do this?"

"As I just said—five years ago. I was in Germany, recovering from injuries I'd suffered in Iraq, when insurgents rigged explosives that brought down our chopper."

"What was your condition when they approached you at the hospital?"

"Guarded."

"How guarded?"

"Enough where I don't remember much at all about their visit."

Gusano thought about that for a moment. "Now I know what those assholes did."

"Then you might wanna consider filling me in."

"They no doubt used their brainwashing technique of persuasion while you were sedated. It's much easier to handle a recruit this way. This was probably when they asked you to join them. I'd bet good money on the fact that they'd implanted you with a tracking device within twenty-four hours of your initial meeting."

"He had one," Erika said.

"Had?"

"I cut it out."

Gusano stared at her. He didn't say anything right off. Then he shrugged. "Just how in holy hell did you find the damned thing?"

Erika reddened and lowered her face.

"Don't ask," Greer said.

Gusano glanced at Greer, then turned back to Erika. He seemed confused, then shrugged it off. "No problemo."

Erika smiled at Greer, reached over and touched his hand.

Greer flinched at the heat of her touch.

Gusano opened another window. "There were actually two of these Agenda 21 human drone-type programs that came right up. One's DS, or Down Scale, while the other's LS, or Large Scale."

Neither Greer nor Erika spoke as Gusano read aloud the new window, which was entitled, *Agenda 21, Down Scale*:

"Recruit small groups of wounded but able-bodied American Veterans, preferably with killing skills, inject them with tracking devices, relocate them to selected key cities to use as human drones to shadow and eliminate immediate enemies of the state."

Gusano sighed and looked up at Greer. "This sounds like your shtick, dude."

***

Greer was unable to reply. His throat was dry, for one thing, and his heart was racing, for another.

He'd always suspected that he was being handled by a Black Ops program. But he just hadn't imagined that the people responsible were connected with anything as sinister or as mind-blowing as a chapter of Agenda 21.

"Nothing comin' atcha?" Gusano asked.

"Nothing that'll make any sense," he replied. "And certainly nothing that'll make me look less like an idiot for going along with them in the first place."

"You had no choice," Erika said. "You were wounded, and all doped up with meds. You probably couldn't think straight for months."

Although she had a point, he knew he shouldn't be let off the hook so easily. "I could still function. My brain was working—not at full capacity, but it was there. I wasn't *totally* out of it."

"But you don't remember much of it at all, do you?" she asked.

"I remember someone coming into my room and talking to me."

"What'd this dude look like?" Gusano asked.

He tried remembering, but all he recalled was a series of blurred gray images. "A uniform."

"What else?"

"He was a guy. Tall, maybe."

"How tall?"

"About half a head taller than my nurse."

"How tall was your nurse?"

Greer shrugged. "I was lying down at the time. And I didn't have a measuring tape with me at the time."

"Nothing else?"

"Nothing that's coming up right now."

Gusano shook his head. "This is classic. I mean total textbook. It's how they recruit for shadow stuff like this. Emphasis on shadow. If you'd been conscious and even partially alert, they wouldn't have wanted to talk to you at all."

"He's right," Erika said. "Don't beat yourself up."

"You wouldn't say that if you knew how many people they made me—"

"You didn't kill *me*." Her eyes blazed. "And you were directly responsible for sparing my parents. That's more than enough for me."

Greer gave her a tired smile. "But where does this leave us? We know who's responsible, directly or indirectly, for pushing my buttons; we just don't know anything else."

"Maybe, maybe not," Gusano said.

"Something up there you haven't told us yet?"

Gusano noisily demolished another tortilla chip. "Could very well be…"

"Care to elaborate?" Erika asked.

Gusano shook his head. "Not me," he said. "Him." He jabbed a fat index finger in Greer's direction. "You can start by telling us everything you remember about all this. From day one."

"Everything?"

"Yeah. That might even work."

"The hospital visit?"

"Every single detail, no matter how small or insignificant."

"I thought I already told you—"

"You obviously missed a spot."

"How could you possibly know that?"

"Because something's clearly dangling out there. Otherwise, this would have started making sense long before now."

"I honestly don't know if I can say with a clear conscience that I—"

"Stop pouring a generous helping of processed bullshit over everything and just start talking." Gusano's expression had turned dark.

Greer sighed. "We might be here a while."

Gusano shrugged a beefy shoulder. "I ain't going anywhere. I don't know if you can tell by my behavior or my wardrobe, but I'm not exactly what you'd call a social animal."

Greer didn't know what to say.

"Besides, didn't this chick tell you? I'm the world's worst conspiracy nut."

Erika nodded. "He really and truly is."

Gusano grinned proudly. "I make those TV dudes like Munch and Mulder look like dyed-in-the-wool patriots." He sat back and clasped his hands together behind his thick neck. "Now you can start telling us things we really need to know."

Chapter 26

Greer's nightmare began five years earlier, just days after he'd spoken to the sober-faced, soft-spoken men at the German hospital. He was sent back to the States just weeks later, with a Medical Discharge. Since he'd been a Central Florida resident when he was first sent to Iraq, his new employers gave him a three-room apartment in downtown Orlando as well as an expense account and an online account with an autopay option that took care of his rent and all utilities.

His first job was dictated to him just one week after he'd settled into his new digs. The assignment was very simple and took less than an hour of his time. He was to eliminate a forty-two-year-old male living in the St. Cloud area. All he was told was that his victim taught fifth grade in one of the grade schools in the area.

"Were you given a name?" Gusano asked.

"Just a description."

"Shrewd. This keeps their asses clean."

"Now you know what I've been facing the last five years."

"One question that's been bugging the tits off me," Gusano said. "Why not just tell 'em to go fuck themselves, leave the state and start all over somewhere else?"

"You don't know how often I've wanted to tell them that."

"Why didn't you?"

"The chip they'd implanted me with always seemed to get in the way."

Gusano sighed. "Yeah, that damned chip thing again. I should have figured. This is definitely Orwell material."

"It was a little more than just that."

"Whenever he did something they didn't like," Erika said, "they just switched him off."

"Howzat?"

"His chip turned him off."

Gusano's eyes grew. "Seriously?"

"Like an on-off switch," Greer said.

"This on the level?"

"It's not something I'd joke about."

"I get it, believe me."

Greer didn't want to tell the big man anything about Erika's special gift but realized he didn't have much choice. If they wanted Gusano's help, they needed to trust him. Gusano was a strange bird but seemed extremely capable. Besides, being strange didn't seem so bad right now. "This lovely young lady found it and cut it out."

"She already told me, but I sorta got the idea that you didn't want to talk about it."

"I didn't," Greer replied.

"What's different?"

"If we want to get anywhere with this, I guess we need to put everything out there."

Gusano turned to Erika. "All righty, then."

Erika returned his gaze. "Whaddya wanna know?"

Gusano sat bolt upright in his chair. "You know what I'm getting at. Those little buggers are *tiny*. I mean *miniscule*. Just a hair short of non-existent, in fact. We're talking about something you could hide in a small shaker filled with rice. How the hell did ya find the damn thing?"

Erika didn't reply.

Gusano's expression, a mixture of confusion and impatience, told them they needed to be straight with him. "You know they don't always pick the same site, don'tcha? I mean, it's not like they have an actual blueprint of the designated area to work with. What fun would *that* be?" He sat back. "What are we talking here? I can't help noticing the bandage on this dude's forearm. Could that be the site? Or are ya gonna tell me he cut himself shaving?"

Greer shrugged. Erika looked sheepish.

Gusano shook his head. "I don't get it. It could've been *anywhere*, for God's sake. The wrists. Neck. Legs. Calves. Then they've got the chest, which gives 'em all sorts of possibilities. And if they *really* wanted to make things interesting, they could've just stuck the damned thing in his ass. And don't forget—there are *two* cheeks we're talking here, and the area—at least, for some of us—is *humongous*."

Erika glanced at Greer, who was watching her closely. He could tell she needed his help.

After the long, awkward silence, Greer said, "What the hell does it matter how she found it? The point is, she managed to pull it out—and without

222

slicing anything important, either. And because of it, she saved my life. So stop the damned third degree and let's just go on from here."

"But how could she possibly—"

"Like I just said, forget about it. Okay?"

"I didn't know you had medical experience," Gusano said to Erika.

"I don't."

"Forget it," Greer said flatly.

"You understand why I can't properly digest any of this, can't you?" Gusano asked.

Greer couldn't blame his skepticism or his confusion. It sounded incredible—no matter how you looked at it. But the big man didn't need to know everything. "Just start focusing on what's really important, and maybe we'll get things going again. There's helluva lot going on here, and concentrating on that stupid chip will only stop any progress we've already made."

"You wouldn't by any chance have that damned thing on ya, would you?" Gusano asked.

Erika shrugged. "I tossed it."

"Why?"

"To keep them from finding us."

Gusano looked pensive. "I guess that was actually a really good move at the time." He gave them a sort of half-smile. "But now? Not so much."

"It was the only sensible thing we could do," she said.

"So now we have nothing? Zilch? A handful of fucking air?"

"Not exactly." Erika reached into her hip pocket and pulled out the earpiece Greer had taken from the assassin. She held it out.

"This was yours?" he asked Greer.

"It's identical to the one they gave me."

"Where's yours?"

"I tossed it."

"Why?"

"I got pissed."

"Can't blame ya." Gusano took it from Erika and studied it. He got up heavily, shuffled back to his computer and started punching keys.

"What are you doing now?" Greer asked.

"I'm gonna trace this nasty little toy to find out if it's military issue."

"Can you do that?"

"Don't ask. Just go back to the couch and watch whatever's on. I've got the Bourne trilogy playing on the widescreen, and also the fourth one Matt Damon made just a couple of years ago, when he gained all that weight and tried like a motherfucker to not look so close to fifty. Remote's on the table. I've got porn on one of my special channels. It's labeled Biology—just in case the folks pay me a surprise visit and wanna get nosey. Have a ball." He stopped typing. "But if you and the chick wanna get frisky, I'd appreciate it if you waited till after you left. I've got a mattress back there behind some boxes, but I really don't wanna hear moaning and groaning or any wet slapping sounds while I'm trying to work. It's totally distracting. I need to focus."

Greer turned to Erika, who was shaking her head.

"He's the best hacker I know," she whispered.

"I understand."

"Believe it or not, he's not nearly as crazy as the others I've met."

Greer just smiled.

**

Twenty minutes later, Gusano got up from his workstation and plodded back to his recliner. He had several scraps of paper in his hand. He lowered himself into the soft, well-cushioned seat and studied the scraps.

"I take it you found something else," Greer said.

"Rightomundo. First of all, that earpiece is definitely military issue."

"I guess I always suspected that," Greer said.

"I'll bet you didn't suspect that it was manufactured the same time Agenda 21 was activated."

Greer didn't reply.

"Also, going by the numbers, this nasty little thingy was implemented during a two-week experiment when Project 21 DS started up while you were in Germany. There were originally fifty DS units implemented all over the country, one for each state, and assigned to the most densely populated area in each. For example, New York City was the one employed in New York State."

"Any idea how many rogues were assigned to each unit?" Greer asked.

"Anywhere from five to twenty. It all depended on the size and density of the area. They didn't want their operatives bumping into one another, but also didn't want them covering too much area and suffering burnout after a couple of months."

"Where's this going?"

"Each earpiece has its own serial number. This bad boy was assigned to the DS unit implemented in Central Florida five years ago."

Greer shrugged. "No offense, but I already gathered that."

Gusano took a few moments before replying. "But did you also know that the program folded three months ago? And that its funding went belly-up two weeks before that?"

***

Greer could not speak. The shock swept right in, voiding his mind of all coherent thought, and he realized that he could not comprehend what the big man had just told him.

The program had folded.

And yet, he was still being ordered to kill people.

What the hell was going on?

He struggled for his brain to start working again, but all he could imagine were the people he had killed during the last three months. And the nightmares. And the countless bottles he'd emptied in a pathetic attempt to rid his mind of what he'd been forced to do.

"Justin?" Erika touched his arm. "You okay?"

He didn't reply.

226

"I realize that was a stupid question," she said. "I just meant—"

He patted her arm and turned to Gusano. "You're sure about this? I mean absolutely *sure*?"

"The program just dissolved. Of course, it had to be phased out gradually because of the sizeable financing for the dudes out in the field, so they gave the program another eight weeks before pulling the accounts. Since the sanctioned killers were still active, they had to keep the payroll in place. Some of the accounts are already in escrow. You're obviously still working, so I'd wager that they've kept you bankrolled until fairly recently. I'd also wager that you're gonna run out of money within the next three or four weeks."

This made no sense. The earpiece. The blackouts. The flat, disinterested voice commanding him. Business as usual.

Most of all, the orders. The assignments.

He stared hard at Gusano. "Could you have possibly made a slight error?"

"I checked and double-checked. I've got a source in the FBI who always seems to owe me a favor. It only took him a couple of minutes to check it out. Dude, your operation's toast."

"In other words, my handlers are no longer sanctioned handlers?"

"The project officially shut down three months ago, in mid-May, and many of their active assets were called in and gradually disbanded due to the suspension of government funding."

"I can't believe this," Erika said.

"Shit like this happens all the time with government programs," Gusano said. "Especially those that seriously compromise the Bill of Rights. I'm not quite sure why this one was dumped, but it might have had something to do with Agenda 21 staying in the crosshairs too long. Maybe one of those mental midgets on Capitol Hill got super-nervous—or simply shit his tighty-whities—and decided to do what those pompous idiots do best—turn tail and let the incoming Administration take the hit. Or turn tail during the mid-terms and start drawing their obscene pensions while they're still able."

Greer sat back and stared at the TV screen, which was playing the third Bourne film.

"I can't believe this," Erika said. "I keep remembering what happened after I caught you scoping out my parents' home."

"That's right." Greer quickly found that he was remembering things. Important things. "You were right there. You never told me what happened after that. Or what you saw."

"You were out cold. It looked like you just went to sleep. I got scared and ran back home, but before I was able to reach my front yard, a cop car had parked behind your Challenger. I hid behind my mother's rosebush. I couldn't see everything, but it looked like the cops weren't actually doing anything. Then a van came by and parked behind the cruiser. Two men in dark clothes got out and talked to the cops. Less than a minute later, the cruiser pulled away and turned off its lights. Right after that, one of the guys got back in the van. I couldn't see the other guy, but I figured he was doing something with you."

"What happened then?"

"About a minute later, both the van and the Challenger pulled out. Nothing happened after that."

"Sounds pretty damn Condor-like to me," Gusano said.

"Did you happen to get a good look at the men?"

"They both looked young."

"How could you tell?"

"They were tall and really slender."

"Could you tell how young?"

Erika shook her head. "Early twenties, maybe? All I noticed was that they were both skinny. I've never really seen too many Government agents or employees that skinny."

The hair on the back of Greer's neck bristled. "The killer we met at the storage facility on Semoran was also skinny."

"He wore a black hood," Erika said. "We couldn't see his face."

"I took out his earpiece. To do that, I had to pull up his hood."

"How much did you see?" Gusano asked.

"Just enough to get a quick glimpse of his cheek."

"Something weird about it?" Erika asked.

"There was hardly any stubble."

Erika's eyes grew. "Does this mean what I think you're telling us?"

"Our so-called killer hadn't been shaving very long."

Erika took a breath. "That makes him—"

"My guess would be no more than eighteen. Twenty, tops."

Gusano shook his head. "That's too fucking young for a government hitter."

"At first I thought I was seeing things," Greer said. "Then I decided he just looked younger than he actually was. We were in kind of a rush, so I couldn't dwell on it at the time. I was afraid he might not be alone. That's why I took the earpiece. Just in case they called back with fresh instructions."

"Were there any?" Gusano asked.

"None."

"Then they either knew what happened or were waiting for the killer to finish up."

"No doubt."

"So how young do you think he was?" Gusano asked.

"*Too* damned young."

"What is this telling us?" Erika asked.

"It tells me that the men who picked me up were probably the same age," Geer said. "And this tells me none of them were Government employees."

***

Gusano went back to punching keys, this time with his headset on.

"What do you think he's doing now?" Greer asked.

Erika sighed. "With him, one never knows."

"Just trying to dig into this from some other perspective," Gusano said as he worked.

"For example?" Greer asked.

"Time frames." *Punch, punch...* "Corresponding news items." *Punch, punch, punch...* "Cross-references." *Punch...* "That squinty bullshit that always makes my eyes glaze over and my head ready to explode."

"I've been doing their dirty work for the last five years," Greer said. "And now you're telling me that the people I've been working for all this time are out of the picture."

"They're still there," Gusano said. "They're just no longer government-sanctioned."

"So you're saying that they've gone rogue?"

"No idea."

"And now they're using *kids*?"

Gusano shrugged.

"This has obviously become some sort of independent operation."

"Once again, no clue."

"You're not helping, you know."

"That's why I'm doing all this goddamned squinty work," Gusano said, frowning.

"Where?"

"The FBI databanks. I've even dipped into the CIA mainframe. I'm also going through every conceivable Black Ops site I can find. Their irritating firewalls are really pissing me off. But at least I'm not going at it alone. I've got two highly reputable contacts who do nothing but explore conspiracy theories. I graduated from high school with both of them." Gusano paused to push a tortilla chip into his mouth.

"Hackers, too?" Greer asked.

"Only the best. They're almost as good as I am."

"This is bound to be interesting."

"I hope you realize that I've just gone really deep. Deeper than shit, in fact."

"Just how deep is that?"

"Let me put it this way—so deep that any normal hacker would be sweating blood under similar circumstances."

"Well, in case I don't get the chance to say this later on," Greer said, "I really appreciate what you've been—"

Before he could finish his statement, the blackness came from out of nowhere.

Chapter 27

Erika dove to the floor and gently cradled Justin's head in her lap.

"What the *fuck*?" His eyes bulging, Gusano got up from his chair and lumbered over.

Erika checked Justin's neck for a pulse. It was rapid, but strong. This gave her hope, but it didn't diminish her rage. "Those bastards…they zapped him again!"

"*Again*? You mean—"

"Just as I said. They zapped him *again*. Those bastards switched him off *again*." She could barely contain the heat raging through her.

"*This* is what you two were talking about?" Gusano gawked at Erika, then Justin, who lay lifeless in her arms.

"We told you about this. You didn't forget, did you?"

"Hearing about it's *one* thing… But actually seeing it happen?" Gusano shook his head. "This is, well, far freaking out! I mean, whacko city! Being turned off and on? Like a fucking *light switch*?"

Erika couldn't stop gazing at Justin's lifeless face. "I just can't believe this! I cut out the GPS in his arm. I thought that's how they were doing it. But I was obviously wrong. Dammit!"

"The one you found was no doubt GPS. Nothing else."

"What about this...this...whatever *this* other stupid thing is?"

"I guess we're talking about a different kind of chip," he said uneasily.

Erika's eyes grew. "*What* other kind?"

Gusano sighed heavily. "One that controls whether or not he's able to stand up. Or stay awake. Or think, even."

Erika didn't reply. She couldn't. This was too much. She could feel her composure deteriorating. "This really and truly totally *sucks*!"

"That basically nails it down, all right."

She couldn't take her eyes off Justin. He looked so frail. So helpless. This was not right. Not right at all. "Gusano, we have to help him. We have to do something about this!"

"I know. But what?"

"Something. Anything. Otherwise, those bastards are gonna kill him. Justin told them he wouldn't work for them anymore. He told me they won't tolerate that. They don't like it when one of their guys quits."

Gusano plodded back to his workstation. "I think I might have something that'll be useful."

While he went through boxes and dumped things in a cluttered pile on top of his work table, Erika continued cradling Justin's head in her lap. *Stay with me*, she thought, gently stroking his face. *Please don't leave me, Justin. We'll find some way of—*

Just then, a distant voice
(the back of his neck)

234

exploded in her head, disrupting all previous thought.

Suddenly uneasy, she looked around the dark room, wondering if someone had snuck up to her. It *had* sounded like a voice, hadn't it? Not a thought, but a voice. That same reassuring voice she'd heard before. And unless she was mistaken, that same voice had something to do with her newly-acquired sensitivities intervening, guiding her.

The back of his neck. Sure. Why not?

Gingerly she turned Justin's head. Using her fingertips, she felt the hard muscle extending down to his trapezius. But after careful examination, she discovered nothing out of the ordinary.

Something else popped out amidst her thoughts

(the base of his skull)

and without hesitation, she pressed her index finger to the area.

And felt a strange *warmth*.

Gusano rushed over, holding a black magnetic wand in his right hand and a small square monitor in his left. He got down heavily on one knee and began moving the wand over Justin's legs, closely watching the monitor.

"Up here." Erika pointed to the back of Justin's skull.

He blinked. "How'd you—"

"Don't ask questions."

He turned back to the monitor and moved the wand up to the back of Justin's head. And stiffened.

"Wh-What *is* it?"

He didn't reply. His jaw dropped as he gaped at his monitor.

"Gusano? *Talk* to me!"

He shook himself. "Shitfire, girl! I don't know what ya did or how ya did it, but apparently you just nailed the shit out of it."

"I did?"

"Fucking A. This dude's carrying around another chip. And it looks like the fucker's buried right there, square in the back of his noggin."

Her sensitivities had done it once again. But how could this help? How could they possibly remove a chip buried so close to the man's brain?

"I'm all ears," Gusano said, his eyes on her.

"What's that?"

"Now *you* get to tell *me* what's going down…"

"I…don't know…what you mean…"

"I can tell your head's doing some serious hoops. Hell, I can actually hear those gears grinding. Talk to me, girl. Tell me what in holy hell is going down!"

She had no idea what to say. Right now, there was nothing she could think of that would make any sense. All she had in her brain right now were questions. Tons of them.

She sat on the frayed Turkish rug, Justin's head cradled in her lap, and all she could think of were the last couple of days.

Did any of this stuff really happen?

Maybe, maybe not. This could all quite possibly be a figment of her imagination. Maybe she wasn't really here. If so, all she had to do was close her eyes for a few moments, empty her mind of all distractions, then open her eyes again. She'd find herself in her own room, sitting at her workstation, working on that stupid term paper. This would be nothing more than one of those silly dreams she had when she was bored out of her skull and yearned to have a happy, exciting life.

But the moment she closed her eyes, Gusano said, "You haven't zoned out, have ya?" and she realized that this wasn't just a dream. It was actually happening. And she needed to do something about it.

She took a breath—a deep one—and told herself that she was bigger than this, stronger than this, and would survive, no matter what. She turned to Gusano and forced herself to focus on more practical matters. "Is there any way of telling how deep down the chip is?"

Gusano had been studying the back of Justin's skull, as well as his monitor. He shook his head. "The image is faint—which tells me it's deep."

"You're sure?"

"The gauge only goes so far. This is an older model. I haven't been able to find a new one at all."

It looked deep, but she told herself they couldn't give up. They had to get it out, somehow. Otherwise, Justin couldn't possibly survive. "We can't just cut it out, then…"

"Without coming a tad too close to his brain? Or damaging anything else? Like the nerves running down his spinal cord?" He lowered the wand. "Listen, girl… I may be a wiseass and all, and the last dude you'd wanna see at a sit-down dinner party, but I tend to sober up like lightning when you start talking brain matter. We're also getting just a tad too cuddly-close to spinal cord involvement and a shitload of other neurological stuff I know absolutely nothing about."

Erika felt herself beginning to freak when something else

(touch it)

suddenly registered in her brain.

But just when she started doubting herself again, the feeling gave her another message

(visualize it dimming)

and before she realized it, she'd pressed her finger firmly to the affected area, closed her eyes, visualized darkness...and the image dimming into nothingness...while holding the position for what seemed a very long time.

Dead silence.

Then:

"*Shitfire!*" Gusano pulled back, nearly dropping his monitor.

Startled, Erika opened her eyes.

"What the *fuck*? W-What did ya—what the *fuck*?" Gusano gawked at her, his veiny dark-brown eyes filling the sockets. Swallowing audibly, he gazed at Justin. "I don't know what the hell's going on with you, girl..." With shaky hands, he moved the wand closer to the back of Justin's skull and held it there.

"What...w-what do you see?" she asked uneasily.

238

He didn't move or take his eyes off the wand. Then he began studying the monitor again. "Girl, going by what I see—rather, *don't* see—I'd say that you just pulled something totally super freaky with this dude's chip."

Had she heard him correctly? Or had her cursed imagination taken over once again? "*W-What* did you say?"

"The image."

"What about it?"

"I…I don't *see* it anymore!"

"W-What happened?"

Just then, Justin began to stir.

***

Greer felt that he was coming up for air after a particularly long, exhausting underwater swim. Everything seemed bright and cold. Then, as he took a deep breath and struggled to open his eyes, things dimmed, turning into patches of darkness intermixed with splinters of bright light.

The heavy scent of weed floated around in the air. Long, slender lights flickered directly above his head. Shadows moved around restlessly in a large screen somewhere on his left.

Erika stared down at him, her large, moist blue eyes filled with worry, her warm hands holding his head in her lap.

What the hell happened?

Why the hell am I lying on the floor?

His thoughts were blurred and seemed very far away. As he tried remembering, everything grew even more hazy. He decided it might be best to focus on his surroundings. Then, as his thoughts looped and flashed clearer images at him, he realized just what had happened.

Another blackout.

The bastards did it to him again.

But how?

A glimpse of Erika holding a tiny microchip in her palm registered amongst the fleeting shadows.

If she removed the chip, how the hell could they have given me another blackout?

More images.

Gusano punching keys. Putting on his headset. Making calls. Punching more keys.

The program folded three months ago. In mid-May. The funding folded...went belly-up.

The program was gone, yet he'd still managed to complete dozens of assignments. Dozens of people killed.

No funds.

Belly-up.

His handlers were no more.

So why was he still killing people?

And, more important, why were they still giving him blackouts?

"Justin?" Erika's soft voice disrupted his thoughts.

It was time for answers. It was also time to face cold reality.

I've been killing people illegally—needlessly—for three months.

That thought alone made him want to purge his guts.

240

"Justin?"

Sighing deeply, he nodded.

"You okay?"

He closed his eyes and fought the nausea. "I don't think...I'll ever be okay again."

"You will be. I'll help you, I promise. But first tell me you can understand me, okay?"

"I understand, believe me."

"They turned you off again."

"I know. I can tell."

"We're just not sure *how* they did it."

The bastards had done it again. Erika had removed his chip, but they still managed to turn him off again. Which told him the worst possible scenario.

"You know what's happened, don'tcha?" she asked.

He looked her right in the eye. It took quite an effort to get the words out, but once they'd left his throat, he immediately felt the anger gushing out with them. "There's another chip."

She didn't respond.

"Erika?"

She sighed. "We...we saw it on Gusano's monitor."

He closed his eyes again.

"Justin?"

He tried pushing away the rage. All he could think of was the hospital in Germany. The doctors swarming around him, dark suits hovering around in the shadows, trying to look invisible... And how he'd thought they were waiting for something, some

241

sort of cue… And that no matter how doped-up he was, he couldn't help thinking that something evil was lurking right there, waiting to be released…

The rage remained, grabbing at him, draining his strength, searing his blood...

Erika touched his cheek. In that one instant, everything dark and cold and frightening dissolved into a soft, warm bed of nothingness.

"Justin? *Please* talk to me…"

"I'm…still here," he said.

Her grim look frightened him. He couldn't help thinking that she had something else to tell him. Something really bad.

"Tell me," he said, sighing.

"You're sure?"

"I'm sure."

"There's another chip, all right. But this one might be impossible to cut out."

"Why?"

She didn't reply.

"Tell the dude." Gusano had moved closer.

Erika turned pale.

Greer struggled to sit up. "What the hell's going on?"

"I…may have done something," Erika said after a tense silence.

Her tone made his flesh crawl. "What…did you do?"

"There's a chip in the back of your skull," Gusano said.

Greer felt a tingle climbing up his spine. It took all his strength to get the next words out. "Is that…it?"

Gusano shook his head.

"I…might have done something…to it," Erika said.

"Keep going." He could feel his throat closing up, his flesh turning cold. "You don't wanna stop there."

She didn't reply.

"Erika?"

She turned away.

"Talk to me, dammit." The suspense was killing him. He had to know—one way or the other. "One of you. I honestly don't care which one it is. Just tell me what the hell's going on. It'll mean a lot, believe me."

Gusano sighed deeply and looked him right in the eye. "I honestly don't know how she did it, dude, but it looks like she might've totally zapped the damned thing!"

Chapter 28

His nerves suddenly jumping erratically, Greer, turned to Erika. "Tell me what I thought he just said."

Erika pushed some hair away from her face with a trembling hand. "I'm...not really sure what...I don't understand...I honestly don't know *what* happened, Justin..."

Greer turned to Gusano.

"I don't get any of this shit, either." The big guy glanced at Erika. "I'm not exactly in sync with implants, but what I saw her do..." He just shrugged.

"You just told me she deactivated a chip in the back of my neck."

"That's basically what she did. Or what I *thought* she did. Or what I thought I *saw* her do..."

"You're sure it's deactivated?"

"Reasonably."

"Not a hundred percent?"

"Dude, I'm not one hundred percent sure of *anything* anymore. Not since I saw that image disappear from my monitor."

Greer couldn't understand why the two of them were acting so frightened. "If it's deactivated, then I should no longer be worried, right?"

"It just ain't that simple, dude."

"What isn't simple about it? Your monitor's working, isn't it?"

"As far as I know…"

"Then why the hell are you acting like someone just shoved a pissed-off hornet down your undershorts?"

"I'm kinda confused and slightly messed up, dude. This kinda shit…this is *Twilight Zone* stuff!"

"What's got you so damned flustered?"

"Everything, dude."

"Start from the beginning. Maybe we'll get lucky as we go."

"First of all, I've got no idea what she just did. Or what sort of chip we're talking about here. Or even why it disappeared from the monitor." He began pacing. "It would seriously help if I knew what the hell we were dealing with. But I'm not, and that scares the shit outa me. If it was just a simple RFID chip we're dealing with, this wouldn't even be an issue. I could just watch our girl, here, make a tiny cut in the back of your neck and pull it out with a pair of tweezers. Then all I'd have to do is place the tag inside a Faraday cage, and the damned thing immediately turns into a worthless chunk of plastic. Or I could just chuck it in a microwave for five seconds and it becomes something my mom would sweep up from the floor. There are other ways, of course, and just about all of them are on the Net. Anyone can look them up."

He stopped pacing. "But like I said, I have no idea what that damned thing is. All I know is that it's powerful. It would have to be for what it's been doing. We're talking government, here. Miles and miles of radio waves, jamming, relays, and all that other highly sophisticated bullshit. Who knows what diabolical minds our country's leaders shacked up with to come up with something like that? But whatever it is, it doesn't matter, because this babe, here, did something that made it dormant. Or dead. Or *some*thing…"

Greer kept his steady gaze on Gusano. "Disregard all that technical mumbo-jumbo and tell me something I need to know. Just tell me why the two of you think Erika deactivated the chip."

Gusano didn't reply.

Greer suddenly discovered that he was frightened. What these two had just told him had quickly become insignificant. What mattered was that he was still carrying around a chip, and the damned thing was imbedded in the back of his skull. This meant one thing—two things, actually. The first little detail was obvious. It meant that even though his program had been deactivated, he was still being played. And used. And manipulated.

And, most frightening of all, he was still killing people.

The second detail was just as obvious. The very thought of it made him want to scream. It told him that if this second chip was imbedded in the back of his skull, it could be lodged dangerously close to his brain. And that meant it was there to stay.

Insurance. It was a word his handlers used quite a bit. A term they liked to toss at him whenever they decided he needed a quick refresher course in loyalty and, most important of all, humility.

Humility. Another word that, thanks to his handlers, he'd grown to despise.

After taking a couple of deep breaths, he tried getting his heartrate back to normal. *Fight this. Forget what might happen and concentrate instead on taking control. Use those resources you needed in Iraq, when you were dumped in that dark, damp, sand-filled cellar and escaped only because the hard-faced guard responding to your feigned coughing didn't notice the rusty ten-penny nail you'd found half-buried in the sand that single crucial moment before you'd shoved it into his left eyeball.*

Feeling more confident, he pulled himself out of his nightmare and into this new one, which had turned abysmally dark as well. And realized that he had to start thinking clearly. He turned to Gusano. "How'd you find the chip in the first place?"

Gusano shot another quick glance at Erika. "That's another thing. This chick here—"

"Her name's *Erika*." He was surprised by the sudden flash of anger. "You already know that. Why aren't you using it anymore?"

"Shitfire...she's *scaring* me, dude..."

"Why? Because she deactivated the chip?"

Gusano shook his head. "Look, guys, I'm the first to admit that I ain't anywhere near normal, okay? Look at me. I don't *look* normal. I sure as hell don't *talk* normally. And everyone—including my folks—knows I don't *act* like a normal dude. I've been living in this garage since I left college. I happen to like it here, and I even manage to make a little money doing what I like to do best. But what I do is some serious shit that would put me away in a federal pen for the rest of my life if someone ever got pissed at me and decided to—"

"What the hell are you trying to say?" Greer asked.

"Ask her, dude. Ask her how she found that damned chip. Like I said, I'm totally clueless here!"

Greer kept his gaze on Gusano. "I don't have to. I already know."

Gusano gawked at Greer, then at Erika. "Dude, what the hell are you trying to lay on me?"

"I'm trying to say that how she found that chip doesn't matter. Not to me, anyway. It doesn't matter to me what kind of chip it was, who designed it, where it was made, or what it was designed to do. And if that stuff doesn't matter to me, it certainly shouldn't matter to you. The only thing I really care about is that I've got a chip in my head, and if it isn't totally deactivated very shortly, it's probably going to kill me when I least expect it to."

"Dude, I honestly don't know if she totally zapped it—"

"Can you find out?"

"Well, *duh*…"

"Shitcan the attitude and do your thing."

Gusano grabbed his scanner apparatus. "Turn around."

Greer did as suggested.

Gusano brought the scanner closer to Greer's head and adjusted the monitor. He made several more clicks, moving the equipment around and pressing switches.

Erika moved closer. "I still don't see it."

"Nope." Gusano squinted. "No sign of the little fucker."

"But it's obviously still there," Greer said.

"I don't think it'd dissolve, dude."

"I've heard some are designed to dissolve after a period of time."

Gusano chuckled. "You actually think the assholes jerking your chain all these years would stick a self-destructive chip in your head?"

"No. I really don't think they'd do something as nice or accommodating as that."

"So where are we, then?" Erika asked.

Gusano shook his head. "I wish I knew."

"Tell me what you *do* know," Greer said.

"Right now? I'm beginning to think I don't know anything."

Greer knew better than let the big man shut down. Too much was at stake. "Then let me ask you this—just to see if your brain has actually turned to mush. If the chip doesn't show up on the scanner, what could that possibly mean? I mean technically."

"That's easy. It's not putting out any signals."

"That means it's dead?"

"I'm not sure."

"Why not?"

"Because I never saw anyone kill the signal by pressing it with their finger. That's exactly what she did. She didn't use magnets, cellophane, foil, radiation—anything that might've worked—under certain specifically controlled conditions, that is. Nothing. Just her finger."

Feeling queasy again, Greer circled the couch and fell into it.

Erika joined him. "What do we do now?"

"There's only one thing we *can* do. We sit and wait."

"For what?"

"To find out if the chip is actually dead."

"We can't do that. Without removing it, we may never know."

Greer's expression turned grim. "Exactly. I either black out again, or black out, collapse and die."

Erika's eyes grew. "And that's *all* we can do?"

Greer gave Gusano a look of desperation.

"I don't think I like that look, dude…"

"When you find out what this look actually means, you're gonna *hate* it."

Gusano paled. "Whaddya talking about now?"

"It goes something like this. Erika and I have reached the end of our rope. This leaves you to finish up."

"I don't follow you, dude…"

"Use that oversized brain of yours in that oversized head and figure this out. Decide why we're here. And what you can do to help us."

Gusano shook his head.

"Listen. And try to keep up, okay?"

Gusano shrugged.

"What do you think comes after all this?"

"All what?"

"Finding a second chip. Finding it too close to my brain to mess with. Seeing it disappear on your scanner and not knowing if it's still active."

Gusano remained looking confused.

Greer began to wonder why hackers, who claimed to be geniuses, failed so miserably when dealing with the problems of normal, less intelligent people. "In simple terms, we can't go anywhere from here, can we?"

"From here?"

"In other words, we can't possibly take this chip out of my head, can we?"

"Not without seriously fucking up a shitload of things I couldn't possibly fix..."

"What's the next step, then?"

Gusano didn't reply.

"You really should have a fairly clear idea where I'm going from here, you know..."

"I *think* I do, but—"

"But what?"

"So far, I've been able to find out just where you and Young stand. And you know damn well that I had to go seriously deep for that."

"We can't just quit. I can't just leave, get back in the car, drive off into the sunset and live happily ever after."

"What exactly do you want me to do?"

"Go deep again."

"You're telling me you want me to get the whole picture?"

"I'd say that would be a pretty safe bet."

"The *whole* picture?"

"Every fucking thing this time."

Gusano didn't reply. He appeared to be calculating.

"Need some coaxing?"

Gusano blinked.

Greer dug into his pocket and pulled out a wad of cash. He thumbed off five bills and handed them to Gusano, who gazed stupidly at what lay trapped in his palm.

"If you need more, I can probably handle it. And if I were you, I'd take this right now. Judging from what you've discovered earlier, I might find out tomorrow morning that I've only got eighteen cents in my account."

Gusano eyed the money in his hand. "You always carry around this much jack, dude?"

"Let's just say I've always had this strong sense to keep as much on hand as possible."

Gusano nodded, then went right back to staring at the money. "I don't usually get paid this much…"

"Then shut up and start earning it."

Gusano pocketed the money. "Thanks, dude."

"Like I just said, you've got to earn it. Otherwise, you'll just piss me off. I'll have to kill you and take back the money, then explain to your mother what I did and why I did it."

Gusano nudged some hair away from his face. "So now what you want is for me to finish this for you."

"I want to finish this myself. I need you to make it so I'm able to. I want you to find out who's been leading me around the last three months and

252

ordering me to kill innocent people. I want to know who these bastards are, where they live, where they work, and who else is involved."

"How soon do you want this wrapped up, dude?"

"Before the chip in my head can activate once again and kill me."

**

Erika could tell Gusano was frightened and intimidated by Justin's demands. So was she, in fact. Now that the grim message had sunk in, she realized the horror they faced.

What Justin had just said was absolutely true. They had no idea if the second chip was deactivated or lying dormant beneath his flesh. Had her strange new powers neutralized the cursed thing when she touched it? Or was she just deceiving herself?

She tried remembering everything that had happened to her since Justin entered her life. The sensations. The emotions. The strange, inexplicable powers. Not to mention her bizarre sixth sense of predicting things and preventing them from happening.

The only thing that mattered was that she and Justin faced serious trouble. It was going to take someone with extraordinary hacking skills to get them out of it. Their lives depended on it. And, if her worst fears rang true, so did the lives of her parents.

She couldn't stop thinking how drastically her life had changed. Just a few days ago, her existence had been centered on her deformed appearance. Her burn scars. The damaged nerves in her cheeks, her neck. The looks people gave her, forcing her to hide her face, as well as her feelings. Withdrawing. Using her computer skills to set up a site that would enable her to earn money without having to leave the house. Becoming a hermit just months before her twentieth birthday. Turning her back on society. And friendships. And any sort of relationship.

All this at such a tender age.

But just when she realized she'd become accustomed to this dismal lifestyle, a man who'd been ordered by the Government to murder her had become a major part of her life, and in spite of the circumstances, she discovered that she was falling in love with him. It was insane. And ironic. And laughable. Yet she found that it was happening, nonetheless. Whether or not Justin felt the same, she had no idea. All she did know was that she'd found herself growing inexplicably fond of the man.

She truly hoped that once this crisis was over, a relationship would ensue. Even if something wonderful didn't develop, she had a strong feeling that, because of this nightmare, this horror, she would no longer have to spend the rest of her life in hiding. Justin had shown her that she was not repulsive. He treated her the way any good man would treat a woman. His behavior convinced her she had value. She was intelligent and attractive— not some disgusting circus oddity. And in spite her disfigurement, she discovered that there actually was one person who considered her beautiful.

Gusano plopped down at his desk and immediately began attacking the keyboard. She wanted to walk over and see what he was doing, but something prevented her from doing so. Instead, she turned toward Justin, who sat stiffly on the couch, watching Matt Damon on the widescreen. And before she realized what she was doing, she sat down very close and covered his hand with hers.

And felt a sudden burst of excitement and comfort when he squeezed her hand in response.

Chapter 29

About twenty minutes later, Gusano finally stopped working, and a tense silence filled the room.

Greer and Erika exchanged worried looks.

"He…stopped," Erika whispered.

"I know," Greer whispered back. "I can hear him not doing anything."

"Whaddya think happened?"

"Either he found something, or—"

"I can hear both of you," Gusano said.

"You're telling us you've got super-hearing?" Greer asked.

"I took off my headset."

"Why'd you stop?" Erika asked.

"I found something."

Greer and Erika got up and went over to where Gusano sat staring at his screen, which was covered with nearly a dozen small black windows. In the center window, an address appeared in tiny white numbers and letters. Gusano was studying it.

"It's right there." His gaze didn't stray from the center window. "Every signal, impulse, or tracking device generating from that earpiece. It's all coming from this address."

Greer's pulse raced as he gazed at the screen. "That looks, well, local."

"It's Casselberry, actually."

"You're sure?"

"I got with two of my guys and we tracked it down. It wasn't easy. Something kept interfering with the orbital jamming. Actually, there was a boatload of interference. I had to have one of the guys do a few loops to disrupt and locate, then try to sniff out the source. But once we did it, we found the connection. It had to be scrambled and unscrambled, and after sifting through what amounted to thousands of miles of cross-device tracking, relays, then filtering imbedded high-frequency messages coming from all over the damned planet, we finally nailed it down."

"In plain English? Please?" Greer was growing impatient.

"This address. Project 21 Down Scale. It popped up every damned time I punched in different codes for incoming and outgoing messages."

"Meaning?"

"I think he's trying to say he found your handler," Erika said.

"Exactimundo," Gusano said.

"You're *sure* about this?" Greer asked after a brief silence.

"Absotively. This is no doubt the address of someone directly involved in the Project 21 program. It was really tricky, keeping it in the scope, mostly because it kept changing codes. We figured it was probably placed in a loop that switched automatically every few seconds. It first came up as DS, then switched to what appeared to be a different program, this one called GW, then more than a dozen other bogus codes that went absolutely nowhere. But it kept up with the DS and the GW at odd intervals. After more tracking, we narrowed it down and got it isolated, and it turned right back into GW and stayed there."

"What the hell's GW?" Greer asked.

"Ghost Watchers." Gusano frowned. "You've never heard of that before?"

"Never."

"Down Scale morphed into Ghost Watchers about two years ago. They're the same program, with different codes and particulars, as well as a shitload of jamming features, most likely to stay out of sight and maintain their changing code status to prevent being hacked. It's the government-sanctioned program that recruits wounded vets, imbeds them with tracking devices, then sends them out in the field to eliminate enemies of the state."

Greer felt the nausea coming back. "And you're sure the address is accurate?"

"Positivo."

"But you have no idea who's involved since the program folded three months ago?"

Gusano shrugged. "I haven't gone much farther than this."

"Then you haven't earned your money quite yet."

"When I find a name and a definite connection, then you'll probably know exactly where to go from there."

"How much longer?"

258

"Give me maybe another half-hour or so. Lemme see what I dig up this time." Gusano put his headset back on and started attacking the keys again.

Greer and Erika went back to the couch. Greer sat back and stared at the screen. Bourne was doing something interesting in a fight scene, but Greer wasn't paying much attention. He couldn't get Gusano's latest find out of his head.

He was being handled by someone in Central Florida. That somehow made the problem much more personal. It also made things easier. If his handlers had been pulling his strings from somewhere farther away, say Washington, D.C., or New York City, this fiasco would be much more difficult to fix. But since it was a local operation, all he had to do was find the man and stop him. And that meant—

Yes. He knew exactly what it meant. He had to kill someone at least one more time. But that's what killers did, wasn't it?

After all, he was a killer. Worse, he was a paid killer. Even worse than that—he was paid by the U. S. Government to kill people. And that alone was what made him hate himself down to the bone.

"A penny for your thoughts," Erika said, and for one moment, Greer found that he was actually smiling. "It must have been a good one," she said. "You don't smile much. Not nearly enough, anyway."

"Before I met you," he heard himself saying, "I never had much of a reason to smile. Or even feel good. About anything."

Erika blushed. And grasped his hand.

Before Greer could respond by tightening his hand around hers, Gusano stopped punching keys again. "I just found a name, dudes."

Reluctantly letting go of Erika's hand, Greer jumped up. "Keep talking."

"I'm pretty sure this is the dickhead who's been responsible for turning you on and off the last five years."

"Seriously?"

Gusano sighed tiredly. "I'm afraid the news is not all good."

"Then tell me the bad part first."

"The man's name is William H. Townes. He was a member of the FBI for twenty years and pretty high up in the ranks. He had all the credentials necessary that led me to a boatload of Black Ops programs, the Agenda 21 platform, even half a dozen undercover operations connected with Iraq and Saudi. I even discovered a couple of super-secret kill-jobs in Pakistan involving the SEALS, with Townes' stamp on them."

"Don't stop there on my account," Greer said, fearing the worst.

"Townes apparently did a couple of tours in Iraq as an intelligence officer and was directly involved in interrogating Iraqi prisoners before being sent to Germany to recruit wounded vets for the Ghost Watchers Project. He was there the same time you were brought in. He was assigned to the Army base and spent nearly six months in the same hospital you were admitted to."

"And that's his address?"

"*Was* is the more appropriate word."

"Was?"

"The dude's dead. Heart attack. He was fifty-two when he croaked."

"When?"

"Four months ago."

"*Four* months ago?" This immediately raised red flags. "That would mean that the bastard died a month before the program was shut down."

"Exactly."

Greer's thoughts began to spin. This was turning into something even worse than what he'd originally thought. "Then who the hell has been handling me all this time?"

"I don't know, but you can probably find out."

"How's that?"

"The dude's address. It seems to be the key to all this."

"But you said—"

"I said Townes is dead. I also said the program has been dead for three months. I didn't say anything about his address being dead."

"Once again? In English, this time?"

"Communications and messages still seem to be coming from that same address."

"Are you telling me what I think you're telling me?"

"I'm telling you this. Whoever has been manipulating you is doing it from that address. Townes' home address."

"Any idea who?"

"Nope."

"You've come this far. Why can't you find out what's going on there?"

"There seems to be boocoo interference and offbeat signals coming out of there, and every time I go on in to triangulate the messages, it puts a myriad of rogue signals out there that sends my feed to a boatload of oddball frequencies, putting me right out there in la-la land."

"What the hell does *that* mean?" Greer asked.

"It means someone is using every damned jamming device possible to block the hell out of whatever I triangulate."

"Someone in the Townes house?"

"I don't even know that for sure."

"Someone could be relaying the messages from that house and sending them somewhere else," Erika said.

"Or taking the messages from the house, looping them, then sending them to Siberia or Australia, or even the North Pole—or some other off-the-wall place—before bringing them back, totally decrypted," Gusano said.

"Or the house could be perfectly harmless," Erika said.

"Maybe," Gusano said.

"Or a decoy," she added.

"That would work, too," Gusano said.

Greer couldn't believe all this. "Now you're both just *guessing*?"

"It's all we can do," Erika said. "We're talking high technology now. It can get seriously crazy at times."

"So this leaves us where?"

"Like I said before—la-la land." Gusano looked and sounded exasperated. "As she just said, the house could be a decoy, but I kinda doubt it. There's entirely too much activity coming from that signal."

"What the hell *do* you know?"

"Dude, it comes down to this. For the last three months, your every move has been manipulated by a dude other than William H. Townes."

"That's it?"

"Absotively."

"So then—"

"You know what has to happen next, right?"

Greer felt the nausea coming right back. "I've got to see what's going on in that house."

Chapter 30

Ten minutes later, Erika sat in her car at the curb in front of Gusano's home, staring at Justin, who sat beside her, gazing at the darkness pressing against the windshield. She sensed that he was obsessing over what they had both learned.

She felt so sorry for him. The man's life had been a living hell ever since he'd come back to the States. She could feel the anger and the betrayal pounding through his veins and knew that whatever he was planning would not be good for the people involved. Although she had no idea what Justin had done in Iraq, she was pretty sure that he'd killed people, and that he'd probably achieved an impressive list of victims by the time he was shipped back home.

Why else would these people—whoever they were—have picked him to do that very same thing over here? It made perfect sense that the Government would select only professional assassins for deadly undercover assignments in the States. No additional training would be necessary. The assassin was already skilled and totally aware of the game plan, as well as the risks involved.

However, she didn't think it would be very bright for a government agency—or anyone else, for that matter—to jerk around an experienced killer, as they'd been doing to Justin the last three months. Anyone with a working brain cell or two would know the risks involved in keeping a paid assassin active even after the program sanctioning him had dissolved.

Erika knew absolutely nothing about the Government, its protocol, or its secret programs. But even so, she strongly feared that what she and Justin faced right now had nothing to do with the Government. What Gusano had recently discovered substantiated that.

"I can't imagine what you're feeling right now." She decided that he needed to know how she felt. "But if it's similar to what I was feeling when I found out that you were planning to kill me—"

"That's what's infuriating about all this," he said. "The fact that whoever has been handling me actually wanted me to kill you and your family."

"You didn't, though, did you?"

He just sighed.

"I'm still sitting here. Alive and well. And my parents are still alive, as well."

He still didn't reply.

"You risked your life to spare mine. *And* theirs."

"I saw no point in hurting anyone innocent. It was bad enough that I've had to kill people I didn't know or knew absolutely nothing about. The bastard pushing my buttons finally pushed the wrong one. He's gonna pay for that."

"I truly understand."

"Everyone has limits. Even killers like me."

She wanted to tell him that he was no killer, but knew that would be a lie. He was definitely a killer—and, judging by how quickly he'd dispatched the armed guy at the storage facility, a really good one. But then she realized that maybe he wasn't as good as he might have been. Justin had a conscience. Most killers she'd read about or had seen on TV were sociopaths—which made it easy—even fun—for them to kill. When you didn't care about someone, it was no problem at all to stay detached.

"I'm glad you've got a conscience," she said.

He turned to her. Even in the darkness of the cab she could see that the anger and the rage had disappeared from his features. She felt a soft, warm tenderness flowing from him, and her previous thoughts about his frightening abilities quickly vanished. She put her hand on his and felt instant pleasure when he covered it with his other hand. His touch was very warm; she could feel the affection coming from him. She wanted very much to kiss him but didn't think he'd have the same urge. Not now, anyway. Perhaps later. Maybe when this was all over. Maybe when they were alone and no longer had to worry about—

"I've got to end this," he said softly. "It's the only thing I can think of that will help me start wanting to live again."

"I know."

"I have to do it very soon. Before they have the chance to turn me off again. I just hope I can get to them before they decide to turn me off permanently."

"I'm here with you." She squeezed his hand. "And no matter what happens, I'll be with you every step of the—"

She wasn't able to finish her statement. In that same moment, he moved closer and kissed her full on the lips.

***

The first twenty minutes of the thirty-minute trip to Casselberry were spent in tense silence. Erika couldn't stop thinking of what had just happened and realized that it was the very first time in her life that a guy had ever given her such a passionate, soul-seeking kiss.

She had been involved with several boys in high school, pursuing a serious relationship during her first year at UCF. However, it didn't take her long at all to discover that Brandon had other things on his mind. His classic '68 Camaro, which he devotedly tended to in his spare time, proved to be his most serious obsession. He also entertained a lifelong passion for football, which kept him totally preoccupied with his friends—as well as pizza, kegs of beer and the widescreen—during the entire NFL season.

To make matters even worse, he'd frequently demonstrated a wandering eye. And during that following spring, when she heard gossip that Brandon had taken his beloved Camaro up to Daytona Beach for Spring Break and hooked up with a stripper working her way through law school, she realized that their romance, flawed as it was, had run its course.

267

It took her several months to recover. To cope, she'd sworn off romance completely, attacking the textbooks with renewed vigor and spending her leisure time watching her favorite movies in her bedroom. For a while, it actually worked. She not only began feeling better about herself, she'd also witnessed a sharp leap in her grades. There were a couple of guys who'd shown interest, but she'd dodged them in favor of a more productive and less complicated lifestyle.

The accident literally tore her life apart, and when she returned to class several months later, she realized just how shallow people actually were. Her small circle of friends acted like they didn't even know her. The others treated her as if she'd done something horrible. The same guys who'd wanted to date her before no longer showed interest, or even acknowledged her existence. It appeared that they didn't want to be associated with a girl carrying around burn scars covering half her face. It made them uncomfortable—or worse, self-conscious. The message they'd sent was that an imperfect female was not exactly what the average wide-eyed young college man had in mind for an enduring romance, or even a casual love interest. And that a classroom filled with cruel, shallow-minded students was no longer the place for her.

Then, after two long, unpleasant years of self-imposed isolation, Justin came along, and an unexpected second chance at life entered the picture. She reminded herself that she was most likely basing entirely too much credence on just one

268

kiss. But by the same token, she could tell something truly wonderful had happened. The way Justin looked at her, touched her, talked to her and treated her showed clear evidence that her scars didn't matter. Justin had scars of his own—which put the two of them on the same level. It also made them a kind of matched set.

It was just a kiss, she reminded herself. *Just one simple kiss, and you're making something extremely wondrous and magical out of it.*

Maybe she was. But somehow, she didn't think so.

A girl was supposed to be able to pick up on such things. Especially a girl like her, whose emotions and intuition had in some way been mysteriously magnified to the nth degree during the last couple of days.

Justin's kiss was no exception. Her senses had swooped in, telling her the simple truth about what really happened. And now, as she drove toward their destination several miles north of Orlando, she found herself smiling and realized that she couldn't stop. But somehow, it didn't matter. She didn't care if she ever stopped smiling again. She knew it was because she fully understood how important that kiss actually was. And what it meant. And what it could possibly mean, from this point on.

It also told her something else. Something she'd suspected before, but wasn't fully aware of.

She had fallen in love with Justin. And, even more important, she strongly felt that he could be falling in love with her.

Ten minutes later, as they pulled onto Red Bug Road and drew closer to the neighborhood where William H. Townes once lived, Justin finally broke the uncomfortable silence.

"I hope that was okay," he said softly.

She didn't reply.

"I…couldn't help it." He sounded nervous and uncomfortable. "I was…well, it had been on my mind for some time. I guess I just let it happen."

She still didn't speak. She was too concerned about keeping her grip on the wheel. Her heart was fluttering wildly, and she feared that, at any moment, it could tear right out of her chest. But at least she knew now why he'd been so quiet during the drive.

"Please tell me it was okay. Please tell me you didn't mind me doing such an impulsive—"

"It was fine," she said quickly. Then she realized just how pitiful the word sounded. Fine? Seriously? Fine seemed to go more with, *Yeah, two sugars will be fine for my coffee*. Or, *I feel just fine, thanks*. Or, *You did a fine job cleaning out that toilet*.

This man had turned her body—as well as her spirit—into earth-shaking fireworks in one passionate moment, and when he asked if it was all right, she said it was *fine*.

Fine? Really?

"*Really* fine." She suddenly felt the irresistible urge to go into excruciating detail. "Better than fine. Much, *much* better than fine could ever be. It was…well, in a word, *wonderful*…"

After several moments of tense silence, he said, "How did you know…what I was talking about?"

She shrugged. "It's the only thing I have on my mind right now."

"The *only* thing?"

She nodded.

"You're not worried about what we're going to do when we reach that house?"

"No…"

"Or what I'm going to do when I get my hands on whoever's been yanking my chain these last three months?"

"Not even that." She still couldn't stop smiling. If only he knew what was going on in her head—as well as her heart…

"Just that one kiss?"

She sighed deeply and hoped that her next statement wouldn't sound as lame—or as tacky—as that first one. Or that it would frighten him, or turn him off. "Justin…it wasn't *just* a kiss…"

He was silent for several moments. Then he sighed. "You're right. It wasn't."

***

Erika turned off the main road and eased down the block, where neat rows of one-story homes lined both sides of the street.

It looked like a comfortable, high-class neighborhood. The houses were probably built thirty or forty years ago, when Disney moved in and caused one of the first of many substantial spikes in Central Florida's population. The homes were all similar in shape and size, many of them a light shade of stucco. Palmettos, palm trees and flower gardens decorated front yards, and trimmed bushes highlighted nearly every front window and entrance.

No vehicles cluttered the front yards, and no junk cars were to be seen anywhere. Only a few high-priced vehicles were parked in front of a garage, and each front yard had been recently mowed.

Since it was late, floodlights illuminated front yards and entrances. A yellowish haze from the streetlamps drifted down each end of the block. Only two living room lights showed from the street.

The Townes house, a one-story yellow stucco isolated by a privacy fence, was completely dark.

Erika stopped along the curb in front of the house next to it. She doused the lights, put the Hyundai in park and flicked off the ignition. Then leaned back in her seat and sat staring at the house, wondering what could be awaiting them inside. It was only then that she realized just how frightened she really was. Frightened of what had been happening and what was bound to happen. Of what Justin was going to do and her being right there, watching him do it. Frightened, but knowing that whatever did happen was something that was necessary, and even if she didn't want it to happen, she couldn't stop it. And even if she could stop it, she wouldn't.

A person living inside that house had been responsible for making Justin's life a living hell. She wanted to look this evil creature right in the eye and ask why this happened. And why Justin was

272

forced to go through this. And what on earth had he ever done to deserve any of this.

She wanted to ask this creature how anyone associated with the United States Government could take a wounded, battle-scarred veteran and subject him to such inhumane treatment. Most of all, she wanted to know how anyone with a conscience could force this severely-damaged man to endure such torture even after the program had gone belly-up.

"I guess this is it." Justin was watching the house.

Erika quickly found that she had no strength in her voice. She could barely nod.

"You okay?"

She felt his eyes on her. She wanted to say no, she wasn't okay. And that it would be quite a while before she was ever okay again. She wanted to tell him that this was the worst moment in her life. This felt even worse than when she'd woken up in the hospital after her accident, her head cocooned in bandages, and was told by the tall, slender gray-haired man in the white uniform that the right side of her face was covered with third-degree burns, and that most of them would probably never fully heal, and would leave permanent scarring over her cheekbone, ear, jaw, and neck. She wanted to say all those things but didn't. It would make Justin uneasy. He was probably already way more than uneasy as it was, and didn't need any additional help. He was going to murder someone tonight. She didn't want to do or say anything that might knock him off-balance, or distract him even a little. She simply said, "I think so," and hoped he wouldn't question it.

"I'll totally understand if you're nervous."

She didn't reply.

He turned silent again. She didn't know if he was worried about her or just concentrating on his plan. She didn't want to make this any harder for him and surely didn't want to complicate things by saying anything that would cause him to worry about her.

After the long, uncomfortable silence, he finally said, "No lights are on."

"I see that."

"That might not be such a good thing, you know. When it's dark and quiet in the house, the slightest noise can awaken anyone living there. Then we've got to worry about possible guns, dogs, a security system—"

"What if there's a dog?" The image of Justin hurting or killing a dog alarmed her. She'd always loved dogs. "You wouldn't…you wouldn't ever—"

"Let's take this one step at a time, okay? And no, I'd *never* kill a dog. I like dogs very much, and they like me as well. I even worked with a couple in Iraq. Actually, I prefer them over people. They're a hundred times more honest than people could ever be."

"What about if…if you're being attacked by one?"

"I was taught a couple of sleeper holds that have been proven highly effective, and they don't really hurt the dog. Not permanently."

She smiled.

"Answer your question?"

"Yes."

"Any other questions you need to ask?"

"What's our plan?"

"Unfortunately, I can think of only one option. I have to go on in and finish this. If I can do this right, and we can get away without anyone seeing us, I might actually be able to lead a halfway normal life."

A halfway normal life…

The prospect of being a victim in a home invasion had always terrified her. But now that she'd found herself on the flip side of what could very easily turn violent, it disturbed her even more. What if there were guns in the household? What if they did encounter a dog? Even if Justin did manage to subdue the dog, what would he do if he stumbled upon a man—or woman—or even a small *boy*—pointing a gun at his face?

She reminded herself that Justin was trained by to face opposition in every conceivable situation. Weapons. Unarmed combat. Concealment. Lies. Booby traps. Explosives. The same man who had given her the best kiss of her life less than half an hour ago had been trained to kill or totally incapacitate someone in a hundred different ways.

"You're so quiet," he said. "Scared?"

She nodded.

"Don't feel bad. I'm scared, too."

She tried to read his expression. Was he truly scared? Or was he just trying to make her feel better?

"Are you? I mean *really*?"

"Ready to come out of my skin..."

"But I thought—"

"You thought that since I'm a killer, I can't possibly be frightened of anything. Right?"

"Well…yes…I think…"

"Here's the simple version. I was trained by the Military to search for, hunt down and eliminate threats to our country. My love for this country has made me what I am today. The killing part of all this started in Iraq, but that was different because I was killing the enemy. Over here, things changed drastically, and I realized that I was killing the very people I'd been protecting all those years I'd served. It gave me nightmares for a long time, and even after the nightmares stopped, I still couldn't sleep because my conscience was killing me. I kept reminding myself that the people I was killing were our enemies. It made things slightly more tolerable, but it still bothered me because I had no way of checking out any of the facts. But since I'd already committed to this, I couldn't back out of it because, as you well know, my handlers were in total control. And when I did try to make any sort of wave, they turned me off as punishment. When I came to, I knew right then that I could do absolutely nothing about my situation. And that they'd always be calling the shots."

She rested her hand on his, flinching at its coldness, its tension. She fully realized just then how much he was hurting. He was a good man. It infuriated her that the United States Government, which was supposed to be the best in the civilized world, could take such a good man and turn him into a cold-blooded killer. "I think I understand now," she said softly.

"I figured you just might. You seem to be able to feel things better than anyone I'd ever met before."

"I guess I do, although I have no idea how…"

"Trust me. I've never known anyone like you before."

She didn't know if his statement was actually a compliment, but she could tell he'd meant it.

"Have you had this gift very long?"

She couldn't respond. How could she tell this man something she could not even understand herself? As far as she knew, this strange power had come the same time Justin had entered her life. And when she struggled to remember if there had been other times when this bizarre gift had surfaced, she encountered a total blank. She could not remember any such occurrence before their frightening encounter at the Mall. "I don't really know," she said, hoping he wouldn't press her further.

"It just comes and goes?"

She nodded.

"I'm glad it's been there when we've needed it."

"So am I."

"I also hope it sticks around a while."

"It probably will." She didn't know why she'd said it. Since she obviously had no control over it, she couldn't make any promises. Or predictions.

"I also hope I don't black out again very soon. I'd hate for them to turn me off after we're inside the house. That'll leave you there alone. In enemy territory. Defenseless."

She sensed no darkness. No fear. No sense of panic. No danger. The only thing she did feel was that things just might turn out all right.

"I honestly don't feel it happening again."

"Promise me that if you're wrong, and I do black out, you'll get the hell out of here immediately."

"Justin—"

"Promise me. Now. Right now. Please?"

He was dead-serious. But she knew that if he did suffer another blackout, she couldn't leave him. If it was at all possible, she'd get him out of that house. There was no conceivable way she could ever turn her back on him.

"*Please* promise me," he urged.

She was going to have to lie to him. But since he wouldn't know what was going on during a blackout, it really didn't matter what she said. "All right. I promise."

He relaxed in his seat.

"You believe me, don't you?" she asked. "When I said I don't think it's gonna happen again?"

"You have a damned good track record. I'm going by that."

"Even if I'm wrong, I'll probably sense it before it happens."

"In that case, I suggest we get this over with. Ready to rock?"

Her heart fluttered. *You can do this,* she told herself. *Justin will be right there with you. He'll be doing the heavy lifting. Make sure you back him up.*

She took a deep breath and nodded.

He squeezed her hand. "Let's do this, then."

Chapter 31

They crossed the darkest section of the front yard, staying close to the line of bushes separating the properties. Greer had his penlight out, but flicked it on only when he needed light to help him maneuver through the unfamiliar surroundings. Erika stayed close behind him, moving so quietly in the grass that he kept glancing behind him to make sure she was there.

He knew she was scared. He also knew she was very brave, and considered himself fortunate that she'd come with him. But he was also keenly aware of his responsibilities. He had to be extra careful and couldn't afford to take his usual risks. He promised himself that he would not do anything that would endanger her in any way. He'd also accepted the fact that if this trip into enemy territory turned deadly, he'd willingly risk his life to make sure she was safe.

Just a few minutes later, they reached the backyard. The hazy floodlight attached to a corner of the roof displayed a deck, lawn furniture, and an above-ground swimming pool at the far end, just a couple of feet from the privacy fence. Six lawn chairs and two white oval tables were arranged in the center of the deck. A large outdoor grill sat off to the side. It was typical outdoor entertainment for the average middle-class Floridian. Looking at it from this perspective, one would never suspect anything illegal or sinister going on in the house.

Greer crossed the deck and crept silently to the storm door in the center of the dwelling. After putting his ear against the glass and listening for about a minute, he depressed the handle and carefully pulled it open, resting it against his left thigh. He tried the door. It was locked.

"What do we do now?" Erika whispered behind him.

Greer pulled out a small leather pouch of burglar tools from his pants pocket and selected two picks. He applied them to the lock, meticulously adjusting their angles and listening closely. After about half a minute, he turned the knob and pushed the door open. He then listened to the heavy silence coming from inside while carefully pocketing his toolkit. Then he pulled out the compact Walther PPK from its holster under his left arm and eased open the door. After listening once again, this time for nearly a minute, he stepped silently into the dimly-lit kitchen.

The instant Erika joined him, he reached behind her and inched the door shut. Then he turned around and silently crossed the kitchen.

The carpeted hall was also dimly-lit. Proceeding quietly, he made it halfway down when he spotted a slender horizontal line of yellow light glowing at the bottom of the door.

He stopped moving. After a few tense moments, he nodded to Erika and pointed. She peered around his shoulder.

The door abruptly opened.

A triangle of hazy orange swept over that section of carpeting. A tall, skinny shadow dressed in a bathrobe stepped out into the hall. Greer watched tensely as the figure turned in his direction, gasped, then froze.

Greer brought up his gun and penlight and flashed the light directly at the figure's shocked face.

The figure cringed, gulped loudly, and took an awkward step back, bumping into the bathroom doorway. The figure's eyes filled their sockets. Its high-pitched voice sounded like the cracked whisper of a child. "Who...what the f-*fuck*...who are *you*? And what the fuck are you doin'...in my *house*?"

The figure was that of a young man around nineteen or twenty years old. Greer's thoughts reeled, but he focused on the business at hand while taking one step closer. And made sure the kid could see his face.

The kid gasped. His eyes grew. He swallowed audibly. His face paled in the haze of the penlight. "You're...you're—"

"Yeah. I know who I am. And, judging by the fact that your eyeballs are just short of popping out and making a gooey mess on their way down the front of your robe, I kinda think *you* know who I am, too."

The boy trembled.

Greer instantly sensed something very, very wrong about all this. The kid looked like he was about to shit himself. "So now you might want to tell me just *how* the hell do you know who I am?"

No reply. The boy's face had grown white as a sheet.

"Let me guess." Greer moved the snub-nosed barrel of the Walther closer to the boy's face. "You know about the program, don't you? Agenda Twenty-One? The Ghost Shadow Project?"

Still unable to reply, the boy swallowed audibly. His nod was slight.

Greer struggled to maintain his composure. *No. This can't possibly be going where I'm afraid it's going.*

William H. Townes was dead. However, the program remained alive. And from what Gusano had discovered, the activity showing up from the Ghost Shadow Project the last few months was coming directly from this house.

Not a good thing, no matter how you looked at it.

"Start talking." Greer kept the gun pointed at the kid's face.

"*Huh?*"

Greer was in no mood for bullshit. It was time for effective scare tactics. After two tours in Iraq, Greer knew how to get people talking.

He moved another step closer and kept the gun trained on the kid's face. He lowered his voice. "Listen to me. And pay careful attention because I'm only gonna say this once. I could blow your head off right now, or I could just bundle you up, stuff you in the trunk of this lady's car, take you out into the woods, tie you to the trunk of a tree, then take my time skinning you alive with my trusty pocketknife. I use my knife to shave with, so I don't think I'll have any trouble slicing you up. And when I'm finished, I'll just leave you there. The coyotes have to eat, too, ya know." He paused. "Which will it be? I'm in a fairly good mood, so I'll let you pick."

The boy continued trembling.

Greer found it difficult to keep his finger away from the trigger. Too many unpleasant memories were zipping past. "All right, then. *I'll* pick. Turn around. We're about to take a nice, leisurely ride—"

"Okay, *okay*!" The boy finally found his voice. "I'll tell you wh-what you wanna—"

"Where were you going?" Greer asked.

"Huh?"

"When you came out of the bathroom. Where were you going?"

"My…my study."

"Where is it?"

Raising a shaky arm, the kid pointed unsteadily down the hall. "D-Down there…"

Greer motioned with the gun. "Lead the way."

"B-But—"

"Move!"

The boy hesitated.

"Kid, I'm not really in the mood for games. Give me one more reason and I'll kill you. If you don't think I'm capable, you're about to learn the hard way. All I have to do is jam the barrel of this gun into your mouth and take my time emptying the

284

mag. Believe me, after all I've been through the last five years? I can do something like this in my sleep."

Trembling even worse, the boy turned and shuffled awkwardly down the hall.

***

The room was quite large. Greer figured that it had once served as the master bedroom. But it had been converted into a computer room and storage area. Shelves covered three of its four walls, each shelf crammed with computer equipment and office supplies. Folding tables, placed end-to-end, spanned the length of the room in two parallel rows. The tables were stacked with monitors, hard drives, transmitters, cartridges, disks, and close-circuit screens. One monitor displayed eight small screens, each showing parking lot and kiosk activity. On the table next to it, another monitor showed six screens, highlighting bar and banking activity. Stacks of graphic comics covered the surface of the third table. Behind it, three shelves overflowed with videos and DVDs.

It was obviously the room of a hacker, and made Gusano's garage setup appear shabby.

"Listen, man..." Trembling, the boy couldn't take his eyes from Greer's pistol. "I'd really like it a whole bunch if...if you pointed that thing—"

"Shut up." Greer kept the gun dead steady. "And sit down. Over there." He gestured to his right, where an ergonomically designed office chair sat in the corner of the room next to a turntable and a pile of vinyl records stacked on the carpet. The boy opened his mouth, but Greer jerked the barrel of his gun. "Just sit down and keep that yap shut. Erika, find some tape. We need to fasten this idiot to his fancy chair."

The boy cringed. "C'mon, man! What the fuck—"

"One more word," Greer said softly, "and you're gonna learn firsthand what a pistol-whipping feels like. Now get that sorry ass of yours over there and sit down. And shut the hell up."

Still shaking, the boy did as ordered.

Erika went over to one of the shelves, where two boxes of packing supplies took up space. She reached into a box and removed a thick roll of clear strapping tape. "This okay?"

"Perfect. Use as much as you want. I don't want this idiot getting out of that chair while we're having our pleasant little conversation."

"Wh-Whaddya gonna *do*, m-man?" The boy's voice had jumped half an octave.

"Shut up."

Erika wrenched three feet from the roll and wound it tightly around the boy's right wrist, which rested on the arm of the chair. She ripped off the end with her teeth, pulled off another long length and fastened the boy's left wrist to the other arm. She then taped the boy's slender ankles together. Just as she moved to the back of the chair to secure his chest, he whined, "C'mon now! Aren'tcha overdoing this just a tad?"

"If I didn't need answers," Greer said, moving closer, "I'd tell her to wrap a couple of yards of that stuff around your big mouth."

The boy groaned and lowered his head.

Erika finished securing his chest.

Greer moved closer. "Who else lives here?"

"No one, man."

"No one? Really?"

"Don'tcha think you would've heard or seen someone else by now? I know it's late, but the walls in this place aren't *that* thick, ya know..."

"That raises a good point."

The kid shrugged. "Besides, why would I lie? You kinda got me in a sensitive spot right now..."

Greer shook his head slowly.

"It's the truth, man..."

Greer turned and approached the door. "Erika, tape his mouth shut while I make my rounds. I've got to find out if this idiot is actually telling us the truth."

Erika ripped off a six-inch strip and slapped it across the kid's mouth. He moaned and dropped his head to his chest.

Greer left the room and went down the hall. Using his penlight, he began checking the other two bedrooms, looking under each bed and, gripping the Walther, carefully opening and examining each closet. This done, he went down the hall and scanned the living room and dining area. After examining the garage, as well as the shiny silver BMW parked in one of the two stalls, he checked the family room and laundry room. Seeing no obvious sign of recent activity, he realized the kid had been telling them the truth. The house appeared to be empty.

"Everything okay?" Erika asked when he came back.

He closed the door behind him and glanced at the pathetic figure taped to the chair. "Apparently this idiot told us the truth."

The boy rolled his eyes.

Greer walked right over and ripped the tape from the boy's mouth, making him wince. "Man, that fucking *hurt*!"

"Get used to pain, kid. It's part of life."

The boy shook his head. He looked like he was about to cry. "Man…"

"Where's your mother?"

"Who the fuck knows? She left when I was still in high school."

"Why'd she leave?"

"My old man was a dickhead."

"That doesn't exactly answer my question."

"His job kept him away for days, sometimes weeks. Then he'd come home and act like a real shit as soon as he stepped through the front—"

"I was looking for something more like divorce, or separation, but I guess it doesn't really matter now, does it?"

The boy sighed.

"Erika, tell me what you see on those tables. I'm curious about all this equipment."

Erika went over to the front table.

"I can tell ya anything you wanna know, man," the boy said.

"Actually, I don't see any reason to trust you right now," Greer said.

"C'mon, man. Give a guy a break!"

"Why should I?"

"Maybe you scared the shit outa me so much that I'll tell ya the truth."

"Maybe…and then again, maybe not…"

"What have ya got to lose? You've got me all tied up here. I'm scared shitless, man! Why would I lie about anything?"

"I have no idea."

"I'm trying to tell ya, I've got no reason to lie."

"And I've got no reason to trust you. That's why I want her to do this for me. I trust her. Enough said?"

"Man…"

"Like I just said, I don't trust you."

"I just told ya no one else was living here—"

"That doesn't mean you're gonna tell me the whole truth about everything else, does it? No matter what you do or say, we're not ever gonna be buds."

The boy groaned.

"This is top-of-the-line stuff." Erika picked up a few pieces and studied them closely.

"Hacking equipment?"

"By the looks of it, the kind the Government would use. It's pricey, to say the least."

"Makes you wonder where this idiot got hold of it, doesn't it?"

Erika glared at the kid. "I honestly don't think he actually bought *any* of it."

"I was thinking the same thing."

"This is a USB value keylogger." She held it up, dropped it on the table and picked up something else. "This looks like a Hack RF One."

"Transmitter?"

"Transmitter and receiver."

"Keep looking."

"This is a mini hidden camera thumb drive." She put it back down and pointed. "That looks like a digital spy recorder, and I also see a network adapter. These definitely look like gadgets the Government would use."

"You're saying our chubby friend doesn't have all this stuff?"

"I'm sure he'd consider going cold turkey on the junk food just to get his hands on some of this."

Greer turned to the boy. "Now, since you seem so willing and eager to talk…how'd you acquire all this crap?"

No reply.

Greer took a step closer. "I asked you a question."

The boy trembled.

"You obviously know who I am. You recognized me the moment you first saw me out there in the hall. You're the bastard who's been pressing my buttons and turning me on and off for the last three months, aren't you?"

The boy nodded once, very slightly.

"You've been watching me on one of those monitors. In other words, you know what I'm capable of."

Another nod.

Greer took one more step. Still pointing the gun, he used his free hand to reach into his pocket. He pulled out his penknife and clicked it open to reveal a gleaming four-inch blade. "As I told you out in the hall, I shave with this thing. I keep it razor sharp. I'm gonna ask you a few questions, and if you don't answer, or if I don't like your answer, I'm gonna slice off one of your ears. And, if you get me *really* pissed, I just might make you eat both of them after I slice them off. Got it?"

The boy trembled. "M-Man…"

"I *said*, got it?"

The boy nodded.

"All right, then. First question: What's your name?"

The boy hesitated.

Greer lowered the glistening blade and rested its sharp edge lightly on the top of the boy's right ear.

The boy trembled and forced his eyes shut. His mouth opened and trembled. His words trickled out softly, in a faint whisper. "I'm…B-Bill…T-Townes…Junior."

Chapter 32

Greer's heart pounded as he pocketed the knife. A wave of nausea tore through him, sending a rippling chill down his back.

He had been correct, after all. The fact that this kid was in this house all alone substantiated that cold fact.

Bill Townes, Jr.

This meant the worst possible scenario. Townes, the bastard who'd been manipulating him the last five years, had died and left his legacy to his teenaged son, who, for the last three months, continued on with the nightmare. The monster manipulating Greer was the smartassed kid taped to the chair just two feet away.

A *kid*, of all people.

A pampered, snot-nosed kid barely out of high school.

Greer wanted to laugh and scream at the same time. He stared at the boy as if seeing something he could not quite understand. Something that made no sense. Something that made him want to heave his guts.

He closed his eyes and tried to think rationally.

"Justin?" Erika placed her hand gently on his shoulder.

Reluctantly, he opened his eyes. He desperately wanted to empty the mag into the kid's skull. At the moment, he thought it would be the most pleasant thing he could ever experience. More pleasant, even, than touching Erika. Or kissing her. Or even sitting beside her, knowing she was right there—

"Justin?"

Her soft voice, as always, brought him right back. He gazed into her beautiful blue eyes. And felt instant relief. And warmth. And surprised that the mere act of looking at her had instantly removed the rage. One look into Erika's eyes and Greer felt in control once again. "Erika," he said in a gentle voice, "this is the asshole who ordered me to kill you and your folks."

Her soft gaze suddenly turned glacial.

Greer decided to let her vent. "If you need to, let him know how you feel about all this. He's right there. He can't go anywhere."

The boy must have sensed the rage coming from her. He began shaking again. "Listen, guys... I was just—"

Her stinging slap reverberated loudly in the room. A high-pitched yelp escaped the boy's lips. His head bobbed; he moaned in agony.

She moved closer and pulled her arm back to give him another one.

The boy lowered his head, gritted his teeth, and braced himself.

She swatted him again. "Why? Why did you want me dead? Was it because I saw Justin at the wrong time? Or was it something else?"

The boy didn't reply.

Erika brought her hand back again. "*Tell* me, damn you!"

293

"I'll tell you, okay? Just don't...don't hit me again...*please*?"

"Then tell me, and maybe I won't!"

The kid took a deep breath. "You went out...with the brother of a friend of mine. A couple of years ago."

"Brandon Wilson?"

The boy nodded.

"So?"

He shrugged. "You broke up with him. Jordan was really worried about his brother, said it got him hooked on some serious meds. It...kinda fucked him up—ya know?"

"From what Brandon told me, his brother was hooked on meds long before we broke up."

He stared at her a few seconds, scowling.

"Something else on your mind?"

"This was way before...before your face...got all fucked up."

"So *this* was why you told me to kill her?" Greer felt the rage coming back, this time for different reasons. "Because of your stupid drugged-out friend?"

"I figured I'd do Jordie a favor—ya know? We caught her on one of our satellites when you two met up. I thought I'd have you do her in. I wasn't sure she'd tell her folks, so—"

"You decided not to take any chances?"

No reply.

Erika remained silent, her eyes on him. She grew tense, and her eyes blazed. "*He* was the one who broke it off, you idiot! Not me—*him*! You

294

stupid asshole!" She swatted him again, this time much harder.

"Man, get her *off* me!" The boy pulled back, squirming and trying to twist out of the chair. "She's *killing* me!"

"My parents, too? Seriously? Are you *totally insane?*"

Greer moved closer. "You've still got questions to answer."

"Ask me, man! Ask me! Just get her the hell *off* me!"

"First, tell me about Ernest Lohman."

"Who?"

Greer had to wait for the rage to die down. "The man whose suicide I placed into motion when you forced me to plant that gun in his bedroom."

The boy didn't reply.

"Want her to slap you again? Or should I start rearranging your face with this gun?"

The boy let his head drop. He looked exhausted. "The old man...he had a run-in with him...a while ago."

"About what?"

"I don't know, man. It was in the old man's book. Something about that old dude getting in the way of one of the old man's investments. I just—"

"Book?"

"The old man kept a book with a list of folks he wanted eliminated. When he croaked, I—"

"You took over."

"I figured—"

"You just decided to continue with the list. Just for shits and giggles?"

The boy just shrugged.

Erika swatted him again. "Mr. Lohman was a friend of my *father's*, you bastard!"

"Man, she's totally *killing* me!" The boy grimaced, moved his jaw, then shook himself. "I can't even feel my fucking jaw!"

Greer gently took her arm and lowered it. "Later," he told her.

"Promise?" she asked.

He nodded and then turned back to the boy. "Why'd you take over for your father? Were you two close?"

The kid snickered. "I *hated* the old guy. He was Mr. Establishment all the way. Got a haircut every fucking week. Shined his shoes all the time. Even wore a stupid *bow tie* to work. Can ya believe it? A *bow tie*?"

Greer sighed tiredly. "How disgusting and totally dorky... Tell me. If you hated him so much, why continue his work?"

"Felt good, man. He had all this *power*—know what I mean? He just pressed a button and *wham!* Someone died or went to prison. I went through his stuff and found all this neat shit. It was a real high. He had three guys he was jerking around—you and two other dudes. It was almost like a video game."

A video game. Greer had never felt so disgusted in his life.

"Justin? We can't lose it now—okay?" Erika sounded worried.

296

He forced a smile. "I'll be fine. Right now, we need to clean this up. For good."

The boy jerked his head. "H-Huh?"

"You heard what I said. This room needs fumigating. You need fumigating as well, but since we can't do that without actually *killing* you... We'll just make it so you're no longer in business."

The boy's eyes grew. "Man...I've got some totally expensive *shit* here!"

"Sorry, but you're about to lose it all. But at least you'll be alive...so to speak..."

"C'mon, man! Give a guy a break!"

"Is he serious?" Erika's eyes blazed again.

"You want a break?" Greer grabbed the boy's little finger of his right hand and began forcing it backward. "How's this for starters?"

The boy gritted his teeth and tried pulling away. "Man, that *hurts*!"

"Like I told you before, get used to it. Pain is part of life. Besides, you need this. In fact, you need a whole bunch more than this for your proper education. You're pampered, spoiled, and worthless. A real tribute to your generation." Greer let go of the boy's finger. He stood very close to the chair, glaring down at the kid. "How old are you?"

"Why?"

He tapped the boy roughly on the top of the head. "I ask the questions. You, on the other hand, answer them. If you don't, I'll get right back to breaking your fingers, one by one."

The boy groaned. "All right! I'm nineteen, dammit. There! Satisfied?"

"And you've been doing all this since your father died?"

A nod.

"You're forcing people to kill. That seems *okay* to you?"

"The old man did it for years."

"He was an FBI agent, you dumbass!"

"So?"

"You really don't get it, do you?"

The kid's expression went blank. "Get what, man?"

"You don't care that what you've been doing has destroyed lives? Careers? Futures?"

"Man, like I said, I've been going into the old man's book, finishing things. He would've approved, believe me. That old dude was radical as hell about his list."

"You're telling me Shooter was in your father's book?"

The kid didn't reply.

"Don't stop now. I'm just beginning to make sense of all this."

"Shooter was taking customers away from one of my buds."

"So *that's* why you wanted him dead?"

"Hey, I had the opportunity…"

"So you decided to make things easy."

The kid gave a weak smile.

"I figured something was wrong when he didn't pull a piece on me."

"Shooter was scared shitless of guns, man… All he ever liked was to get high."

Greer felt his blood turning cold. He wanted to vent, but there were still questions to be answered. "You've been doing all this all by yourself?"

"Fuck, no, man. A few of my buds come in a couple times a week to help me out. They also do things for me out in the field. It works out well for all of us because they've all got assholes they wanna deal with, too. Sometimes they don't even have to come over. They hack, too, so they can actually work outa their own digs. And they don't mind moving you around—like that time we had to put out your lights outside this chick's house."

"How do you get past the cops?"

He laughed. "We've got a shitload of ID's and a bunch of other good shit the old man used. No problemo, just flash a badge and the cops back off. Cops are stupid, man. My buds show up in dark jackets, flash badges, and the cops just evaporate. Cops never wanna fuck with the Government. My buds are good at what they do. Like I told ya, we've got two other dudes we've been moving around besides you, and it's been pretty smooth going."

"Who was that dirtbag I killed at the storage facility on Semoran earlier?"

His eyes bulged. "You...ended *Artie*?"

"If that was his name..."

The kid swallowed audibly.

"You honestly didn't know he was dead?"

The boy shrugged. "I...kinda wondered why the dumb fuck didn't call back in. Artie liked his snort, so I figured he did a couple lines after he'd wasted you two, then got it on with his favorite hooker before he decided to call back for his sit rep." He went silent, then straightened in the seat and glared. "He was a *bud* of mine, shithead. Why'd ya do it?"

"Oh, I don't know. Maybe it was because he was trying to kill me. I take stuff like that personal these days."

The boy shook his head.

"By the way…how'd you manage the small matter of that voice trick?" Greer asked.

"Whaddya mean?"

"You don't sound at all like the bastard who's been giving me orders the last five years."

"He's got a voice altering program here." Erika was sorting through a stack of disks.

"Really?"

The kid looked confused. "Man, where the fuck have *you* been? That program's been around forever…"

"It's simple," Erika said. "He did a match with whichever voice he wanted to dupe, then programmed it into the system. Every time he activated the program, he spoke into the mike, and it automatically morphed the moment it connected with your earpiece."

"Like I said, man…it's been around forever."

Erika was still checking things out. "He also has a gender altering program, courtesy of YouTube."

"Why would you need that?"

The kid shrugged. "Comes in handy."

"When?"

No reply.

"You'd better answer us..."

The boy looked sheepish. "I like to mess with people's minds."

"There's an adult site here." Erika had logged into one of the monitors. "With a long list of email addresses, credit cards and phone numbers. Ask him what he's doing with it."

Greer slapped the kid on the forehead. "You heard the lady."

The boy pulled away and glared. "*Watch* it, man! You don't have to keep up the rough stuff. I'll tell ya what you wanna know!"

"Then start doing it. Now would be a dandy time."

"Looks like guys call in and ask for a certain female operator, and he uses the program to say nasty things to them," Erika said, studying the monitor. "There's a long list of female names, plus several different subjects listed here. BDSM, rough sex, S&M—stuff like that."

"Classy," Greer said, scowling.

"It's just a *game*, man..."

Greer felt his self-control crumbling. "This is all a *game* to you? Conning people? Taking their money? Making them do disgusting things? Making them *kill* people?"

"Like I told ya before, Pops was doing it..."

"That program was shut down *three months ago*!"

No reply.

Greer wanted to beat this idiot to a pulp but reminded himself what this was all about. He'd killed too many people already, many of them because of this pampered twit. It was over. It had to stop. And he was the only one who could stop it.

"Tell me about the blackout program."

"Huh?"

"Are you trying to piss me off again?" He moved closer to the chair. "The program where I black out? Because I did something you didn't like? Remember now?"

The boy perked up. "That's a cool program, man. A real turn-on."

Erika groaned.

"You mean for the one pressing the button," Greer muttered. "*Not* the poor schmuck on the receiving end of the shit…"

"Pops only liked using it in emergencies. He said there was a danger of brain damage if you did it too often, so I figured—"

"You figured it would be fun to do it anyway." Greer felt the rage growing, his skin heating up. His hands were clammy.

"It's really cool, though." The boy's face lit up. "Like one of those games where you've got this warrior you wanna waste, only he's got this advantage, and to make sure he doesn't use it, you've got to—"

Greer's slap was much more brutal than any Erika had delivered. The boy's head was wrenched viciously back, nearly cracking his neck. His high-pitched wail made the walls of the room shake. His

302

head dropped. He slumped forward, moaning quietly.

Greer moved closer. "This isn't a *game*, you piece of shit. This is life. With living, breathing people. People with families. And lives. And feelings. Get it? It's obvious that you're living in your own safe, insulated little fantasy world, but can you possibly for one moment grasp the concept that there are actually other people walking around out there just as real as you are?"

The boy's expression suggested that Greer had just spoken a foreign language.

Struggling to keep his rage in check, Greer lowered the pistol, until the snub-nosed barrel rested firmly on the boy's unprotected groin.

Cringing, the boy tried to pull away, but the tape held him fast. "What the *fuck*? C'mon, man! Now you're gonna *shoot* me? In the *nuts*? Just because you're *pissed*?"

Greer knew right then that the boy obviously hadn't heard a word he had said, or just couldn't understand what was happening. *William H. Townes,* he thought wildly, *I never knew you, but judging by what I'm seeing right now, I can safely say that you failed miserably raising your boy.*

"*Talk* to me, man!" The boy sounded desperate.

Now was the time to get the answers he needed.

"Tell me about the blackout program. Now, before I lose my head and decide to waste you right now, while I'm in the right mood for it."

"You *can't* shoot me, man! Everyone in the neighborhood'll hear the shot. They'll call the cops, and before you can—"

Greer increased the pressure on the boy's crotch.

Gasping, the boy heaved back, nearly upsetting the chair. "Man, that really *hurts*!"

"By the way, this is your dead bud Artie's gun. Want me to show you the silencer I unscrewed from the barrel and stuck in my pocket?"

The boy swallowed loudly.

"Know what a silencer does? You seem to know everything else. At least, you think you do."

His gaze still glued to his crotch, the boy nodded.

"But if you're really that concerned, I guess I can tap my resources for a different method of persuasion." With his free hand, Greer reached into his pocket and produced his penknife once again.

The boy let out a trickle of high-pitched whimpers when he saw the gleaming blade shining in his face. "C'mon, man...*please* don't do anything to...*please* don't cut off my—"

"Tell me about the blackout program," Greer said calmly, "and I'll stop all this."

"Wh-Whaddya w-wanna know?" he asked in a strained voice.

"Where is it?"

"You mean the program?"

Greer moved his hand closer, bringing the knife less than a foot from the boy's groin.

Another gasp. "It's...over th-*there*, man! O-Over there! That m-monitor in back! Next to the b-box!"

"Erika, check it out."

Erika went over to the monitor and start punching keys. "Looks like a simple Windows program."

The boy nodded eagerly. "Th-That's it!"

Erika punched more keys. "It's locked. I can't get in."

Greer pressed the tip of the knife to the boy's groin. "The ID and password. *Now*."

The boy began stammering incoherently.

"Is there a thumb drive for the program?"

The boy nodded.

"Is it hooked up to the monitor?"

The boy mumbled something they couldn't understand.

Greer could tell the boy was quickly entering the panic mode. It wouldn't be long before he became totally incoherent. He walked over and put the knife and pistol on the table. "Erika, grab all the USB's you can find and drop them in a pile over here."

She pulled the thumb drives out of the monitors and tossed them on the table. Greer did the same, collecting six while Erika had added more than a dozen to the pile. When they'd finished, Greer said, "Find a bag."

She went over to one of the boxes on the shelf, reached in and rummaged through it. Moments later, she found a plastic Walmart bag. She came back over and, opening it, placed it on the table. The two of them scooped up every thumb drive they'd collected and dumped them into the bag. Greer picked up the bag and handed it to her. "We're taking this with us."

"Man, you can't…can't *do* that! That's my *personal property*!"

"Shut up." Greer pocketed his knife and grabbed the pistol. He turned to Erika. "Go on over there and stand behind that idiot's chair. I don't want you to get hurt."

Once she'd done as he said, Greer grabbed a monitor, raised it over his head and smashed it viciously to the floor. It broke open in several jagged parts, bits of plastic debris and glass flying everywhere.

The kid was shaking his head wildly. "Man, what did ya do *that* for?"

Greer stomped what was left of the monitor until its pieces covered the floor in an impressive pile of jagged glass and plastic. He then grabbed the tower, slammed it to the floor and made sure everything was reduced to useless, irretrievable pieces. The boy began screaming again. Greer paused. "Erika, slap a few yards of that tape over his big mouth."

The screaming was immediately muffled, replaced with a series of high-pitched whimpers.

Five minutes later, the floor was covered with scattered piles of plastic strips, shattered glass, and other debris. Greer stood among the wreckage, catching his breath. He turned to Erika. "Think that did it?"

She walked over to the tables. "I'd better check to make sure there isn't a CD or anything else still intact. The way it looks right now? Yeah, I'd say you pretty much destroyed his stupid blackout program."

"I wonder if there's a kill program around here somewhere."

"You can try asking him, or we can just destroy the rest of this stuff and call it good."

"I'd hate to think he's got anything else stashed away in a different place." Greer glared at the kid, who moaned and sobbed as he gawked numbly at the mess.

"I don't think he'd trust anything that valuable with anyone else," she said. "He's too arrogant and narcissistic for that."

"To be safe, check out what's left of these monitors and hard drives. I'll go through that desk to make sure he doesn't have anything valuable on hidden disk or written down that could kill me anytime in the future. That should take care of everything."

"What about...him?" Erika asked, her voice almost a whisper.

"What about him?"

"You're not gonna...are you...Justin, are you gonna—"

"As much as I'd really and truly love to, I'm not gonna kill the stupid son of a bitch."

"You're not?"

"No. I'm not."

"Why not?"

"You *want* me to kill the little bastard?"

"Well, no, but…"

"But what?"

She shrugged. "I just thought—"

"I'm a killer? Killers kill people? Therefore—"

"It's not that."

"What *is* it, then?"

"I just thought that, going by what he's done to you and by what he almost had done to me—"

"I told you the killing stops tonight, didn't I?"

"Well—"

"Erika, I'd never lie to you. Nothing would make me feel better than capping that asshole. But I'm tired, disillusioned, and thoroughly disgusted. I'm through with this crap. I mean it. The killing stops with him."

Chapter 33

Erika's thoughts raced as she and Justin went back outside.

Although furious about what had happened, Erika discovered that she couldn't help feeling sorry for the boy. Having known several privileged people in high school and in college, she realized that even in spite of their conceit and obvious condescension toward everyone, they were simply living the only way they knew.

"Do you really think we should've left him like that?" she asked as they got back into the Hyundai.

"Yeah. I really do."

"Justin…he's taped to a *chair*. He's completely helpless. And there's no one around to cut him loose."

"So?"

She thought about what he'd said before they'd left the house. Justin was through killing people. That was commendable—especially since the kid taped to the chair had been responsible for destroying so many lives. And she could tell by the intense anger raging through him that he'd really and truly wanted to murder the boy just to end the problem. But even though the kid had nearly succeeded in getting her and her parents killed, she still couldn't help feeling sorry for him. She hated herself for having these feelings, but she couldn't ignore them. "What I'm trying to say is this. If no one goes in that house in the next few days, he could die of starvation, thirst, or—"

"What's your point?" When she didn't reply right off, he said, "Listen to me, okay? And try to understand what I'm feeling right now. That dickhead played with me. To him, I was no more than just another stupid video game. How many of the people he ordered me to kill in the last three months were actually enemies of the state? That arrogant jerk was forcing me to kill people he didn't like. There could very easily be a kill program in this mess—" he shook the bag of USB drives he held in his lap "—that he most likely would have activated if we hadn't gotten there when we did."

She clearly understood his anger. "I guess we both have a right to be—"

"I almost killed you, Erika. And if I hadn't convinced him otherwise, your parents would also be dead." Justin's words, though soft and contained, resonated with a simmering anger. "That pathetic little bastard should be grateful I didn't blow his head off."

Erika didn't respond.

"I hope he needs to use the bathroom. I also hope his idiot buddies don't come over until hours after he's crapped his undershorts."

"Do you regret what you did to all that equipment?" she asked after some thought.

"Why?"

"Evidence, in case we wanted to take him to court."

310

"I've got no faith whatsoever in our judicial system," he said flatly. "If we did go to court, you can be damned certain the Government would get involved, and it would go south from there almost immediately and keep its downward plunge, possibly for the rest of our natural lives. Anyway, I wouldn't want that damned kill program to get into the wrong hands."

"You were right, then. This way, we've got all the evidence, and once we destroy it, it can't hurt you anymore."

They remained silent for several blocks, watching the haze of the headlight beams straight ahead as Erika drove.

"Now that we're talking about it," Justin said a few minutes later, staring at the pile in his lap, "I just hope we got it all. I really wouldn't want that stupid shit to have a kill program hidden anywhere else in that house."

"I don't think you need to worry about that."

"How can you be sure?"

"I have this strong feeling that everything we need is right there, in that bag."

He didn't reply.

"You believe me, don't you?"

"If I didn't, we'd be back there, tearing that house up."

She drove the next few blocks in silence. The darkness had thinned, turning gray, then silver, and after a few minutes, the gradual shimmering of a hazy dawn beckoned, coaxing in a new day.

Later, as the fresh daybreak cleared away remnants of the previous night, she sensed something strange. Something that made her think of the accident. And the hospital. And, of course, what happened during her long, excruciating recovery.

"What's wrong?" Justin asked.

"I suddenly have this strong feeling that we need to be somewhere else."

***

Justin was silent as Erika turned off the main road and coaxed the Hyundai past the open gates leading to the cemetery. She could tell he was watching her as she inched the car down the paved drive, which veered around a stone fountain and a beautiful flower display before curving back to the nicely-trimmed lawn that led to the straight path separating the many rows of gravestones. She knew he was going to ask her questions; she just didn't know what she could tell him.

"Why'd we come here?" he asked after she'd eased the car to a stop.

"I'm not quite sure."

He sat back and stared straight ahead as she put the car into park and flicked off the ignition.

Her pulse fluttering, Erika leaned back and closed her eyes. And surrendered to the feelings and emotions that had brought them here.

Flashes of her accident quickly took over, turning hot and bright as always, and she soon experienced the same pain, agony and terror she remembered so well when the dark-blue Camaro

312

had burst from out of nowhere, viciously tearing into her the moment she'd taken her car through the four-way intersection on green, at South Orange Blossom and Holden Avenue.

The nightmare exploded in one savage, sizzling flood, and she felt her hands go totally numb as they tightened into fists. Her body went stiff, turning cold as the horrific images swept past the cloudy gray picture-screen in her head. Her eyes squeezed shut the instant the sickening crunching sound of her beloved Honda Accord gave way to the heavy vehicle slamming viciously into the passenger's side, spraying shards of metal, plastic and glass at her while forcing her left side into the door panel, breaking her upper arm, jolting her spine and cracking her jaw as her face smacked into her window, breaking the glass and knocking her unconscious.

The unconsciousness immediately turned black, then bright red in just moments, as a heavy gush of gasoline splashed the right side of her face, neck and shoulder a split second before igniting and turning everything into an agonizing inferno.

Her screams seared her lungs as the flames hungrily ate through her unprotected flesh, making everything blindingly white, sizzling and excruciating just seconds before the blessed unconsciousness returned, this time sustaining solid blackness until she was able to open her eyes an eternity later, in the hospital. And as she drifted in and out of consciousness, she could never forget the flurry of silent white uniforms hustling about, carefully tending to her.

Justin's soft, soothing voice flowed into her consciousness, gently bringing her out of the muffled gray cocoon smothering her. "You went back, didn't you?"

She opened her eyes.

She was sitting in the Hyundai, the steering wheel directly in front of her, the gray sheen of early morning resting softly against the windshield. Justin sat close beside her, watching her, a worried look on his handsome face.

You went back...

She hadn't said a word, but he knew. Of course he knew. He'd been through hell himself, had seen and done things most everyone else would never know—or even believe—in their lifetimes. He'd seen death. And horror. And monsters. People who had spent time in hell shared things no one else could even begin to comprehend.

It took her considerable effort to find her voice. "You knew, didn't you?"

His smile made her feel a little better. Justin hardly ever smiled. When he did, it always meant something important. "Same thing happened to me in Iraq."

It took her only a moment to understand what he'd meant. "You were burned, too."

He nodded.

She didn't want to take him back there but realized that she needed to know what happened.

"Talk to me. Please? I really need to know. I *have* to know."

He sat back and stared at the windshield. Then, after a bit, he turned back to her. "Mine was mostly shrapnel, but I'm also carrying around a splatter of burn marks on my back and sides. IED stuff, mostly. They shot down our chopper when we were about twenty feet up, getting ready to land. Our guess was that it was an artillery shell treated with gasoline and set with a detonator. I also have a couple of bullet holes in my right thigh. And a stab wound in my left tricep. It was pretty deep, but it only seems to bother me when the weather's really humid."

She suddenly felt things for him that she'd never felt for anyone else. She wanted to hug him. And pull him close. And feel his heart beating against hers. And tell him how badly she felt for what he'd gone through. And that he should have never been forced to endure any of that. And, most of all, that what she had gone through had been nothing compared to his nightmare.

Then she realized that she could not say or do any of those things. Not now, anyway. Right now, all she could do was sympathize. And hope he understood that she meant every word she said. "Your scars are probably *much* worse than mine."

He shook his head. "The only difference is that I can hide mine much easier."

She nodded. Justin once again proved that he could make her feel better with just a couple of well-chosen words.

"So…what brought us here?" he asked after the silence.

She stared numbly at the neat columns of gravestones. And tried once again to rationalize why she'd driven here.

And once again drew a blank.

But just then, she found herself focusing on one of the markers. This one sat about fifty yards away, in the sixth row on the right, three down from the long path separating the rows.

It seemed to be glowing. And, as she continued gazing at it, she noticed that some sort of hazy golden halo had encircled it.

Was it glowing because the early morning sun was shining on it? She realized right off that it couldn't have been. The sun hadn't shown itself yet. Besides, it was the only marker that seemed to be glowing.

Suddenly dizzy, she rubbed her eyes. When her vision cleared, she stared at it again.

"Do you…*see* that?" she whispered.

"See what?"

"Can you see anything different…about that one marker?"

"Which?"

She knew right then that what she saw was visible only to her. "You *don't* see it?"

"What are you talking about, Erika?"

She sat in nervous silence, wondering how she could tell him without sounding crazy.

"You can tell me anything," he said softly.

His statement gave her the confidence she needed. "I see a slight golden haze floating directly above that gravestone."

He turned back to the windshield, stared straight ahead for about half a minute, then shrugged. "I don't see anything."

She found that she could not reply. She also found that she could not look at him. She didn't want to see disbelief—or fear—on his face.

"I believe you," he said, watching her. "I honestly believe you see a golden haze."

"You do?"

"Of course."

"Then why...why don't *you* see it?"

"I don't know. Something tells me there's probably a valid reason. But not necessarily one we should be able to understand."

She stared at him and felt, once again, a closeness she'd never before felt for another human being. He believed her. No one else would have, but he did.

And now you truly need to find out about this, some other voice inside her said.

Pulling her gaze away from Justin, she forced herself to start thinking clearly. Her pulse sputtered as she reached for the door handle. "I have to check this out."

Chapter 34

The gravestone was marked, simply:

Madelyn Jane Gordon
B. 2/10/1971
D. 10/05/2018

Erika stood stock-still in the trimmed grass, staring in shocked silence. The golden haze highlighting the stone seemed to be hovering quite close to the top, nearly touching it. She wanted to reach out to see if she could actually feel it, but her arms had turned to lead at her sides.

Her eyes lowered, returning to the marker. A flurry of images rushed by, this time more urgently, making the memories of the accident more frighteningly real than ever before, and she shuddered.

Madelyn Gordon.

Oh my dear God.

This sweet, lonely lady died just a few days ago...

"Erika?" Justin had moved closer. "What's going on? Do you know who this lady is—or was?"

It took her a while before she discovered she could speak. A lump had gathered in her throat; a strange coldness enveloped her.

"This lady...she was the mother of the guy...the guy who slammed into me...my car...on the Trail." She was surprised that the anger and the hurt consuming her for the last two years had suddenly diminished in intensity.

"This grave is fresh," Justin said.

"I know."

"She died just last week."

Erika didn't reply. Her gaze remained locked on the woman's name.

"Did you know her?" he asked.

"She…came to see me. Two years ago. At the hospital. While I was recovering." She took a deep breath. "She came every day. Every single day. Michael, her son, had died in the collision, but all she seemed to care about was that he almost killed me, and that I was lying in Intensive Care with tubes and my head covered in bandages."

"Did she talk to you?"

The memories remained just as clear as ever. "Whenever they let her. They didn't want to—not at first. My parents didn't want her to be in the same room with me. They didn't even want her in the hospital. The first day, they called for Security to escort her out of the building. But it wasn't long before she showed everyone that she was totally devastated about what had happened. After a while, they reconsidered, and let her come in to see me."

Justin placed his hand on her shoulder.

"Just a few days later, my folks started talking to her. It didn't take very long before they said they actually liked her." Erika smiled. "She was really a very sweet person. Honest. And sincere. You couldn't hate her even if you tried. Her son's accident nearly destroyed her, and anyone could tell by how she looked that she hadn't slept or eaten for quite some time. She told us all about Michael and his substance abuse problem, the many times he'd been in trouble, and how she'd been forced to go into serious debt to bail him out."

"Was there a father in the picture?"

"Judging by what she told me, he'd been gone for several years. I don't know exactly what happened, but from what she said, her husband was a drunk, an abuser, and had a wandering eye. One day, he just left without a word. Madelyn was a medical transcriptionist, but she wasn't making much money, and had to find a second job to add to the budget. Michael couldn't hold down a job of his own, and this put even more pressure on her. And since he was hooked on coke and pharmaceuticals, and frequently took money out of her purse and her checking account to support his habit, she could barely make the mortgage payment. It wasn't long before she had to give up the house and move into a small apartment in downtown Orlando. Since she had very little money, she was forced to move to a bad section."

"What happened with her son?"

"He was arrested for burglary not long after their move, then later caught mugging an elderly woman for drug money. The car he was driving when he hit me was stolen, and when they autopsied his body, they found coke in his bloodstream, as well as a blood/alcohol content of .24."

"Damn. Nearly a quarter of the blood in his system was alcohol."

"He probably didn't even know what was happening when he slammed into me."

"How old was he?"

"Twenty-one."

Justin shook his head. "Poor lady went through one hell right after another."

Erika's head continued swimming with images—the dear woman standing beside her bed, her head lowered, tears streaking her cheeks. Erika remembered the many times the lady had covered her hand with her own…and how warm it had felt.

Erika could never forget the strange sensation of actually feeling the woman's pain when their hands touched.

"Each time Madelyn came to see me, she sat down next to the bed, took my hand in hers, and said in a very soft voice, "I'm gonna make this right, dear, sweet Erika. I don't know how, but I will. I've been told all my life how sensitive I am, that I can actually feel the emotions of others. I've never figured out exactly what all of it means, but that really doesn't matter. All I care about is that I will somehow make this right. Michael's worries are over, and I thank God for that. Yours, unfortunately, are not, but I swear with all my heart that I'll find some way of helping you any way I can… Even if it takes the rest of my life to do it…"

Oh my God… The senses. The new emotions.

Most of all, the reassuring voice she kept hearing, telling her things, warning her of danger…

Erika felt her skin turning cold again.

"Erika? Are you all right?"

She couldn't pull her eyes away from the name on the marker. Or the golden haze hovering above it that had dimmed slightly. "She...actually did it," she whispered, a lump filling her throat. "She fulfilled her promise."

***

Greer managed to coax Erika from her spot in front of the grave. He put his arm around her waist and led her back down the grassy path, where her car was parked.

He could tell she was confused and quite shaken. He also knew that even in spite of what he himself had gone through, he had to focus on her pain and try to make some sense out of all this.

His main concern was getting her back to her car. She needed to relax and let her mind clear. Only then could he try talking to her.

Minutes later, she sat behind the wheel, her head back, her eyes closed. She no longer trembled. Her breathing had become more regular.

After giving her a few more minutes, he decided the time was right. "Do you really think she was right?" he asked. "About her fulfilling her promise?"

Without opening her eyes or looking at him, she said, "I honestly think it's been her all along."

"How so?"

"She died just a few days ago. That was right about when I started getting all these strange feelings, these emotions. These senses and all those other things I'll never be able to explain."

"You honestly think she was the one doing all this?"

"I really and truly believe she was. I believe I even heard her voice talking to me."

Greer had no idea what to say.

"She felt so badly about how things had turned out. It devastated her. Since we lost contact with her when I left the hospital, I can't possibly know for sure, but I remember my mom hearing from someone that Madelyn went on heavy meds not too long after my accident. But as far as what she told me? I figured she just felt so guilty about what her son had done that she wanted desperately to say or do something—anything that would make me feel the tiniest bit better. Neither I nor my parents could possibly know what she had in mind. I just let her go on because I had the feeling that she was somehow easing her own guilt a little by offering to fix things."

"But you obviously feel differently about all this now."

"One of the last things she said to me really stuck in my mind."

"Which was?"

Erika turned to him. "When she told me she'd find some way of helping me, she ended it by saying, "even if it takes the rest of my life to do it...""

"What did your parents think of all this?"

"They were going through a lot back then. My accident hit them nearly as hard as it hit me. After all, I'm their only child, and I always showed promise in everything I did, even as a little girl. The accident nearly killed me, and I could tell that they really believed I would die. But as I said, they eventually warmed up to Madelyn when they realized that she'd been going through her own personal hell for such a long time. They even had lunch with her a couple of times at the hospital and told me what a warm, caring person she actually was." She paused. "This reminds me of something Mom told me, though. Strange that I hadn't thought of it before now."

"What is it?"

"It's really hard to put into words. Mom said that Madelyn seemed to have a special brightness about her. She said that when she and Dad were talking to the lady, they both felt a strange uplifting. It was as though they could actually feel something good was going to happen."

"You said you felt the same thing when she came into your room, held your hand, and talked to you."

"The strange thing is, I still feel it."

Greer sat trying to absorb what Erika had just told him. And also trying to dismiss it in spite of the fact that he knew he couldn't. He'd seen and heard of many bizarre things, most of them during his time in Iraq. And one of the most important things he'd learned was that many of life's greatest wonders were things people could not see or understand. And that many of these incidents should not have happened in the first place. Lastly, they were things that could not possibly be explained or believed.

But in spite of all this, he knew that he needed to maintain a fresh perspective. Erika was directly involved and saw things only subjectively. He, on the other hand, should maintain a clear head. "So then, I guess you're pretty certain it was her spirit helping you?"

"Nothing else can explain any of this. I never had any hint of ESP or premonition before. I played the LOTTO three separate times and quit forever because I didn't even get one number right." She shook her head. "No, nothing else can convince me otherwise. It was Madelyn. I sensed her presence, and like I said, I even heard her voice. I'm sure of it."

"Then you obviously believe in life after death?"

"Don't you?"

"This really isn't about me."

"Justin, you're just as involved in this as I am. Don't you realize how many times my strange feelings saved both of us?"

He didn't reply.

"Oh my God!" Erika froze in her seat and stared straight ahead.

"What's wrong?"

She swallowed audibly. "The golden haze shining over her grave."

He gazed at the markers. "What about it?"

"It's *gone!*"

Chapter 35

The drive back to Lake Underhill was spent in tense silence.

As he gazed at the sidewalks and driveways sliding past his window, Greer could tell Erika was totally confused and overcome with emotion over the episode at the cemetery.

Some strange phenomenon had obviously taken place. Although he hadn't actually seen a golden glow above Madelyn Gordon's gravestone, he was certain Erika's eyes hadn't been playing tricks. However, he could hardly explain its appearance, or even why it had disappeared by the time they'd gone back to the Hyundai.

He wondered if it had something to do with the approaching sunrise. Or maybe the angle of the trees reflecting the new light of day.

Or had Erika been right in her evaluation?

Had Madelyn Gordon come back to the mortal world in spirit form to guide Erika through the forbidden path the two of them had been forced to endure the last couple of days?

Was it possible to conquer death to fulfill a promise? To postpone passing over into the Afterlife to repay a crucial debt? To perform one ultimate selfless act in a final effort to cleanse the soul before approaching its final resting place?

Did the Hindu belief of redemption through personal liberation from guilt or sin apply in this case?

Or was he just imagining all this?

He knew he wasn't imagining anything. He strongly felt that such a phenomenon had truly happened.

Erika had inexplicably manipulated him at the Mall. She had somehow sensed what he was doing and unknowingly cashed in one of her minor miracles to stop him. And from that point on, she'd sensed and predicted things that had eventually saved their lives.

It hadn't been imaginary. It had happened. And, as he thought more about it, he was forced to admit to himself that he actually did indeed understand what had taken place.

Just as he had followed her outside and into the parking lot, he'd heard a voice in his head. He couldn't remember what it said, just that he shouldn't go through with the hit. At the time, he'd thought it was his conscience talking to him, warning him that this was all wrong. Then, as he agonized more about it, he found that he couldn't concentrate. And before he realized what was happening, he'd taken a misstep and stumbled, hurling himself to the rough pavement.

Was it actually his conscience warning him, thus sabotaging his mission?

Or had he actually heard Madelyn Gordon's voice?

"You never saw it, did you?" Erika asked, staring straight ahead as she drove.

Her voice forced him to shift back to the present. It took him a moment or two to realize what she was talking about. "No."

"Then it disappeared. But since you couldn't see it in the first place, did you think I was just—"

"I truly believe you saw something."

"You're not just saying that?"

"Of course not."

"Then why couldn't *you* see it?"

"Maybe Madelyn wanted you—and you alone—to see her sign. This *was* a personal thing, wasn't it?" He saw no reason to tell her his version of what happened at the Mall.

She drove in silence. But he could tell her mind had shifted into overload. And that she was desperately trying to process it all.

After a while, she said, "It was like…well, as if she wanted me to see the marker. She'd already sent me a message to get me to drive there, but it wouldn't have mattered much at all if I couldn't find the marker. Once we found it, her work was done. It was like she was telling me what had really happened. And that she had fulfilled her promise."

"That's one way of looking at it," he said.

"You sound skeptical."

"I truly believe you saw something."

"But you're not sure."

"Since I couldn't see it? No. I'm not. Not totally, anyway."

"What about the rest of it? Those feelings? The perceptions I kept getting?"

"I'm not exactly sure. I kind of believe in just about everything nowadays. I've seen and heard a lot of weird things in my life. No matter who you are or what you believe, you just can't dismiss all of them. You either accept them or turn your mind off to everything in life that you can't see or hear."

"Is this all because of what happened in Iraq?"

"And, of course, all that I'd gone through. And what I saw. And what I thought I saw."

She was silent for a few moments. "Are you thinking about what was happening to me?"

This made him wonder if her powers were just as sharp as before. "How'd you know?"

"I just guessed. It's probably because I'm thinking about everything that's happened, and I'm pretty sure you're doing the same."

"And what have you figured out?"

"The only thing I truly believe is that Madelyn Gordon came back to help us through this."

He tried once again to imagine how things would have been if Erika's explanation was wrong. It was pretty clear that things would have turned out much differently if Erika's senses hadn't influenced them when they'd needed immediate guidance.

She reached the end of the block and stopped at the intersection of Wayfarer and South Conway. Then she turned to him. "I have this strange feeling that the senses and premonitions I'd been getting for the last two days are all gone."

"You're feeling nothing now?"

"I feel like something's missing. It's like when a relative or good friend who's been staying with you leaves after several days, and you're all alone again. There's a vast emptiness. I actually feel alone again. It's as if no one is watching over me anymore."

"That *is* strange."

More silence as she made the right turn that took them down Rockledge, which led to her parents' home. As she slowed to make the turn, he stiffened and wondered once again if their relationship could actually be a good thing. After all, they'd been thrown together through a series of truly bizarre events. But now that everything was over, he feared that their feelings for one another might not be strong enough to endure a permanent relationship. He couldn't help wondering if the warmth and closeness they felt for one another right now would be enough.

Or would they simply pull away from each other and return to their former lives?

Erika went up the paved drive and stopped a couple of feet from the garage door. She put the car into park and switched off the ignition. Then turned and stared at him in a way that made him feel nervous and extremely vulnerable.

He wondered what she was feeling right now. If she could see into his soul, his heart. If she could honestly sense how much he cared for her, how much wanted her. How much he loved her.

Finally, she said, "You're nervous."

It took him a few moments to find his voice. "I'm just…well, I'm thinking about all this."

"What about it?"

"I'm thinking that…well, I'm kind of—"

"Kind of what?"

"You know I'm several years older than you, right?"

"So?"

"And that I have issues? Lots of them?"

"I kind of think I've got a bunch of them, as well."

He hadn't expected her to say such a thing. But she was right. Absolutely. If anyone had issues, it was Erika.

"Are you finished?" she asked. "I mean, with the age thing? And the issues?"

He nodded.

"Is that all you wanted to tell me?"

"Not exactly…"

"Okay, then. I'm still listening."

He took a breath and thought about what he would say next, but his mind kept blanking out, and all he saw was Erika. The two of them together, loving one another, laughing, making love. Sharing a life together. Doing things he never thought he'd ever be able to do again. Then he noticed the bag of thumb drives in his lap. One of them held the key to the main issue that he could not ignore. The program that could activate the chip imbedded in the back of his head. The lethal one. The one that could give him a blood clot. Instant death.

"It can't be activated if the program isn't opened up." Erika was obviously reading him again. "And if it isn't opened up, the chip is useless. Just a foreign body that will eventually be absorbed by all the antibodies your system can produce."

He couldn't reply. Once again, she was right.

"I'm still listening…"

For a moment he'd forgotten what they were talking about. Then he remembered. He'd been trying to put up a barrier that would separate them, maybe convince her that they had no chance together. But the more he thought about it, the more he realized that there really wasn't that much of a difference between them. And that they could actually make a go of it.

But it did bother him a little, knowing that when he was in Iraq, interrogating enemy prisoners, Erika was a beautiful young girl in high school, just a handful of years away from being disfigured in a serious accident that would forever change her life.

"Then it's okay with you? Our age difference? The fact that I came back from Iraq with serious issues?"

Without warning, she moved closer and pressed her warm lips to his. He closed his eyes and felt her arms closing tightly behind his neck, pulling him against her and making the kiss even more passionate. He relaxed and felt his body responding, growing hotter.

When she finally pulled away, he imagined that he'd just slipped into her soul and had become part of her.

She gazed at him, her deep blue eyes devouring him. Then she sighed. "Justin, I wouldn't care if you were fifty. Or eighty. What I feel for you is something I've never felt for anyone ever before."

He didn't reply.

She tilted her head. Her thick red locks slid down her shoulder. "Please tell me you feel the same as I do."

He realized at that moment that he'd never wanted a woman as much as he wanted Erika. "I do. I really do."

Erika smiled and reached for his hand.

He took it and clutched it tightly. But he still felt uneasy. This seemed like one of those wonderful, surrealistic things that could not possibly be real. Something so fragile that it could easily fall apart. "What about your parents?"

"What about them?"

"They're probably only a few years older than I am..."

"I really don't care. Not at all. Not one damned bit."

"Will *they*?"

"Like I just said—"

"I just don't...I don't want to alienate you from them..."

"My parents will love you. Just as I do."

It took him several moments to realize what she'd just said. "You...*love* me?"

"Very much."

"You're sure?"

She smiled. "I'm sure."

"I mean, are you…positive?"

She nodded.

"What I really mean is—"

"Justin?"

"Yes?"

"*Please* shut up."

It had been years since a woman had told him she loved him. Sharon had said it, but only during sex, and even then, she'd never said it with the same conviction that he'd just heard in Erika's voice. Erika meant it; he felt it and truly believed it. The moment he felt it, he realized how much he loved her as well.

"Are you all right? You look…funny."

"I *feel* funny…"

She reached up and touched his cheek. He closed his eyes and enjoyed the sensation. Moments later, when he opened his eyes, he saw her sitting there stiffly, staring at the windshield.

"What's wrong?" he asked.

She didn't move. Her eyes were distant. "I just…I just had this strange feeling…"

"What sort of strange feeling?"

"I don't know how to explain it."

"Try."

"Suddenly I feel that everything will be okay from now on."

"Everything?"

She nodded.

He thought of Madelyn Gordon. And her promise to Erika. "Do you think it might be her? Again?"

"I don't know. It was a very warm feeling, and I suddenly feel content and secure."

"Anything else?"

She closed her eyes and fell silent. A few moments later, she opened her eyes and smiled. But it was a sort of sad smile. "It's gone now."

"The feeling?"

A tear rolled down her cheek. "The feeling's gone, but the warmth and contentment are still there."

"That's a good thing, then."

"Yes. It really and truly is." She kissed him again, this time lightly. Then she pushed open her door. "I think it's time for my parents to finally meet you."

THE END

ALSO BY DAVID BERARDELLI

338